FRACTURED REDEMPTION

PARAMOUNT SCHOOL OF ARTS SERIES
BOOK 2

SASHA-MARIE MARSHALL

FRACTURED REDEMPTION

PARAMOUNT SCHOOL OF ARTS SERIES
BOOK 2

SASHA-MARIE MARSHALL

To YAHUAH, my Father.

For those on the path to healing and true self love.

Chapter One

LUCAS

"Hey, let's change the note here. E minor gives a more emotional effect," I suggest, stopping mid-song and switching to said chord on my guitar.

"Dude, we don't want the lower notes to overpower the music too much," Ricardo, one of the bass guitarists, chimes in. He looks at me through the overgrown black fringe almost cloaking his eyes from view.

"I'm with Lucas," Michelle agrees. "I think E minor makes the most sense here."

"Whatever," Ricardo says in defeat.

"Our other lead singer has spoken," I say confidently. Michelle carries this one. What she says holds a lot of weight.

We're a small group within the much larger Paramount School of Arts Music Club. We've been practicing together all summer, having written a few songs in preparation for our senior showcase at the end of the fall semester.

When it comes to music, I geek out.

I play on PSA's varsity football team, and although that's

been a pretty big part of my life, music is my core, my foundation. Without it everything else just kind of falls apart.

We make another attempt at playing through the entire song, but this time Michelle stops us. "Could we speed up the chorus?" she suggests. "And play harder when it gets to the end. That way it'll make for a deeper contrast with the softer, slower second verse."

I notice Ricardo's irritated look, but I don't comment.

After making the necessary changes, we practice for another half hour, thoroughly fleshing out the song.

At least for tonight.

With only one week of summer remaining before school starts, we wanted to get at least four more sessions in. I need them, because I don't look forward to choosing between football and my music. I have a strong feeling it'll come down to that this year.

As I place my guitar in its case, my phone starts vibrating. I pull it from my pocket and look at the caller ID.

Oh great.

It's only nine, too damn early for this crap.

"Yeah, this is Lucas," I say. "I'm on my way." I don't even give the guy on the line a chance to explain. I already know where I'm needed. I look to the others and nod. "Hey, I'm out. See y'all tomorrow."

"Later, Luuuke," I hear Michelle call back.

I face her, walking backward and winking as she flips her long auburn hair over her shoulders. She smiles widely, her eyes inviting.

I grin in response, holding up my phone as a promise I'll call her soon.

When I get to my truck, I throw my guitar on the back seat and quickly climb in. I back out of Ricardo's driveway and head straight over to The Lilac Alehouse just twenty minutes across town.

I make it there in ten.

As soon as I get inside, the owner spots me and gestures over to where a woman in a black dress and red stilettos is slumped over on one of the barstools.

That *woman* is my mother, Laura Moore.

She had me when she was a teenager, having married my dad not too long after she'd found out she was pregnant with me. Less of a love marriage and more of an *encouraged* one.

That kind of stuff is common where I come from.

Got to love the South.

I approach my mom and place one of her arms over my shoulder. "Come on. Let's go."

"He … ruined me," she whines, her words slurred. She reeks of vodka, her breath, her clothes, her hair. "That man, he … he's making my life … hell. Lucas—"

She stops up short as I open the passenger side door of my truck and start lifting her in.

I don't know who she's talking about. It's not Dad. That's for sure. He died a few years back of a drug overdose.

I don't touch that stuff, *ever*.

My mom, however, never had an alcohol abuse problem until she lost her position at her company last year. She'd been a supervising manager, and some case with an important client went sour. He'd threatened to pull out of some contract with the company if she wasn't released from her duties.

It isn't like either of us have to work. I've inherited enough money to take care of the both of us for the next two lifetimes. But that didn't matter to Mom. She prides herself on being an independent woman.

"Nooooo," Mom groans. "I don't want … to go home."

I ignore her protests, place her down on the seat, and buckle her in. Swinging around to my side, I hop in, secure the door locks and drive away from the bar. I don't bother trying to lecture Mom, because she won't listen nor hear it for that matter, not in the inebriated state she's currently in. I've tried asking her to see a therapist, someone, *anyone* she trusted enough to talk to about her troubles. This habit of drinking herself into oblivion is deadly, and I don't want her ending up like Dad.

When he died, I took over the helm as the man of the house.

I care for my mother, even though sometimes it can get stressful. Like tonight, where I have to go collect her from Lilac's.

I'll probably hire a professional who makes home visits. I know damn well my mother won't willingly leave this house to see anyone. Except maybe that bartender at Lilacs. That jerk would gladly hand her the next drink.

I get it. Dude is under no obligation to her.

I click to open the wrought iron gates that stretch to about twelve feet high, and drive up to the entrance of our two-story mansion. It's been in my family for the past four generations. Its Gothic architecture makes it look like something from the *Addams Family*.

I park my truck in the circular driveway and hop out. As soon as I get to my mother, Keenan, one of the guys we'd hired as a live-in groundskeeper, is already there to lift her out.

"Good evening, Keenan," I say to him in greeting. "You know where to take her."

He nods, reaching in and lifting Mom's sleeping form from the truck.

I close the passenger door and fall into step behind them. When we enter, Keenan brings Mom up to her room in the mansion's east wing. He's proven trustworthy, so I'm never suspicious of him where my mother's concerned.

I go to Dad's former study, now mine, and I pick up the phone to call our secretary.

Yeah, we have one of those too.

To be fair, Mrs. McCall was formerly Dad's secretary whom we kept on to handle our family's affairs.

"Good evening, Mr. Moore," Mrs. McCall says. "To what

do I owe this phone call so late in the evening?"

I detect a slight annoyance in her voice.

My eyes instantly shift to the old mahogany wall clock directly across from the office desk in the study.

I hadn't realized that it was almost ten. "I'm sorry, Mrs. McCall, but I need you to find someone who can help my mom."

"Oh dear. Did it happen again?" Her annoyance evaporates, quickly replaced with genuine concern.

"Yeah, and I don't think I'm equipped to affect any sort of change anymore."

"OK. You don't worry yourself, young man. I'll be on it as soon as possible." We hang up, and a sense of temporary relief washes over me.

I head up to my room on the west side of the house. Stripping down, I slide into the shower.

I should probably move into one of the rooms on Mom's side of the house, just so I can monitor her more easily.

I'm the kid, but I've had to become the parent for my parent. Life sure knows how to throw curveballs.

The warm water flows over my hair until it sticks to my forehead. I make a mental note to ask Mom about the guy she mentioned tonight, the one out to *ruin her life*.

Allowing my mind to mellow a bit as the water soothes and relaxes my muscles, it's not long before lyrics come to me, and I etch them in one of the fogged-up sliding doors of the shower.

As soon as I get out, I wrap a towel around my waist and head across the hall to my bedroom, grab my notepad and jot down the words and the music accompanying them.

> *With you by my side, pretty girl,*
> *We're up for a wild ride*
> *'Cause the downs of this life*
> *With you as my wife*

I pause and scratch out the last line, because what the hell?

Shaking my head, I send a few ringlets of water splashing against the page. I quickly wipe the notepad on my towel before reaching for my guitar.

"Damn it!" I left it in the truck.

The system signals movement at the front door. Going over to the intercom next to my bedroom door, I see my best friend's face on the screen.

I'm not surprised Beanca is here this late. She'll probably be staying the night.

I push the button that unlocks the front door to allow her in, and then I press on the speaker. "Hey, Bee, could you go over to my truck? I left my guitar on the back seat."

"Lu-cas," she whines, rolling her eyes before heading over to my truck.

I grin, loving the way she says my name. I watch her in the camera as she opens the back door and retrieves the hard case.

I'm about to head downstairs to meet her, when I remember that I'm only in a towel. I throw on a pair of sweatpants, not bothering with a shirt.

By the time I get downstairs, she's already hauling my case in. "Why is this thing so heavy?" she complains as she hands the case over to me. "And where are the rest of your clothes?"

"My house, remember, my rules. I'm allowed to be in any state of undress. You're lucky I even have these on," I tease, tugging on my sweatpants.

"Ugh, you're so gross, I can't even." She steps past me and takes her blonde tresses out of their customary ponytail. Her hair falls to her back, almost reaching her waist. Staring at it, I walk past her and tug on a few strands.

"Gosh. You're so annoying," she says, wincing before slapping my arm. "Anyway, I started *The Alchemist*."

I immediately swing around to face her. "Seriously? How far'd you get?" I told her about the book a couple of days ago when I'd read it. I'd also recommended it to our other best friends, Jones and Shepherd.

Shepherd probably hasn't gotten to reading it. He and his girlfriend have been on a road trip for the better half of summer. On the other hand, Jones is still in Baltimore with his family. He went there for summer and won't be back until school starts next week.

"I read most of part one," Beanca replies. "I think it's one of the best books I've read recently and that's saying a lot since I'm not even finished." Her gaze shifts to my chest, then back up to my face. When she catches me grinning at her, she rolls her eyes and reiterates, "Put a shirt on, Lucas."

"See something you like, Bee?" I wriggle my eyebrows at her teasingly. Grabbing her duffle from her shoulder, I place it over mine, watching her eyes widen.

"Oh shut up. As if."

We head up to my room and I place the duffle bag on the floor as she takes her laptop out of her satchel.

"I'm staying over tonight." She doesn't ask, doesn't have to.

I won't ever deny her. I've never denied her. I guess I always figured she needs space away from home, so she stays at my place.

"My sister's back and my parents are being total dweebs about it. It's like I don't even exist," Beanca says in annoyance, dropping onto the edge of my bed. Her fingers fly across the keys on her laptop, and I bend close, looking over her shoulder at what she's searching up.

"Scholarships?" I ask, turning my face toward hers.

She turns to me, our noses practically touching, and instantly leans away. "Whoa, Lucas. Personal space, please. And for the *last* time, put on a shirt. Gosh."

I straighten up, go over to my drawer and pull out a black T-shirt before dragging it over my head. "Happy?"

"Whatever," she replies, waving me off. "Anyway, I'm

hoping to get enough scholarship money to pay my own way through college. I don't want to depend on my parents."

Something about the way Beanca says it, raises my hackles. I walk back over to her and sit beside her on the bed. "Did they tell you they're not paying for your college?"

"No, not in so many words. But I'd rather be safe than sorry," she says evasively. "I'm hoping our school invites top-notch music school recruiters to come out during my recital. With any luck, I don't even have to apply to school. They'll just scout me on the spot."

I frown at the thought of all of us splitting up next year as everyone goes off to college.

"Where were you thinking of going?" Beanca asks, distracting me by placing a warm palm against my thigh. "Are you hoping to get a football scholarship?"

I spring from the bed, frowning as I walk toward one of the windows in my room. "Nah, I'm not interested in playing college football. I'm trying to focus more on my music."

"Seriously?" she asks excitedly. "What if we end up at the same school?"

Her words make me feel better, but I don't think I'm interested in studying music at a university either. "I'm thinking more along the lines of continuing with the band, you know, doing my own thing," I reply as I turn to face her, needing to see her reaction.

She looks glum, but plasters on a smile. "That's cool too."

"Bee, I know you want me to come with you. Just say it."

When she says nothing, I grab my guitar from its case and go over to the bed. Looking down at the notepad from earlier, I start playing the chords to the lyrics that had come to me in the shower.

After a few minutes of playing, Beanca starts humming to the tune. She doesn't even know she's doing it. The corners of her lips turn up and her head bobbs from side to side.

Feeling happy and super energetic all of a sudden, I play harder, gazing at her as I sing the lyrics in my head.

"Is that a new song?" she asks.

"It kind of came to me tonight," I admit.

"Sounds pretty awesome. Does it have lyrics yet?" She closes her laptop and slides closer to me, her face curious.

"No," I reply too quickly, shooting up from the bed, snatching the notepad and pocketing it.

"OK." She looks at me through narrowed eyes. "You've never been this secretive with your songs."

"Well, there's a first time for everything," I say, brushing a hand through my hair. I have no idea why I'm hiding the stupid lyrics.

"Whatever." She picks up her duffel bag and takes it across the hall to the bathroom.

When she returns a few minutes later, she's sporting a pink rabbit onesie. Throwing herself onto the bed, she crawls over to the side she's grown accustomed to and pats the other side.

"You wanna reread some of *The Alchemist* with me?" she asks, excitement etching her features.

I don't hesitate. "Hell yeah." I place the guitar on the corner stand in my room and go to her.

These shared readings have become a tradition of ours, and it's never awkward or uncomfortable when she sleeps next to me.

We read through part one of the story for the next hour and a half. I try not to spoil any of it, because Beanca will kill me if I do. And I want to at least make it to my senior year of high school.

When I notice the book faltering in her hand, I look over and see she's fallen asleep during my portion of the read-aloud. I gently remove the book from her grasp and place it on the nightstand.

Bringing her head against my chest, I hum along to the tune of my new song until I fall asleep.

Chapter Two

BEANCA

*S*enior year.

Hands down *the* best year of the high school experience. We're the ultimate upperclassmen and are pretty much catered to by staff and administration. Their goal is to see us graduate. Our goal? Making sure we enjoy the hell out of our final year.

Piano is my first period of the day and I wouldn't have it any other way. It makes me look forward to the school day.

When I get to the class, only nine chairs are organized in a semicircle, with the instructor's chair facing them. It's a small class. Smaller than the ones I'm used to. Usually, there are at least fifteen students. So far, there are already three people here, and I only recognize one of them, Jazmin, a sophomore. I only know her because she's my sister's friend. They met last year, and she's been over to our house on more than a few occasions.

"Hey!" Jazmin squeals as I sit beside her.

"

"I didn't know you'd be in this class." Seriously, I thought only seniors could take this advanced class.

"I had to audition for it."

"Oh, wow." That makes sense.

"Yeah."

The instructor arrives shortly after the rest of the students have taken their seats. My eyes wander over to this guy I've never seen before at our school. His chestnut hair is styled in an undercut and slicked back at the top.

During our class icebreaker, I learn his name is Vincent and he's also a senior. He's so handsome it's painful. When he stands, he's super tall with a swimmer's body.

"Where are you from, Vincent?" one of the other students asks.

"South Africa," he replies, his voice confident. "I moved here over the summer."

I don't want to be *that* girl so I stop myself from staring at him too much.

When class ends, Jazmin starts up a conversation with him. I head over to our piano teacher.

After speaking with him, I'm making my way to the class-room door, but chance a glance over to Vincent. Only to find him still in conversation with Jazmin.

Well, those two are hitting it off.

I tamp down on my disappointment. Yet another guy interested in someone other than me.

Leaving the class, I head to my locker.

"Yo, Bee, we have science together again this year." One of my best friends, Jones, slides up next to me. With dark eyes, a fade, and smooth dark skin, he's got a lot of girls at PSA vying for his attention. If Jones ever decides to get serious with one of them, the rest will be in for a world of hurt.

"That we do," I reply, turning to him. "I'm not taking all the notes for you again. You have to help this time. I have a lot on my plate already."

"Come on, Bee. I need the help. You know how much is riding on me getting scouted," he fake whines, before winking and grinning at me, dimples on display.

"Whatever. Let's go." I hook my arm through his and we head to chemistry.

As soon as I enter the class, I stiffen.

Sitting along the back row is Shepherd, our other best friend, and a bunch of the other football players. Jones yells over to him and he looks at us.

I want to disappear.

I made a mess of our friendship last year and almost cost him his relationship with Evelyn, his girlfriend.

Jones walks us over to the guys and we take two nearby seats.

Shepherd shocks me when he says, "What's up, Jones? Beanca?" There's no malice in his voice, no animosity rolling off him in waves toward me.

I'm speechless.

Jones nudges me, and I jump. "Hey, Shepherd," I say, my voice wavering.

"Bro, you lived for the rest of us this summer," Jones says, slapping hands with him. "That trip you took with Evie looked epic. No hard feelings, even though I saw her first."

"Dude, come on," Shepherd says, smiling. "This again. You might've known about Evelyn first, but I liked her first." The two bicker among themselves before Shepherd glances at me.

I smile, then look away.

I'm happy for him. He's found someone he genuinely loves. And even though Evie wasn't into him initially, it's evident she cares for him a lot now.

"How about you guys?" Shepherd asks Jones and me.

We each take turns filling him in on what he's missed. Although the friendship between Shepherd and me isn't quite the same, I'm happy for this small step in the right direction.

A few hours later, we all meet up with Lucas in the school cafeteria for lunch.

"I'm jealous," Lucas complains, sticking his fork into his lasagna. "All three of you are in Simmons's chemistry class together, and I'm stuck taking bio by myself."

I look over at where Evelyn's seated next to Shepherd. As Shepherd's girlfriend, she's now a permanent fixture at our table. When she looks up from her tray, I instantly look away.

"Yo, don't we have math together?" Jones asks, directing his question to Lucas.

"Dude, yeah. But I still feel shafted since three of the four musketeers are in with Simmons and I'm left out in the cold." He looks at me, then says, "Bee, why are *you* so quiet?"

"I'm not any more quiet than I usually am," I protest, frowning at him for calling me out. He should know better, especially when he's aware of the current situation.

"What does that even mean, Bee?" he teases.

This is the side of Lucas that annoys me, when he tries to get a rise out of me, especially with others present.

"Nothing, Lucas. It means nothing."

"Then why'd you say it?"

"Say what?"

When we start bickering, Jones interrupts us. "Well, would you look what Paramount's halls just dragged in."

Everyone's eyes follow Jones's line of vision as we all look over to where Vincent is standing. He apparently joined the lunch line and already, a group of girls flock to him like he's the sun in their sky. All he does is smile at them, and they all start flipping their hair and hanging on to his arm.

It's embarrassing.

I narrow my eyes as I scrutinize his face, attempting to gauge if he enjoys all that attention. Upon closer inspection, I find his smile is fake and doesn't seem to reach his eyes. It's subtle, but I can spot it.

I smile like that at home.

Vincent probably wishes they'd all leave him the hell alone.

"What's got you all smiley?" Lucas asks, eyeing me. He then looks between Vincent and me, an idea taking root in his head. "Oh, does *someone* have a crush on the Vincent kid?"

"Shut up, Lucas," I snap, refocusing my attention on the food in front of me.

"Bee? You have a thing for Mr. South Africa over there?" Jones asks, looking curious.

"Oh my gosh. Just because someone finds someone else attractive, doesn't mean they have to automatically be into them." I sound defensive; all I can do is stare into my food.

"Well, at least now we know she's moved on from you," Lucas says, tapping Shepherd on the shoulder.

Seriously?

It gets quiet and awkward.

I don't dare look in either Shepherd's or Evelyn's direction. Lucas can be so annoying, it's a wonder sometimes that we're friends. If it wouldn't look weird as hell, I would get up and leave right now!

I don't say another word for the rest of lunch.

When I'm finally done eating, I get up to throw out the contents of my tray. But I run into Vincent at the trash receptacle.

"Beanca, right?" he asks, startling me.

"Yeah," I reply, my stomach doing backflips.

"Vincent. From first-period piano class," he replies.

As if I could forget. "Oh yeah, right."

"I wanted to officially introduce myself," he says, holding his free hand out.

I accept it after placing my tray in the receptacle.

He throws his trash out, and when I turn to leave the cafeteria, he falls into step beside me.

"I know it might seem strange me coming up to you, but you just seem friendly," Vincent says.

That's the first time *anyone* has said that to me.

"Well, that makes one of us," I say.

"What?" His brows knit together in obvious confusion.

"I'm not generally thought of as a friendly person. But, I'll accept your compliment for what it is. Thank you."

"You seem that way to me," he says.

We turn into the entrance of the stairwell leading to the classrooms on the second floor.

"Anyway, I was thinking," he continues. "Since we have piano together, we should get to know each other. I noticed you glancing at me during class. I wanted to let you know you don't need to be shy around me."

Whoa! He'd noticed that? How freaking embarrassing. Now the guy probably thinks I'm interested.

Just great.

"Who says I'm shy?" I counter. "I'm *the* furthest thing. I go after what I want." The fake confidence I infuse into my last statement surprises even me.

"You're feisty. I like it," he says with a wicked grin. "Here, let me get your number." He pulls his phone out.

"Who said I'm willing to just hand my number out to you? I don't even really know you, remember?"

"That is true." He frowns, drags his bag off his back and then pulls out a pen. He rips a sheet of paper from one of his journals and jots something down before offering it to me. "Here's my number. Whenever you feel comfortable, text me yours."

"Seriously?" I ask, incredulous.

This guy.

"*I go after what I want,*" he says, repeating my words. He then takes my hand, places the paper into it, then closes my hand in his. He then squeezes my fist, releases it, and leaves me standing on the steps.

LUCAS

This Vincent guy rubs me the wrong way.

I don't know if it's some vibe he's giving off, or if it's the singular way he went after Beanca when she left the cafeteria the other day. It seemed calculated in some way, and not completely without artifice.

It hasn't even been a week, and all the cheerleaders are already singing his praises.

Which makes me more skeptical.

This guy waltzes in here our senior year and *already* he's the talk of the town. Something's up. I don't know what it is yet, but there has to be something.

"Hey, what do you guys think of this Vincent kid?" I ask John and Dudley, a few players I'm friends with, as we hang back in the locker rooms after football practice.

"He seems cool to me. Why?" John replies.

"I don't get it," I say, my aggravation evident. "It's only been a few days and he's already risen to King Simba?"

"Cut him some slack," Dudley says. He always wants to see the best in everybody, when sometimes there's just no good to see.

"I can see what you mean," John says. "But girls can be basic. They see a good-looking guy who can hold a conversation and they're ready to drop trow. I mean, that's how I get 'em." He laughs and Dudley shakes his head, chuckling along.

"One day you're gonna wish you learned how to value these ladies," Dudley says to John as he sobers up. He walks away, heading to the showers.

Maybe I'm too suspicious.

I head over to Ricardo's for tonight's jam session. I have only two hours to burn. I need to go home afterwards and ensure my mom is situated.

"There he is," our drummer, Mickey, says as I approach Ricardo's makeshift garage studio.

It's not like Ricardo's place isn't big enough to hold us in one of its many rooms. Dude chose the garage for its acoustics.

"Lucas," Mickey continues. "We're like half an hour behind schedule no thanks to you."

"He had football practice. Relax," Michelle says, in my defense. "How many of you play a sport after school?" she asks. When no one answers she gives them all a look. "Exactly. Since Luke is here now, let's just start."

We practice for the next three hours, and by the time I'm heading out it's already eight thirty. When I check my phone I notice I have a missed call.

Oh hell.

I redial the number and it goes straight to voicemail.

"Guys, I've gotta go."

"I swear, you're always heading out as soon as we're done," Michelle complains.

"Sorry, it's an emergency," I say, jogging over to my truck. I call the number twice more and it still goes to voicemail.

When I finally start up the engine, I notice two unopened voicemails. One is from our secretary, McCall, and another is from some guy at Lilac's. It's another one of those dragging-Mom-from-the-bar nights.

After listening to McCall's voicemail, I could hug a tree. She's finally found a therapist who makes house calls. According to her, not only is he well-sought after, having had success with a majority of his clients, he's apparently a decorated author of bestsellers on healing a fractured mind.

I'm elated and in a way better mood than I usually would be having to retrieve my mom yet again from Lilac's.

My mood instantly takes a nosedive, however, when I enter the place and notice an older gentleman sitting next to her at the bar. I can only see the back of his head, but he's pretty big, though, with an athletic build. I can tell he's well-off by the expensive cut to the suit he's wearing.

Whatever he's selling, we're not buying.

I make a quick beeline over to them. "Come on, Mom." Placing an arm around her waist, I help her up from the stool, paying no attention to the guy.

"Lucas … why are you here?" she asks, her words slurred. "Isn't it … a school night?"

"Do you need some help?" the man in the suit asks, his voice an exact match of his stature. He rises and reaches an arm out to steady her. "I can carry her to the car."

"No," I say. "Thank you, but I think we're good."

The moment my mom stumbles, the guy instantly lifts her from grasp. He carries her out of the bar without breaking a sweat, and like a toddler, I'm left to follow behind them.

I should be grateful for the assist, but I'm irritated. "I said we didn't need your help, sir," I say to his back.

"Where's your car?" he asks, ignoring my statement.

"Right over there," I reply. The sooner he drops her into the truck the sooner we can leave.

When he places her in, he's so gentle with her that it gives me pause.

Who is this guy?

"I'll leave my card," he says, damn near reading my mind. Taking a business card from his wallet, he places it in my truck's console before turning to me. "The name is King Bridges. King works fine." He holds out a hand to me and I shake it. "Make sure she gets the card when she sobers up. Once you let her know King helped her, she'll want that card."

Some other dude, in an equally expensive black suit, appears by his side and whispers something to him. I warily observe them both, ready to defend myself in case either of them tries anything.

When King turns and leaves with the other man, I briefly watch them before jogging over to the driver's side of my truck.

That was … odd.

Who was the other guy? And how important is King Bridges anyway? Does he have security on retainer?

As soon as we arrive home some time later, Keenan gets Mom from the truck and I head straight to the study. I hop on the computer and start looking into King's identity.

I stagger back when I find article after article about him. The guy is a business tycoon who owns real estate worldwide. Over the years he's made some pretty impressive investments that have skyrocketed his global status and financial standing.

To say he is a billionaire is an understatement. Dude makes money just by breathing.

I sit back in the office chair wondering what the hell a guy like that wants with my mom.

Chapter Three

BEANCA

"*B*eanca!" Dad yells from downstairs. He sounds upset, which is his customary mood where I'm concerned.

I wonder what I did this time. "Yeah, I'm on my way down!"

I get downstairs and am mortified to see Vincent standing beside my dad.

It's been about three weeks since school started and he and I have been hanging out on campus after school, practicing our music for our upcoming recital. He's an amazing piano player and we collaborate well together. I've helped him improve his pacing with the more classical pieces, while he's helped me highlight parts of my performance for when I get in front of recruiters.

I have no earthly idea, though, why he's at my house.

How does he even know where I live?

"This young man says he's here to see you." Dad's eyes

bulge as he glares down at me. He's managed to keep a neutral tone in front of our uninvited guest.

I want to defend myself. Tell him I don't know why Vincent decided to show up here. But I think better of it. My explanation would be useless. He would still find some way to make this another one of my many shortcomings.

I smile at Vincent's friendly hazel eyes, then turn to my dad. "Thanks, Dad, we'll be in the study."

I usher Vincent into the study, then close the door before turning on him.

"What are you doing here?" I ask.

"Going after what I want," he replies, nonchalant.

I roll my eyes so hard I almost lose them. "Vincent, that's not funny."

"Who says I'm trying to be funny? Look, Jazmin told me how to get here. I thought, why not just call round to your place? She's friends with your sister, Beverly, is it?"

"Yeah," I reply, trying to keep the frustration out of my voice. "Vincent, look, you can't do this again. It's not cool. My dad was only being polite just now," I continue. "Why did you come to my house?"

"We didn't get a chance to practice today, and I remembered you saying you have a Steinway at home. I thought why not practice here?" he explains, strolling over to the piano.

"Call or text next time. Don't just show up to another person's house without notice or an invitation. I don't know how they do it in South Africa, but here in America we call first."

Grinning at me, he sits at the piano and gestures for me to come over to him.

I do, unable to stop myself from returning his smile as I sit beside him.

"Play something. Anything," he encourages, placing my hands on the keys.

I think for a few seconds before playing Waltz No. 2 by Shostakovich.

A moment later, Vincent takes over for the right hand and I continue playing the left. He's doing pretty well with pacing, and I look over at him, genuinely enjoying his company.

The study door opens while we're in the middle of *Swan Lake*, and I look up to find my sister there.

I immediately stand. "What is it?" I ask, walking over to her.

Beverly's blonde hair, a lighter shade than mine, hangs in loose curls just below her shoulders. Her eyes, a bright blue, shift over to Vincent.

I turn to look in his direction. "Hey, I don't think you two know each other. Vincent, this is my sister, Beverly. Beverly, this is Vincent."

She nods over at him as he pops up and comes from around the piano to greet her.

"I've heard a lot about you," he says, coming to stand beside me.

"Not from me," I say when Beverly looks at me through curious eyes.

"No, not from your sister. Jazmin's told me about you," he admits.

"Nice to meet you," she says politely before returning her gaze to me. "Can I talk to you for a second?" She pulls me along with her through the door.

"Vincent, give me a second," I say, as Beverly ushers me out into the hallway.

I don't know what she'll say and I don't want Vincent overhearing family drama, so I pull the door closed behind me. Just in case that's what this is about.

"When I ask you this, don't get all suspicious OK?" she says.

Which automatically puts me on guard, because what the hell?

"Is Jones … dating anyone?"

I look at her in confusion.

"I'm only asking because he's been acting weird around me lately. Like he doesn't want people thinking we're together."

"You *aren't* together, though," I say, wondering why she's even concerned with how Jones acts around her. They're hardly ever in each other's company without me around.

"I know that, Beanca," she says in frustration. "You know what? Forget it. Forget I asked."

Before she walks off, I stop her, responding truthfully to her initial question. "No. From what I know, Jones hasn't told us he's even into anyone let alone dating anybody." When she still looks worried, I continue, "For what it's worth, if he's acting differently around you, it's probably because he values you as a friend. He doesn't want his groupies getting any ideas about how close you two are. Those girls can get mean."

She smiles, relieved. We've known Jones since grade school, so it's understandable that she doesn't want anything to change between them now.

"What's that Vincent guy doing here?" Beverly asks, changing the subject.

"We're practicing. He's in my piano class."

"Are you sure that's all it is? You guys seemed pretty close when I walked in."

"Beverly, please don't. It's not like that."

"*He* probably wants it to be. The way he was looking at you—"

"Shh!" I say, putting a finger to her mouth.

She arches a brow and backs away, heading to the stairs. "*Whaaatever.* You heard it here first," she says grinning, her blonde curls bouncing over her shoulders as she climbs the stairs.

When I reenter the study, Vincent returns to the piano.

I rejoin him there and we continue playing *Swan Lake*. This time he's on the left. We play several other classical pieces up until dinnertime.

"I would invite you for—"

"No worries," he says interrupting me. "I showed up unexpectedly. I doubt your family would have known to cook for an extra mouth to feed. There's always a next time, right?"

He's so matter-of-fact, I can't help but tease him. "Who's to say there'll be a next time?"

I walk him to the front door.

"She's right, you know," he says abruptly.

"Who is?" I ask, unsure of the *she* he's referring to.

"Your sister," he answers, smiling down at me. "She's right. I'd like to be close to you. Or I should say, *closer* to you. I'd like that very much." His smile fades as he lowers his head, his face inching closer to mine. His lips are a breath away from my own when my dad clears his throat.

I startle, turning around to find him glaring at us.

"Beanca, please tell your *friend* goodbye and come see me. You know where I'll be." He stalks away, leaving a chill in his wake.

"I'll see you at school," I tell Vincent as we walk to the front door. I'm already dreading the rest of the evening.

He brushes a feather-soft kiss against my cheek before I can react. Turning, he practically skips down the driveway to his car.

I watch him drive away, and then close the door.

Mom's not home yet, and I can hear Beverly's music faintly coming from her room upstairs.

My feet are heavy as I make my way to my dad. Maybe if I walk slowly enough, Mom'll be here before I get to him.

As soon as I get to his den, Dad gets up from the sofa, walks past me and closes the door.

I stiffen.

"Some things never change do they?" he asks as he comes closer, removing his belt.

I don't look at him because I know it'll make him angrier if I do. He always says I'm a defiant little green-eyed devil, ignorant of how to respect adults.

"Why can't you be like Beverly, huh? She wouldn't dare invite a boy over to our house without asking!" he yells.

I flinch when he clamps down on my upper arms, the buckle of his leather belt imprinting into my skin.

"Stop it, Dad. You're hurting me." I squirm, trying to get him to let go of me. But that only makes him squeeze harder.

"It *hurts*? Well, Beanca, how do you think I feel when you repeatedly threaten the reputation of this family. Were you really going to kiss that boy out in the open like that? In *my* house?!"

I don't know why he's acting like our neighbors would have seen anything. We have house help, but they're not even here. He's clearly trying to find something to argue about. His day is never good unless he finds something to insult me over.

I know I only have to put up with this for one more year, but the thought of that doesn't make it any easier to deal with.

"Dad, we didn't kiss." I don't know why I said it. I know to remain silent when he's on one of his ego trips, but he's being unreasonable.

He removes his hands from my arms and squeezes my jaw in one large, roughened palm. "Not if it weren't for *me*. Let me tell you something. If you want to be a little whore, save it for when you're no longer under this roof. You got that?" He shoves my face, pushing me away from him.

"Don't call me that," I say through clenched teeth, daring to meet his gaze. He can call me whatever he likes, but I draw the line there. I've never even had a boyfriend.

"What the hell did you just say to me?" he asks, stalking after me as I back up, trying to distance myself from him. "Don't think I don't notice that you don't sleep here half the time. Since you haven't come up pregnant, I haven't made a fuss about it. But don't you ever dare summon another one of your *playthings* under my roof again."

"Are you serious? You think I'm going out sleeping with boys. I don't stay here because I can't stand the way you always look at me!" I scream. "The way you treat me! You're the reason I hate being in this house! You're the reason—"

He whips a hand up and slaps me across the face. "You bitch! Don't you ever talk to me like that! Knowing what I know, you're lucky I kept you under this roof. You're not even—"

"Baron. No, please."

I whirl around at my mother's voice as she dashes through the now open door.

"What are you two doing?" she asks in horror, looking between Dad and me.

"Your daughter has started inviting boys over to my house," he replies angrily, scowling at me.

Mom's gaze trails over to me, and I can see the sadness behind her eyes. I know she won't defend me.

"Your slut of a daughter has been leaving our house almost every other night going God knows where. Acting like a little whore, she comes home the next day without explanation of her whereabouts and we're expected to what? Act like we don't notice? She's a disgrace to this family. Always has been and always will be. I look forward to the day she leaves this house." He stalks out of the den.

Trust me I'm looking forward to that day, too.

Mom approaches me, touching a hand to the corner of my mouth. I wince, reaching up to touch the area. When I look down at my hand, there's a tinge of blood in my forefinger.

Dad's never hit my face before. But then I've never made it a habit of talking back to him. I guess the thought of eminent freedom loosened the chains that held my mouth imprisoned these past few years.

The older I get, the worse his temper becomes.

I may have to move out before I graduate.

The moment I turn eighteen, I'll leave this house for good. I don't see how we can both coexist under the same roof when he despises me this much.

"Mom, why does he hate me?" I ask quietly, not looking at her.

"He doesn't hate you, Beanca," she says, smoothing a palm against my cheek. "He's just upset. He doesn't mean any of it."

We both know that's a lie.

Instead of arguing with her, I brush her hand away and head to my room.

It's like a dam breaks as soon as I open the door to my bedroom. I cry silently, curling into a ball on top of my comforter.

I don't eat dinner and I don't change out of my clothes.

I try to find solace in sleep.

Chapter Four

LUCAS

I'm at the usual house party at Chase's place. We're in the back room where several other cheerleaders and players from our team are congregating.

I rode with Shepherd, Evie, and Jones, our designated driver for the night.

Spotting Michelle, I go over to her, passing a few people playing beer pong on the way.

"Luuuke, there you are." She reaches up, placing her arms around my neck. "I was wondering when you'd get here." Her auburn hair is in a top knot and her sapphire eyes dance as she smiles up at me.

"I told you I'd come," I say grinning at her. "I wouldn't miss one of Chase's parties. Are you kidding?"

She gets me a can of soda, and I pop it open and take a swig, the cool liquid making its way down my throat.

Chase comes over to us, and looks around in confusion. "Where's Bee?" she asks, when she only notices Michelle beside me.

"She didn't pick up when I tried calling her," I explain.

Beanca's been busy lately, hanging out with King Simba, and ignoring her friends.

Well, she hasn't been ignoring us, per se. She's just been spending more time with Vincent than with us.

Whatever makes her happy.

"That's strange," Chase says, her brows furrowed. "She said she'd be coming here tonight. You think Vincent showed up at her place again? Hopefully, he at least texted her this time."

"What?" I ask in surprise. What the hell would he be doing at Beanca's?

"She texted me that she was with him," Chase explains. "I thought when they were done they'd come straight here. But I guess they have more important things to do." She grins at us before returning to the group at the beer pong table.

Dude went to her *house*?

I've been to Beanca's house several times, but that's been for parties and little events her dad's *allowed* her and Beverly to have friends attend. I'd never, *ever* just show up at her place. What the hell was this guy's problem?

Excusing myself from Michelle's company, I leave the back room and head into the hallway.

I call Beanca, but she doesn't pick up, so I naturally call three more times.

"Lucas?" she finally answers.

Alarm bells go off when I hear her voice. She sounds like she's been crying.

"What happened, Bee?" I ask softly.

"Where—where are you?" she asks, and I can tell for sure she's been crying. She's avoiding my question.

"I'm at Chase's place. She said you were supposed to be here, but you weren't answering any of our calls," I say before continuing with my questioning. "She said Vincent showed up at your house again. Is that true?"

Her voice hitches, but she doesn't answer me.

"Beanca, I swear … tell me what happened to you." I lose my patience when she doesn't say anything. I know damn well something's wrong with her.

"Luuuke," Michelle says loudly, peeking out at me from the back room. "We miss you, come on back."

"You … should go back to them," she says before hanging up on me.

"Bee, no—" I clench my fist around the phone, rubbing my other hand against my neck. How the hell am I supposed to enjoy myself when I know she's hurt?

A thought comes to mind and I quickly follow through with it. I dial the number and the other end picks up almost immediately.

"Hey, Lucas, what's up?" Beverly asks cheerfully.

"Do you know what's up with Beanca? And did that Vincent kid have anything to do with it?" I don't have time for pleasantries.

"Huh? What's wrong with Beanca? Why do you think there's something wrong with my sister?" she asks, clearly confused by line of questioning. "Sure, she didn't eat dinner with us tonight, but she often doesn't. She's been in her room the whole time," she explains. "And no, I don't think Vincent caused anything. Why do you think that?"

"It's nothing," I say, not wanting to raise any unnecessary suspicions about the guy to Beverly.

"Why'd you think there was something wrong?" she asks.

"Never mind, Beverly," I say, avoiding her question. "Good night."

When we hang up, I frown. I'm pretty sure Beanca was crying, so what was it about if it wasn't to do with Vincent?

Michelle walks out of the back room, grabs hold of my arm and pulls me back inside. "Seriously you just got here and you're already not even here. Put the phone up and enjoy the moment," she pleads.

When the music gets louder, Michelle starts dancing on me. Placing my hands on her hips, she sways in front of me. I dance with her feeling myself relax a little.

"I want you to have some fun tonight," she says, covering my lips with her own. I return her kiss, absentminded.

There's this nagging feeling that something isn't right.

Not with Michelle. No, she's gorgeous.

With Beanca.

Beanca wouldn't have answered me had I not kept calling like a maniac. She's always hanging out with Vincent, and now she's crying herself to sleep. I remember her looking into scholarships and grants to pay her way through college when I know her parents are loaded.

Beverly seems just as clueless as I am.

However, I'm not a complete idiot. One of the perks of having an analytical mind is apt intuition. And my mind tells me something's off about what's happening in that house. Beanca is very private about certain things, so I don't know how I'll get it out of her.

I get home a few hours later, but I'm not tired so I head into the study. A few messages are waiting for me. I listen to them one after the other. My ears perk up when I hear a familiar masculine voice. I've only heard it one other time a few weeks ago at Lilac's.

My mother hasn't returned to the bar since that night.

Surprisingly, I think King unwittingly had a lot to do with her improvement. Of course, her therapist plays a significant role in her recovery process. Once she sobered up and I showed her King's business card, it was like a bucket of ice water was dumped over her head. She didn't explain how she knew the man, only that he'd been the client who had unceremoniously gotten her fired from her company. When I explained that he'd helped me get her out of the bar and into my truck, she'd looked at me with the oddest of expressions, a mixture of shock and wariness. She'd walked away then, mumbling something about sociopaths.

Since starting her sessions with the therapist, Dr. Spaulding, over the past few weeks, she's been doing great.

I listen to King's voicemail, and it's like the guy becomes even more of an enigma now than he was a few minutes ago. He's responsible for getting my mom fired, yet he turns around and offers her a position at *his* company. Couldn't he have thought about this a few months ago when she'd started spiraling?

I sit there wondering if he has some sort of savior complex, when Mom strolls into the study.

"I thought you were already asleep," I say, sitting up.

"I was trying to sleep, but decided since my body isn't tired, I'd come down," she explains. "Did you just get in?"

"About fifteen minutes or so ago." I rise and head over to her, then think better of it. "There's a message you need to hear." I turn the speakerphone on and start the voicemail playback. I cycle through the messages until I get to King's, allowing it to play out.

"That *bastard*." She begins pacing the floor. "Of all the asinine things to suggest."

"Mom, did he go out of his way to get you fired? Or was it something the company decided to do because he threatened to pull out his investments?"

"Does it matter?"

"Yes. If it's the former then he's got some kind of angle, some game he's playing. If it's the latter, I'd say he's acting out of remorse."

"Honey, I think it's likely a touch of both. I can't say if he knew *I* was a part of the team that got let go. I only know he wanted the senior manager out for negligence, and I happened to be that senior manager. I think if he'd truly known it was me, it might have given him pause. Either way, he caused more than a few people—people who weren't directly involved in his case—to lose their jobs, and that was a jerk move to make. Offering me a position now is a clear attempt at atoning for that mistake." She continues pacing.

I smile because I know my mother. Even though it'll initially crush her pride to work for the guy, she'll eventually cave.

Chapter Five

LUCAS

When I see Beanca at school the next day, it's not during our lunch since she skipped out on that. It's at the end of the school day, in the stairwell leading to the parking lot.

"Beanca!" I call out.

She's pretty much tried to avoid all of us today, which is impossible since she has second period with Shepherd and Jones. They both told me it didn't seem like anything was up with her. But they don't know about last night.

"Hey, Bee, wait up!" I yell again, catching sight of her signature ponytail, bobbing along as she goes down the stairs. Beanca swiftly disappears around one of the bends in the stairwell.

When I get to the landing, I notice she's racing down the stairs.

I'm sure she heard me.

"Beanca!"

She hesitates, then decides to keep moving.

At this point, I'm leaping down the stairs after her. How the hell are there so many of them? It's like they double up, multiplying each time I take a step down.

I know for a fact Beanca heard me, but she just doesn't give a damn.

I jump from the last step and pick up speed, running after her.

When I finally get to her and grab her upper arm, she winces, and I immediately let her go. "Didn't you hear me calling you?" I ask, looking into her vivid green eyes. They're my lie detectors. Anytime Beanca lies, her pupils dilate.

"Do you need something?" She tries to evade my question, but I refuse to be deterred.

"Beanca, you seriously didn't hear me yelling your name just now?" I narrow my eyes at her.

"I heard you," she replies, resuming the path to her car. "But I'm kind of in a rush right now. I can't talk."

"Why? What's up?" I walk alongside her. Her car isn't very far away from us, and I grow impatient when she ignores my question. "What the hell is your problem, Bee?" I ask, blocking her path.

"Don't talk to me like that!" she yells, before shoving me out of the way and stalking the rest of the way to her car.

I go after her.

She's upset. And the last thing she needs is me picking a fight with her. Usually, when she's in a mood like this, the sane thing to do is to let her be.

Usually.

Today, I'm not feeling particularly sane.

I get to her car, and as she clicks open the doors, I pull open the passenger side door and slide into the pink Mini Cooper.

"What are you doing, Lucas?" she asks, starting up the engine and purposefully not looking in my direction.

"What's wrong?" I ask, softening my voice.

"Nothing I won't get over in a few days." Her vague response gives me pause. She could be referring to her time of the month. I'm aware girls PMS at times. I have a mother.

But this isn't that.

"It's more than that," I say, more so to myself. "You've been avoiding me all day. You didn't show up for lunch and deliberately ignored me on the stairs. You were crying last night. Did something happen to you? Did that Vincent kid do something that got you in trouble?" I question, playing Sherlock Holmes.

When all she does is clamp her mouth shut, I sit there praying to God for patience, because the thin line that's left is fading fast.

"Beanca, what happened to you?"

When I touch a hand to hers where it rests on the gear shift, she removes her hand shakily and brings it to her mouth, covering it.

At the first sign of tears against her cheek, my chest seizes, and I reach over to hug her. My mind races as I try to figure out what I said or did to cause this.

I feel low as hell.

I hug her over against her seat, not knowing what to say.

She shakes against me with the force of her sobs. Still through all of it, she barely makes a sound.

After a few minutes, she sniffles and I release her. Kissing her forehead, I lean back and watch her, not daring to ask any more questions.

I bring my hand to her face, using the pad of my thumb to wipe at the residue of her tears. I search her face, and my gaze narrows on a scar at the side of her cheek. She must have used makeup to cover it because it's barely visible, but there all the same.

My jaw tightens and I want to break something. "How did that happen?" I ask, my voice quiet now because I don't want her to get defensive.

"It was my fault," she says. "I was rude, and I knew better than to talk back. It's nothing really. I was acting out of character." She says everything so quickly, so smoothly, I think she actually believes she deserved whatever her parents obviously did to her. "It's senior year and I guess I'm ready to be out of the house already."

Even though I'm relieved that it wasn't Vincent who did this—because I would have knocked his teeth in—it isn't any better knowing that it was her parents' doing.

"Nothing you said or did warranted this. It's—"

"I'm fine," she defends, interrupting. "It was barely even a cut."

"Oh yeah? And I guess that's why you had to use makeup to hide it, huh? I guess that's why you were missing in action all day and couldn't get out of here fast enough." I'm upset and I know this isn't helping the situation.

"You know what, Lucas? Get out of my car," she says, turning away.

When I make no move to leave, she moves the gear into reverse and backs out of the parking space. When I still don't move, she puts the car into drive, glides down the parking lot a few yards, and then stops the car.

"Get out," she deadpans, putting the car in park.

I stare over at her, resignation on my face.

This pisses her off and she's full on shoving at me. "Get out! Get out, Lucas! I said get the hell out of my car!"

I grab her wrists into one of my hands and raise her arms above her head before placing her fists against the headrest behind her. She glares at me through stormy jade eyes, made darker by her rising temper.

"Yes, Bee. You should be angry. But not at me." I place a palm against her cheek. "Whoever dared do this to you," I continue, sliding my thumb to her scar, faintly circling it, "they deserve your anger, not your tears." I drag my gaze back up to her eyes. "Only, if they put their hands on you again, they won't be facing just your anger. They'll have to deal with mine." I cup her chin, placing my lips on her cheek, on the scar there.

After a beat, I release her.

I don't think about why I felt the need to kiss her, and I don't question it either.

Getting out of her car, I watch as Beanca drives out of the parking lot.

BEANCA

"Chase, can I stay at yours tonight?" I ask, holding the phone to my ear while I pack.

She threw a house party at her place last night so I know there won't be another one for at least another week. I can't stay in my house tonight, they're having people over and it's exhausting pretending we're one big happy family.

"Sure! Bee, you know you don't have to ask," Chase replies. "I'm having a few people over for a movie night, remember? You can invite Vincent too, if you want."

Ugh. I forgot about the movie night.

"Chase, didn't you have people over last night?" I ask wryly.

"So? Listen, I get my work done and my parents don't care as long as we're responsible." Chase has an interesting family dynamic. She's the only child and her parents are rarely ever home. They hired a woman who comes and checks in on Chase from time to time, especially when they're gone for an extended period of time. It's crazy, because the woman drops in spontaneously, but Chase always seems to know when she's coming.

Her house is an estate home on one of the huge hills over-looking Paramount. Yeah, her parents are old money. A lot of their financial holdings are from owning land and crude oil.

I hang up with Chase and text Vincent.

Me: *Hey are you up for a movie night tonight?*
Vincent: *Sure, your place?*
Me: *Hell no. I'll be over at my friend Chase's place. I can text you the address.*
Vincent: *Perfect! You bringing anyone with?*
Me: *Like who?*
Vincent: *No one in particular lol*
Me: *Yes, three people in fact. I'm bringing me, myself and I*
Vincent: *Touché*

My sleeping arrangements for tonight handled, I set about packing my duffle bag.

I get my stuff into my car and am heading back toward the house when a black Bentley pulls into our driveway. I look over in alarm and quickly stride over to my front door.

Were the guests already arriving?

Damn it! I wanted to be out of here before they showed up.

Curiosity getting the better of me, I pause at the door and watch as a man in an ebony suit exits the driver's side and goes to open one of the back doors of the car. A taller middle-aged gentleman with light brown hair steps out from the back seat. He is very good-looking with an overall demeanor that screams importance.

He starts walking toward the house, and I hurry inside. I dash upstairs in search of my cell phone, retrieving it from where I forgot it on the bathroom counter.

By the time I get back downstairs, I can hear the maids talking in hushed tones.

"I've only seen him once, some years ago when Mrs. Carlyle first moved in here," one of the them says.

"I wonder why he's stayed away this long," another one chimes in.

I hop off the last step and when they notice me, they scatter, continuing on with whatever they'd been doing before their conversation.

I walk to the front door, but Dad stops me.

"You won't be leaving the house this evening, Beanca," he sneers. "There's been a change in the guest list, and it would be in your best interest to attend tonight's formal dinner."

I have no intention of staying here tonight. I'll risk the tongue-lashing from him if it means escaping this hellhole on a night like this. I'm not a thespian. There's no use in me sticking it out as part of the clown show.

Without a backward glance, I make a quick escape, slipping outside. I jog the rest of the way and am halfway to my car, when a hand encircles my arm.

Damn!

I didn't even hear Dad come after me.

I flinch, expecting to be slapped. But when no heavy hand falls, I look over my shoulder.

My jaw slackens when I find myself face-to-face with the wealthy gentleman I'd seen exit the black Bentley earlier.

He looks at me oddly and slowly releases my arm.

I absentmindedly rub where he held me, waiting for him to introduce himself.

"Were you leaving?" he asks instead, his manner now completely under control, his face a mask.

Up close, he's even more ridiculously handsome than I thought. His face is an exact replica of one of those Grecian statues of antiquity.

When I don't respond to his question, he looks directly into my eyes .

Those eyes.

They're the same shade of green as mine.

The fact endears me to him, giving him an air of familiarity. "Yes, I have other plans for the evening," I say, smiling up at him.

"That makes two of us," he says, before looking toward the entrance of the house. Anger emanates from his body as he watches my dad staring daggers at me from the front door.

I walk around to the driver's side of my car, remembering my mission to avoid being trapped here tonight. "Well, I hope you enjoy your evening, sir," I say politely before getting in. "I know I sure as hell will, away from this glass house," I mumble, pulling out of the driveway.

The closer I get to Chase's house, the more I dread having to return home eventually. I know Dad is going to lay into me. I try to put the consequences of my actions out of my mind, instead focusing on this temporary reprieve.

Chase lets me through the huge security gate to her multi-car driveway. I park and instantly notice that Vincent's car is already here, among others.

Free from the birdcage that is my house, I damn near skip to Chase's front door.

"Hey, Bee! Finally!" Chase says. "We're out back."

She ushers me to her backyard where there's a projector set up. I recognize some faces. Dudley and John, two of PSA's football players. Lexie, one of the girls Shepherd used to mess around with before Evelyn. And, of course, Vincent.

I immediately go to him.

"Well hello, gorgeous, nice to see you've finally made it here," Vincent says, embracing me in a tight bear hug. "I've missed you."

"Vincent, I just saw you yesterday," I counter in a teasing tone, gazing up at him.

"That's the problem, isn't it? And now it's the weekend. As in it *ended* my opportunity to gaze at this beautiful face of yours," he says, gently twisting my cheeks between his fingers.

They must learn how to master the art of flirting in South Africa. That coupled with his accent has my heart pounding away, setting cadence to the butterflies in my stomach. I eat up his words, feasting on them like some starved creature.

We move over to where everyone's lounging about. Some people are in their own lawn chairs, others are seated on patio furniture. A few are laid out on towels they've spread over the grass.

"I've already got our spot right here," Vincent says, leading me to a large towel, closest to the screen. It's also closest to the back entrance area of Chase's house, and in full view of everyone behind us. "You can use me as your human pillow," Vincent adds, patting his chest.

He's attentive and showers me with so much attention, I'm on the wings of the wind right now. He's also really cute. I have to look away sometimes because it can be a bit over-whelming.

"You two an item now?" John asks, seated in one of the lawn chairs not too far from us.

"If she'll have me," Vincent says before winking at me.

I'm about to respond when Chase announces she's putting the movie on. It's an old Western flick Dudley's been dying to see apparently. He and Chase have been getting closer this year and the movie choice tonight makes it even more evident.

"Did we miss anything?!" Lucas bursts through the back door a few minutes later. Michelle and some of the other members of their band file out from the doorway as well.

I don't miss the way Michelle is hanging on to Lucas's arm.

"Chase, rules were you don't start the movie until we're all here," Lucas says when he notices the opening credits are already rolling.

"*Rules are*," Chase says, putting air quotes around his words, "that you'd be here by eight thirty."

"Seriously?" Lucas lifts a wrist, indicating a silver watch. "It's only eighty forty. You could've given us a fifteen-minute courtesy." He then angles his head down to where I'm cuddled up near Vincent. "What's up, Bee. Vincent." His greeting is lackluster, and I don't miss the way he slides a hand over to cover Michelle's on his forearm.

She whispers something to him, and he turns to her. His

sudden smile dissolves whatever momentary annoyance he held about Chase starting the movie prior to their arrival.

I shift my gaze back to the screen, trying to find anything to look at but them. Michelle's made it obvious she doesn't like me. I haven't said anything about her nor have I ever done anything to her. But in this world I've learned that people didn't need a reason to dislike you.

Everyone gets situated as Chase restarts the movie.

After the first half hour, some people decide it's not their cup of tea, so they either head inside to talk or leave.

During one of the more boring parts of the movie, Vincent bends his head to my mine. "So, will you have me?" The look in his eyes is a mixture of hope and steady determination. "Don't think I didn't realized you still haven't answered."

A part of me wants to say yes, but the other part, the fearful side, believes that the moment he becomes my boyfriend, he'll eventually get bored and discard me. He'll find out I'm unlovable and he'll toss me aside like some washed-up toy. I don't think I can handle someone I'm interested in seeing the raw side of me, and then deciding to end what we have because of it.

I turn my head up to his, intending to make an excuse for why we should probably wait. But his mouth clashes with mine as he firmly covers my lips. My eyes widen and I'm about to lean away, when Vincent holds my face to his.

I suddenly become self-conscious, as he moves his lips across mine. I place a hand against his chest, and it's not long before he releases me, staring down into my eyes.

"I guess I have my answer, Bee," John whispers.

Vincent grins over at him then hugs me to his chest, before kissing the top of my head.

After the movie ends, we file into Chase's living room. I don't miss Lucas heading straight to and through the front door instead of remaining with the rest of us.

"Hey, Lucas, are you heading out?" I ask after him.

He doesn't acknowledge my question.

It's not like him to just ignore me, so I follow him out. When I finally catch up to him, he's halfway to his truck.

"Lucas." I grab on to the back of his shirt, tugging at it. "Are you leaving?"

He twists around to face me, his features tense, and his eyes a hard mask.

I'm not in the mood for another fight so I don't comment on his attitude.

"The movie was like two hours long, Beanca." He looks behind me at someone before continuing, "Plus, you seem to be doing just fine without me. Why does it matter if I leave?"

I turn to see Vincent striding over to us. Michelle also exits the house and quickly jogs past him.

"Luuuke," she whines, stepping between us, her back to me. "Where are you going?"

"I'm not going anywhere," Lucas says, smiling at her. His voice is mellow and in stark contrast to the sharp tones he employed with me a few seconds ago. "I just came to get my phone." He walks the rest of the way to his truck and pulls out his cell phone before holding it up and waving it at Michelle. "See?"

He could have just told me that.

I jerk when Vincent suddenly takes my hand. "It's a pretty night out, and we can actually see the stars up here. Would you like to go for a walk?"

We've been outside for the past two hours. Besides, I'm not in the mood for a walk. But Vincent is eager, so I'm hard-pressed to turn him down.

"Sure, why not?" Turning away from Lucas and whatever scene Michelle is trying to create, I clasp my hand tightly in Vincent's as we turn and walk along Chase's driveway. It's pretty big and we decide to walk the length to the entrance gate and back.

"Tell me about your family," Vincent says.

I want to groan.

I inwardly roll my eyes since my family is the last thing I would ever choose to talk about. I grin and bear it, choosing to talk about the one member of my family I can actually stomach.

"My sister, Beverly, is pretty sweet."

"Is she?" he asks, sounding genuinely interested.

"Yeah. We rarely argue and that's saying a lot considering our family dynamic."

"Is she also allowed to date?"

I'm caught off guard by the question.

"Yeah. Why wouldn't she be?"

"I don't know. It seemed like an issue when I came round to your house. Your dad wasn't—didn't seem—" It's as if it's hard for him to get the words out without offending my dad. "I thought if he acted that way when his eldest daughter had a guy friend over, he'd probably have a fit if the younger one wanted to do the same thing. Am I wrong?"

He's so far off base but I don't have the energy to correct him so I shake my head. The reason my sister is allowed to do anything she wants has nothing to do with me and everything to do with the fact that she is Beverly. She's the opposite of me, and that's why she *is* allowed to date.

"How about your family? Tell me about them," I say, steering the conversation away from me.

Vincent tells me about his childhood in South Africa. He doesn't have siblings but he'd lived near his extended family. "Plenty of cousins to roam around with. We were always getting into little spats though. That's where we differ from you and your sister. Speaking of, does she also play an instrument? What with PSA being an arts school and all."

I chuckle. "I'm pretty sure you've observed by now that not everyone who attends our school is there for the arts program."

"I notice. Strange that."

"It's not that strange actually. There are plenty of schools where it happens. At least here in America anyway. But to answer your question, Bev doesn't play any instruments. Although she does like the piano, among other instruments."

We talk for a few more minutes and make our return trip up to the house.

"I've got to head home," he says. "I live a good whiles from here, so I'll see you Monday." Vincent hugs, and then kisses me before adding, "I'll miss you tonight, beautiful."

He slides into his red Camaro and disappears down the drive.

Chapter Six

LUCAS

My mom started working for King and I don't know if it's the wisest decision she could have made.

Sometimes she comes home even later than me, which says a lot. I'm usually done with the band between nine and ten o'clock. She leaves the house at seven in the morning. That's more than a sixty-hour workweek, and I think it's starting to take a toll on her.

She's barely at home on Saturday mornings, when we usually go horseback riding together, enjoying creation and nature. And forget about seeing her on Sundays. That's her *beauty rest* day. The day she uses to catch up on all the sleep she's missed during the week. If I'm not up in Tallulah Falls, this awesome hiking and camping site, I'm usually busy with the band on Sundays.

Lately, I haven't been spending much time with my mom. For some people that might be OK. For me, it's not. When we go horseback riding, I get to pick her brain, reconnecting with her after a long week. I find out where her head's at and discuss personal stuff I can't talk about with my friends.

I've had a lot on my mind that I need to talk to her about and I'm hoping she'll be up for going to the stables with me today.

I knock on her bedroom door and when I don't get a response, I push in. "I'm coming in, OK?"

Her bed is empty but I hear the sounds of her shower running.

Good, she's already up. That's a good sign.

I tap her bathroom door next, just so she's aware I'm waiting in her bedroom.

When Mom emerges, she has a towel wrapped atop her head and she's in a purple robe. "Lucas, I know you want us to ride together today, but unfortunately I'll need to take a rain check." At my dejected expression she continues, "*But* I promise that this upcoming Saturday, we'll be back on schedule."

"Mom, but next Saturday I'm heading up to Tallulah with everyone."

"Oh that's right," she says, hitting her palm against her forehead. "There's so much going on, honey. I'm having a hard time keeping up." She ruffles my hair and heads back into the bathroom for her blow-dryer. "Was there something you wanted to run by me?"

"Yeah. Where are you going today, though?" I ask, noticing a white skirt and blazer hanging by her wardrobe.

"King has a business function this morning, which he told me about *last night*. I was of a mind to refuse, but in the end here we are."

"Wow. You're working on the weekend, plus you're on a first-name basis with him now?"

"You know, King and I have known each other since high school. It was awkward calling each other Mr. This and Mrs. That. Of course, we use the titles when others are around, but when it's just us we leave those off." She starts the blow-dryer and I can barely hear anything she says.

I wait for her to get done before continuing. "Mom, I have to ask you something."

"Mm-hmm, go ahead." She's seated at her vanity, flat ironing her wavy chestnut hair, hair the same texture and color as mine.

"Is it normal to feel annoyed at your best friend for hanging out with other people?"

She looks at me through the mirror of her vanity, contemplates for a little, and then says, "I suppose *some* jealousy is to be expected, especially if that friend starts to spend more time with those other people than with you."

"Mom, I said *'annoyed,'*" I state, correcting her. "I'm not in the least bit jealous."

She passes the flat iron through her hair. "Did you tell your friend how you're feeling?"

"I'm still trying to understand it myself," I reply truthfully.

"Well, honey, how do you know you're … annoyed?"

"I feel like ignoring her. I'm mad at her for spending so much time with this guy. Mom, she doesn't call or text to hang out anymore."

"Is this Beanca?" she asks, correctly surmising who I'm talking about. "If that's the case, then it's normal you'd feel this way. If she doesn't communicate with you and spends all her time with this new guy, you have every right to be somewhat upset about it. Why don't you talk to her about how you feel? I'm sure she'll understand." She turns to me after placing the flat iron on her vanity. "The one question I want you to ask yourself is, would you feel the same way if this were any other friend? If they treated you the way Beanca is now, would it affect you as much?"

I frown in confusion, contemplating her words.

"Let's take Jones, for example," she continues. "If he got a new friend and started hanging out with them, started texting you less, hanging out with you less, would you want to ignore him and feel as upset about it?"

"Well, I wouldn't be—," I say, raking a hand through my hair in frustration. "I don't know, maybe. Or maybe I'm just expecting too much from her. That's it. That's what it is."

"Honey, I think your feelings are valid," she continues, offering more advice.

When she reenters the room after getting dressed, she gives herself a once-over in the room's long standing mirror.

"Listen, don't overwork yourself, Mom," I warn.

She looks over at me as she pulls down the white blazer off a wooden hanger. "I'm not, honey, I promise. This upcoming week I'm not doing any more long hours. I'll be back in at about the same time as you."

By the time Friday evening rolls around, Mom has kept her promise. She really did make it home around the same time I did all week, even returning earlier than I did on some evenings. I hope this sticks because I hate seeing her strung out with no real time to enjoy life, smell the roses now and then.

I put my truck in park as Michelle, Ricardo, and Sloane, the girl he's invited, hop out. I step down from my truck and instantly inhale as I look up at the trees overhead.

Tallulah Falls.

It's not fall yet, but the trees signal that the season will change pretty soon.

"It's so beautiful," Michelle says, coming around to hug me. "Seriously, nothing beats this. Thanks for inviting me, Luke."

"*Us*," Ricardo adds. "He invited *us*."

Michelle side-eyes him and rolls her eyes.

I invited the whole band, but a couple of them already

had other plans for the weekend, so only Ricardo and Michelle were able to make it.

We unpack our gear and hike down to the river. Usually, the whole group meets here before participating in the first planned activity for the weekend.

We're evidently the first ones here, because when we get to the river, none of the guys from our football team are there.

"Let's go for a swim," Sloane suggests. She and Michelle strip down to their swimsuits and head into the water. Ricardo and I join them not long after since there's nothing much to do but wait around for the others to arrive.

After about an hour of swimming and playing around, we head back to the meeting spot.

I spot Shepherd and go over to where he's standing with Evie. We slap hands as he removes his shirt.

"Hey, Evie. He better be on his best behavior with you," I tell Evelyn, teasing her.

"He is," she says, laughing and giving me a side hug.

Shepherd reaches for her, placing a light peck against her neck before lifting her onto his back. The two head down to the river.

There are a lot of people here.

Michelle grabs hold of my arm as I look through the crowd. I find Jones, Dudley, John and a few other players and head over to them, leaving Michelle and the others to their own devices.

I chat with the guys, my eyes searching the other groups. I spot Chase, Lexie, and some of the other cheerleaders.

I frown when I notice Chase is here, but there's no sign of Beanca.

I want to take my phone out and text her to figure out where she is, but I think twice about it. If she'd wanted me to know, she'd have contacted me.

"Hey, where's Bee?" Jones asks Chase, when he also notices her absence.

"She says she's on her way," Chase replies. "She'll be here soon."

I try to put Beanca out of my mind. She didn't text our group chat to tell us she'd be here later than usual, and honestly, I don't care where she goes or who she decides to spend her time with anymore.

"Guys versus gals tug of war!" John yells out.

"Dude, no," I counter. "That doesn't even make sense. We'll easily smoke the girls, and you know that. Let's mix it up."

Dudley and the rest of the guys nod in agreement.

"Whatever. You guys are lame anyway," John says.

"Shut up," Lexie says, scowling at him. "You're lame for making such a ridiculous suggestion." She returns the finger he shoots at her.

With everyone back from the river, we figure out the teams, and start playing. The victor of each round goes against a new team until there's only one team standing.

My team is in the third round and we're winning. I'm giving it my all when Michelle places her arms around my waist, instead of on the ropes.

"What are you doing?" I ask her, mid-pull.

"The rope's starting to burn," she complains.

"Well then, go to the back of the line, but you can't pull *me*, or you're gonna make us lose." When she doesn't move, I warn, "*Michelle*."

She finally takes the hint and goes to the back of the line.

We keep pulling and after about another five minutes, we finally win.

"Hell yeah!" I growl out.

"Can we join?" His accented voice stands out among the crowd, and I instantly shift my gaze to ascertain Vincent's whereabouts.

I spot Beverly first before my eyes take in Beanca standing at his side. She's wearing jean shorts that fit her to perfection and her red silhouetted tank top draws my attention to her slim waist. Vincent's hand tightens against her there, hugging her against him.

I grind my molars together, my eyes narrowing as I see how Beanca's looking at him.

"Yeah, you can probably get on Lucas's team," Lexie suggests.

"No, we're almost done," I state, bridging no arguments. "We've only got one more round, so it doesn't make sense for you to join now. You just got here."

"Bro, you good?" Jones whispers to me, as we set up to battle the final team.

"Yeah. Why?" I ask. When he narrows his eyes, I say, "They *just* got here. Why the hell would they even want to participate in a game that's just about done?"

The final round is a cakewalk, and we win in under two minutes.

"We won," I say. "I call first dibs on the food."

Whoever wins the first activity of the trip gets to choose which communal item they get to control for the weekend. Everyone always choses food, because who gives a damn where we sleep?

We get to the campsite and set up the fire. I mosey over to where the food's laid out. I choose the hamburgers and s'mores for Michelle and me, and the rest of our team picks out what they want as well. I'm smirking by the time I sit around the campfire, feeling pretty good about my life right about now.

I try not to, but my eyes slide over to where Beanca and Vincent are sitting. Their chairs have basically morphed into one and he's holding her hand.

Shepherd was right when he told me last year that the moment Beanca found someone she liked, she'd move on from us.

I scowl.

Vincent squeezes her thigh and leans over to kiss her. I avert my gaze. For someone who's just entered a relationship with the guy, she sure as hell doesn't stop him from public displays.

Irritated, I train my gaze on the flames.

"Let's play two truths and a lie," Chase suggests. "Lucas, our rules please."

Grateful for the distraction, I go over what is and what isn't off limits.

"I'll start," Chase says.

"You always start, Chase," Shepherd argues. "Let someone else go first for a change."

Dudley defends, "If she wants to start there's no one to stop her. Go ahead, sweet—Chase."

I know I'm not the only one who heard that slip, but it's not like we all don't know they're dating.

"I'm a princess. I don't like cheerleading, and I'm a shoo-in for Stanford when I graduate." Chase grins, looking around at everyone.

"Easy, you're not a princess," John says.

"Duh," Chase laughs. "OK your turn."

The game keeps going until it finally lands on Vincent.

"I'm in love. I'm from South Africa, and I'm into music."

Everyone's quiet until Beverly says, "Vincent, it's two truths and a lie. One of them has to be a lie. You've never played this game before?"

"I'm aware of how to play the game. One of the things I've said is a lie."

I look at Beanca to gauge how she's taking this, because this dude is a moron.

She turns her head to him, and deliberately masks her expression. "I don't expect you to love me, so that's … the obvious lie."

"Bro," Dudley and John say in unison as they shake their head.

"What?" Vincent looks over at Beanca questioningly. He looks around at everyone and says, "The lie is that I'm from South Africa. I'm *not*."

Everyone looks at him confused.

Vincent clarifies. "I was born in England, Leeds to be exact. Then my father moved us to South Africa when I was about three."

He'd purposefully done that. But why?

I glare at him because I'm starting to believe he truly has issues. What was his angle? Because he clearly had one.

Beanca quickly rises to her feet and walks out of the circle. Vincent gets up to go after her, but I stop him. "Dude, stay right the hell there."

When Michelle gets up as if to follow me, I give her a quelling look before going after Beanca.

BEANCA

"Beanca, wait up," Lucas says.

My path is a blur. I left the campfire because I wanted to be alone. I don't want to talk to anyone, least of all Lucas.

"Leave me alone," I say, trying to keep my voice neutral.

Vincent hurt me. I don't know if he intended to, but he did.

Was he trying to find a roundabout way of telling me he loved me? Because I don't believe it, and I wouldn't have believed it even if he'd come right out and said it.

"Stop." Lucas spins me around. When he sees my tears, he hugs me to him without another word.

I don't want him or anyone else seeing me like this. It's embarrassing. I try to get my emotions under control as he holds me tighter, closer.

When he tugs gently on my ponytail, I lift my head from his shoulder but keep my gaze trained on his chest. I realize he's shirtless. He flexes his pecks and I immediately look up at him.

"Like what you see?" he asks, grinning at me. Leave it to Lucas to joke at a time like this.

"You're ridiculous." I smile, despite myself. Taking my arms from around him, I swipe at my face.

His hands remain on my lower back, anchoring me to him. I feel a sense of security in that. Security I didn't feel when Vincent suggested he loved me.

"Beanca," Lucas says after a while, his voice low.

I don't want a lecture from him so I place my arms around his neck and hug him again, hoping to delay the inevitable.

He hesitates for a second before smoothing his palms up my back and around my torso, holding me against him.

I need this right now, him holding me like this. It makes me feel … calm, like I'm back to myself again. Maybe that's why I've been so emotional. I probably just missed my friends. I've been MIA of late and I haven't been going to Lucas's for our shared readings or sleepovers. I don't even know what's going on with Jones or Shepherd. Instead, I've been juggling my time between spending it with Vincent, practicing for my recital, and applying for schools and scholarships.

"I'm sorry," I say.

Lucas releases me with a frown. "For what?"

I start absentmindedly playing with one of the loops in the waistband of his Levi's. "Because. I've been a sucky friend. I wasn't intentionally ignoring you guys. It just sort of happened with all that's been going on."

"What's been going on?" he asks, gently covering my hand with his. He doesn't let go, but hauls me next to him so we're both side by side, looking out to where the trees meet the darkness of the horizon. There are a few stars out tonight and glancing over at Lucas, I notice how the cool breeze tousles his hair, whipping it ever so slightly against his face.

I fill Lucas in on what's been going on. It's more of the

same really. The only change is the amount of time I realize now that I've been hanging out with Vincent. Most of it is after hours at school, since I never dared invite him to the house. We'd practice for a few hours then we'd just do homework and talk. We're still not official, even though he'd like us to be. I have my hang-ups, and what he did tonight made me more reluctant to be his girlfriend.

I don't expect Vincent to love me, and I told him as much. Real love carried weight, responsibility, staying power. In my life, love has proven itself fickle. When applied it can be powerful. I witness that in the devotion my parents have for Beverly. But when lost, it's damn near gone for good.

I've lived that.

I am living that.

"Why were you crying, Bee?"

"Because, I don't want Vincent to love me," I reply.

"What do you mean? W—Why?" Lucas squeezes my hand and turns me to face him.

"Because it doesn't last."

When he doesn't say anything, I attempt to pull my hand free from his, but he tightens his grasp.

"Beanca, that's … not true." He takes my chin and turns my face up to his. His expression is an odd one I can't place.

"Yes it is, Lucas. Sooner or later I'll end up doing something that'll make him not love me anymore. That's just how life is. Why do you think so many people end up breaking up, divorcing?"

His grip slackens slightly, and I let go of his hand.

He's silent for a beat before continuing. "Love is deep and long-lasting. You don't have to *do* anything to earn someone's love or to keep it. It's freely given." He looks away from me, then adds, "It isn't based on whatever flaky idea you have of it or what you've learned from some show you've watched."

Leave it to Lucas to ruin a perfectly good conversation.

"You're such a jerk." I turn to go, but he grabs hold of my elbow.

"Are you serious? I'm not a *jerk*. That douchebag you rode in here with is sure as hell one though."

I've called Lucas a jerk before and he's never reacted like this. I'm upset and I should just yank myself free and head back to the others.

"Are you OK?" I ask instead, using sarcasm in an attempt to understand his overreaction. "Did I hit a nerve?"

When he doesn't answer, but releases me and looks away, I've got my answer.

"Is this about Michelle?" I ask.

He shifts his gaze back to me, his face confused. "What does Michelle have to do with this?"

"I don't know. You looked pretty annoyed with her during your little tug-of-war tournament. Did you two have a fight? Is there trouble in paradise?"

"Why do you care how I feel about Michelle? *You* have Vincent."

"Oh I *don't* care actually. You can go marry her for all I care."

"Whatever, Beanca," he says, turning. "I'm heading back to camp."

"Well that makes two of us." I stalk past him, then quicken my pace when he catches up to me.

Chapter Seven

BEANCA

*I*t's the day of my piano recital and everything that could go wrong, has already.

First, my dress didn't arrive on time. So I had to buy one from our local department store. And now, the recital has been pushed forward an hour due to some hiccup in venue scheduling, so some of my friends may not be able to catch my performance. I've been a nervous wreck all day and I haven't eaten anything but a measly cereal bar I tossed into my bag this morning.

I'm the next performer.

From my position backstage, I peek into the audience, searching for my parents. Out of everyone invited, I want them here tonight. They've heard me practicing at home, but a stage performance isn't the same. My dad is a lost cause, but a part of me still wants him to be proud of my accomplishment.

When I don't spot my parents, I search for Beverly's mop of blonde curls. I don't find her either, so I head back to the dressing room to retrieve my phone. Smoothing my hands down the scarlet silk of my gown, I then run them lightly through my hair. The soft locks fall in waves down the skin of my back, concealing the open cut of the dress. Dad hates it when I wear my hair this way, but he would hate it even more if he saw my back uncovered.

If the dress I ordered had arrived on time, I wouldn't have to improvise like this. I wanted to wear red. The other dresses I saw at the mall didn't cut it, so I had to get this one. It's important for me to leave a lasting impression tonight.

My future depends on it.

Our school's music department heads told us there'd be recruiters present. Tonight is a pretty big deal.

I grab my phone and dart out of the dressing room, returning to my original spot backstage. Peeking out again, I smile when I find a fully occupied row with my friends. Chase, Lucas, and Jones were all able to still make it, even with the last-minute time change.

I still don't see my family. I quickly text Beverly to find out where they are and why they're not here yet. It's almost my turn to perform.

The audience erupts in applause when Jazmin completes her performance. She did an amazing job playing Piano Concerto No. 20 by Mozart.

"Jaz, congrats! That was awesome," I say.

"Thanks. Will someone help me with these?" She unloads a few bouquets to the staff. "My family can be a bit overkill sometimes." She laughs, taking a few single stems out and sniffing them.

It dawns on me that Beverly just missed her friend's performance.

"Our next performer is Beanca Carlyle," our teacher announces.

I hand Jazmin my phone and step out on stage, walking slowly. I attempt to stretch out the seconds in hopes that my family, by some miracle, will appear in the front row. My entire performance is forty-five minutes but I want them here for the whole thing.

I try to search the audience one final time, but am hindered by the stage lights.

"Beanca is a senior in our program here at PSA. She will soon be eighteen and enjoys performing classical, fast-paced pieces. Some of her favorites are by Mozart and Beethoven. She graces us with two pieces from the latter this evening." Our teacher exits the stage, gesturing for me to start.

I take my seat, looking out into the room again. The audience is an ocean of darkness, and I give up trying to find my parents. Inhaling deeply, I caress the piano's keys, feeling their coolness beneath my fingers. I close my eyes, letting the music take over as the notes become me. Beethoven's *Moonlight Sonata* permeates my being.

After fifteen minutes, I end the first piece and transition into my second, Beethoven's *Sonata Pathétique*. I glide and sway as the music moves me. There's no one in the room but me and this piano. At the first sensation of water against my cheek, I become a vessel on the leading strings of the music.

Half an hour goes by easily, and I rise to my feet, bowing as the audience cheers. The staff collects the flowers from the edge of the stage as people bring them to the front.

I walk off stage and head back to my dressing room.

"You were amazing, Beanca!" Jazmin smiles as she hands me my phone. A few others touch my arm offering their congrats and words of praise.

"Thanks, guys." I rush past them and into the dressing room.

My reflection is ghastly as I give myself a once-over in the mirror. Dark mascara lines streak down my face. I reach for one of the makeup wipes and clean them away.

Finally checking my phone, I find two missed calls and a few texts. Mom tried calling me about twenty minutes ago.

I check my texts first.

Beverly: *So sorry. Dad brought us to some restaurant.*

Beverly: *I don't know what's happening, but he's ordering food.*

Beverly: *I'm trying to catch an Uber, because this is beyond ridiculous.*

Beverly: *Almost there.*

Beverly: *Here.*

Beverly: *You're amazing, Bee!*

I quickly listen to the voicemail, hoping that my parents made it too.

Mom: *Beanca, I'm sorry, darling, but we can't make it tonight, OK. Something's come up and …*

I slowly collapse into the dressing-room chair behind me. The phone slips from my hand and crashes against the floor tiles.

I bring my gaze up to my reflection.

My eyes are dry.

They stay that way as I grab the phone off the floor and collect my purse.

Something in me hardens like granite.

"Beanca, where are you going?" Mrs. Smith, one of the music teachers from our school, asks as I stalk past her.

Technically, we're not allowed to leave until after the final performance. "I'm just going to the audience restroom. The one back here is occupied," I lie.

She doesn't give me grief as I exit the backstage area and head into the hallway.

"Hey, beautiful, where're you off to?" Vincent asks, blocking my path. I was wondering where he went. He'd disappeared right before I was about to go onstage.

"I have to get something from my car." The lies come easily now.

"Would you like me to come with?"

"No," I reply instantly. "Uh, you didn't perform yet."

"I don't perform for another hour," he counters.

"Vincent. Thank you, but I'll be right back."

I take one of the emergency exits to avoid any other potential obstacles.

I breathe easy when I'm finally outside. I walk to the back parking area but pause when I recognize one of the cars. It's the same black Bentley that came to my house the evening I escaped to Chase's movie night.

The Bentley is parked in the VIP area near the right entrance of the building. The green bridge logo on the front plate is a dead giveaway. There's no mistaking it. That's the same car.

That man is here?

Whatever.

I keep it moving and shoot a text to the group chat.

Me: *Hey thanks for coming, guys.*

Shepherd: *Evie and I just got here.*

Jones: *Dude, you're so late. Bee already performed.*

Shepherd: *Damn! Sorry, Bee.*

Me: *You're OK.*

Lucas: *You were beautiful tonight, Bee. Sounded even better.*

Me: *Thanks, Lucas.*

Jones: *I second that!*

I change as soon as I get in the car, pulling on a pair of jeans and throwing on a white tank top. I pull out of the parking lot not knowing where I'm going exactly, but I don't care. I'm feeling impulsive.

Some minutes later, I drive by a beauty salon, and a thought occurs to me.

I go for it.

I park, hop out and head inside.

"Good evening, dear," the hostess says as I enter.

"I'd like to change my hair color. Can you guys fit me in?"

"Oh, but you've got such gorgeous hair. Why ever would you want to change it? You know blondes are all the rage."

"Black. I want jet-black."

I don't want to be *anything* like them. Even though I can't do anything about my face, I *can* do something about my hair.

My mom and dad are blondes, and my sister inherited my dad's curly hair. My mom's hair is bone straight, and mine is somewhere in between.

At the woman's shocked expression, I say, "Look, if you guys can't do it, I'll just go somewhere else."

"No, no. We can do it. It's just why ever would you want to—"

"I'll take you right over here, miss." A petite brunette stylist ushers me over to her chair, while giving the hostess a stern look.

"You said jet-black?" she asks politely.

"Yes, please."

"It'll actually contrast well with the paleness of your skin," she compliments.

That's not why I'm dying my hair, but whatever. I'm aware that in this line of work, compliments keep clients.

She works on my hair for the next two hours, and when she's done and I look at myself in the mirror, the image looking back at me is so striking, I barely recognize myself. My green eyes stand out like crazy now and my skin is almost translucent against the stark contrast of my hair.

I smile. "I love it!"

"You look great!" the brunette says.

My parents wanted a black sheep, well now they've got one. I have no Fs to give anymore.

Still acting impulsively, I walk down the strip to find a tattoo parlor not far from where I parked. There are two artists available when I enter the parlor. All the other chairs are occupied, with some people behind privacy curtains.

I have an idea of what I want.

Green-eyed devil.

That's what my dad had called me on several different

occasions. I'll show him how much of a green-eyed devil I can be.

"I'd like some musical notes behind my left ear. Can you make one green? I want it the same shade as my eyes."

"Got you," the guy doing my tattoo says. He pulls out a portfolio and flips through a couple of pages. "Choose which notes you want."

By the time I leave the tattoo parlor, I feel so liberated. I want to keep chasing the high.

They don't deserve your tears.

Lucas said those words, and I can finally understand them. I can finally embody them. My parents would never love me the way they love Beverly, and the sooner I come to terms with that reality, the better.

When I return to my car, my cell phone vibrates in the console.

It's Beverly but I don't answer. I'll text her later. What I want is a drink. I call Chase but she doesn't answer. I dial her again.

Still no luck.

My phone vibrates and I'm excited because I think it's Chase. It's not. It's a text from Lucas.

Lucas: *Where'd you run off to?*

I notice a string of other texts he's sent me before this one.

Lucas: *Did you leave?*

Lucas: *Where are you?*

Lucas: *Beanca.*

Lucas: *??*

The group text shows another few messages.

Jones: *Hey, Bee, I just checked backstage.*

Shepherd: *Bee, you left?*

Lucas: *You left?*

Guilt creeps into my conscience. I should've told them I was leaving when I did. But I wanted to be alone, and I know they would've come after me.

Me: *Sorry guys. Yeah, I left. It's a long story.*
Jones: *No worries. Bev is trying to reach you.*
Me: *Are you with her now?*
Jones: *No.*
Shepherd: *Evie and I left not too long after it ended.*
Me: *I'll call Bev later. Thanks for coming, guys. It means a whole lot.*
Lucas: *Where are you?*
I text Lucas next.
Me: *Hey I'm coming over tonight.*

There's no way in hell I'm going home. And since Chase isn't picking up, Lucas's place it is.

I groan.

Lucas hasn't kept alcohol there since his mother's struggle a few months back.

I get to his place about half an hour later but he isn't there. Keenan, one of the groundskeepers, lets me in.

Not even ten minutes go by before Lucas arrives.

"Beanca, I can't believe—" He stops short when he sees me.

I self-consciously rake a hand through my hair, my heavy tresses cascading over my shoulders and back. I've decided to wear it this way from now on. Not because my dad hates it, but because *I* like it better this way.

"What did you do?" Lucas asks, his eyes widening.

"You hate it," I say, a little dejected.

"No. I—I love it. I think you look great," Lucas says. "Do *you* like it? 'Cause that's all that really matters."

I bite my lower lip and smile, nodding my head. "I actually love it this way." I go over to him and flip my hair away from my left ear. "Look," I say pointing to the adhesive covering my new tattoo. "I just got my first one."

"Whoa," he says, placing his hand against my neck. He turns my chin up with his thumb then folds my ear back, trying to peer through the adhesive. He carefully lifts a taped edge, then puts it back in place. "Music notes." He smooths his fingers over where the adhesive meets my skin before releasing me.

The familiar way Lucas touches me has never made me feel odd. But somehow what he did just now felt intimate. "Yeah," I say, trying to sound nonchalant. "One of them is green."

"It's cute," he says, walking past me and over to the office desk in his study. "So this is what you were doing all these hours? Dying your hair and getting tattoos." He sifts through mail. Lucas in this room, like this … seems so mature. He's so unlike his age. So much more like … a man.

Feeling like some rebellious teenager, I fidget and look away from him.

"While everyone was sitting there after your performance, waiting for the show to end, you were already gone." He sits down. "Like I said, you played beautifully. I just wish you told us you were leaving." There's a hint of agitation in his voice. "Why did you leave?"

I bring my attention back to him as he opens a piece of mail. Lucas is still in formal attire, a charcoal suit and white button-down. His short chestnut hair falls over his forehead. At my lack of an answer, his head comes up and his blue eyes connect with mine.

My stomach does this strange flip and I immediately tear my gaze away because what the hell? Lucas is my friend. We're friends. That's it. Right?

"Because my mom and dad decided they'd rather have an early evening meal than come to my recital. I didn't want people asking for them when everyone else's parents were there. It's embarrassing."

He doesn't respond.

I continue. "You're the one who said they didn't deserve my tears. If I'd stayed, they would have had them. I wanted to go *anywhere* but stay there tonight. Do something that *I* wanted to do."

"So the hair, the tattoo? Beanca wanted to do those things?" he asks, rising from his office chair. "It has nothing to do with the guy you're involved with? Changing for him in some way?" He approaches me, searching my face.

"What?" I frown up at him. "Why would I change for some guy?"

"I don't know, Beanca. Maybe because you haven't really paid much attention to the rest of us for a while now, which isn't like you. Even after we talked about it, nothing really changed now did it? It's not that far-fetched to think you'd do this for him."

By him, he means Vincent.

"Just because Vincent and I are interested in each other doesn't mean I'd do all this just to please him. We're just friends," I explain defensively. "Look, did you hear the part where my own parents didn't even show up today?"

"I did, but I guess I missed the part where that had anything to do with changing your hair color and getting a tattoo," he replies. "Unless of course you think this will turn back time and get them to show up."

I don't get it. How did a perfectly good conversation turn into this?

I shake my head. "And I guess *I* missed the part where you turned into an asshole." I turn away from him and walk to the door.

I don't get a chance to leave the study, because Lucas strides ahead of me and blocks my exit.

Chapter Eight

LUCAS

After the recital we went searching for Beanca backstage. She and Vincent were conspicuously missing from the stage when all the other students took their final bow.

We found out from a couple of instructors that the two had left before the show ended. It frustrated me that she left without saying anything to us. I mean, how could she have left when she was the one we came there to see? It was incredibly selfish on her part.

I brought flowers for her. I wanted to capture the memory in videos, photographs. Beanca looked so beautiful tonight. She played with such passion. I *felt*, rather than listened to the music. There were a few moments where everyone else disappeared, and all I saw was her, her movements, and her emotions with every shift in the music. She teared up on her second piece, causing my chest to seize up. I wanted to go to her in that moment.

But then, she left without saying anything.

With Vincent.

When she reached out and said she was going to my place, I was tempted to reject her, tell her my house was off limits tonight. But I didn't have it in me to do it.

I was with Michelle at the time. She called me about needing a jump start because she was stranded outside of town. I ended up calling a company to tow her car and paying for a loaner she can use. In all that time, my mind kept going back to Beanca leaving with Vincent.

On my way home, I came up with a million different ways I'd tell her about her selfishness. But when I entered the house and saw her, her newly dyed hair, her tattoo, and how excited and happy she was, I faltered.

But then I ask her about why she left and she gives me some crap about her parents not showing up.

Jones, Chase, and *I* were at her recital.

"And I guess *I* missed the part where you turned into an asshole." Beanca turns away from me and walks to the door.

I brush past her and block her path. "I am not an *asshole*. Take that back," I grind out.

"You're sure as hell acting like one," she replies, folding her arms in front of her and glaring up at me.

I chuckle at the irony of her words. "Trust me, Beanca, you're the last person to call someone an asshole."

"What the hell does that mean?"

"Do you even care that you left the rest of us at *your* recital, while the whole time you were off traipsing around town getting your hair done and doing God knows what else with Vincent?"

Her expression changes to incredulity.

"And don't even mention your parents not showing up because it's been established that they're flaky where you're concerned. If it was family you wanted there, what about Beverly?"

"I don't need this," she says, attempting to get around me and to the door.

I back up against it, closing it behind me.

"Get out of the way, Lucas. I'm leaving." She curls her hands into fists at her sides.

"Not until we finish our discussion," I counter.

"Oh, was this a discussion? It sounded more like one of your lectures to me." She sighs, looking exasperated. "Look, I didn't come here to fight with you."

"*I'm* not trying to fight with you."

"So what are you trying to do?" she asks, raking both hands through her hair. "And for the record, I didn't go anywhere with Vincent."

"Don't lie to me, Beanca," I warn. "It's not like you, and it's completely unnecessary."

She may ignore me from time to time, but I draw the line at outright lies.

"I'm not lying!" she yells, scowling at me before going over to stand by the sofa beside my desk. A few seconds later, she then starts pacing the room, detailing everything she's done since she left the recital.

Apparently, she left Vincent there and was by herself the whole time.

"I didn't even know he left until you said it. Why would I lie about that?" She stops, facing me again, her eyes earnest.

I believe her.

And I guess she's right. There's no reason for her to lie about being with Vincent.

"I'm sorry," I say.

"I don't like it when we fight, Lucas," she confesses, pouting as she walks over and places her arms around my neck, hugging me.

I squeeze her to me, my palms smoothing against her skin where the crop top doesn't cover her lower back. I get a whiff of her fruity, vanilla-scented shampoo, and my nostrils flare.

The smell is addictive, and I try to take in more of it. I unwittingly turn my nose into her hair.

In my attempt to place a light peck on her cheek, Beanca moves to release me. My lips then connect with the side of her mouth. Instead of leaving my arms, she turns her face toward mine, causing my mouth to fully cover her softer one.

On instinct, I move my lips slowly over hers. The kiss feels so natural between us that I don't register what we're doing. I palm the hollow of her neck as we both deepen the kiss. I hold her firmly against me as her fingers steal into the hairs at the nape of my neck.

I slide both hands up to and through her thick hair, touching it the way I wanted to when I first saw it tonight. Bringing my hands down to cup her face, I touch my tongue to hers, and my body reacts. I know she feels it too, because her eyes instantly flash open and our gazes lock, her greens on my blues.

Realization hits at the right time because voices filter through from the foyer, and within seconds, someone pushes against the door of the study.

Beanca and I instantly break apart, creating a much-needed distance between us.

"Lucas, I brought—" My mom stops short when she notices I have company. "Good evening, Beanca," she says, looking over at where Beanca now stands by one of the bookshelves.

"Hi, Mrs. Moore," Beanca says. And I'm impressed, because if I hadn't been the one kissing her a few seconds ago, I'd have thought she really was in search of something to read.

"Mom, you were saying?" I can see King standing behind her, his gaze shifting to Beanca.

"Yes. Well, King just happened to be on this side of town this evening and invited me out for dinner. I thought I'd let him in for a minute."

King steps to her side. Still staring at Beanca, he reaches out his hand to her. "We meet again. King Bridges."

I frown. "You know Beanca?"

In her pretense of searching for an abandoned book, Beanca brings her full attention to King. Her eyes widen with recognition. "You know Mrs. Moore, too?" she asks while shaking his hand.

He nods politely.

"You two know each other?" Mom asks in bewilderment. "How?"

"I wouldn't say we know each other. I saw her briefly at the Carlyle residence not too long ago," he replies. He cocks his head to the side and frowns. "Although, I remember you being blonde at the time."

"Yeah," Beanca confirms, laughing shyly.

"What is it?" King asks when he notices the odd way Beanca looks at him.

"Nothing," she replies. "It's just rare to find someone else with the same eye color as me."

"It's a trait I inherited from my father, and he from his father," he explains. "I reckon you inherited them from your father."

"No one in my family has green eyes," she states. "I'm the anomaly."

"Enough talk about eyes," Mom chimes in. "Beanca, love the new hair color. We'll leave you two to continue where you left off." Mom turns to usher King out. "Lucas, don't wait up."

King hesitates, then follows my mom out, "It was lovely officially meeting you, Beanca." He looks at her, then remembers I'm here too. "Lucas, be responsible."

When he walks out and we're alone, I turn to Beanca. "He was at your house? When?"

"You think it's strange too, huh?"

I nod.

"He came for a dinner party my parents were throwing. It was the same night Chase had that movie night." She lowers her voice. "And today, I'm pretty sure I saw his car at the recital."

"Do you think maybe one of his kids goes to PSA?" I ask, curious.

"That's a possibility. Unless of course, he's a recruiter. Otherwise, why else would he have been at the recital? "

"That doesn't make any sense, Bee. He and my mom work in real estate."

"A girl can dream," she says, grinning mischievously. "Anyway, maybe he was at my house to talk about real estate then. That's the only thing that makes sense."

I don't know.

There's more to this King Bridges than meets the eye. I just haven't figured it out yet.

We head up to my room. Beanca showers and changes across the hall. I use the bathroom further down the hall to do the same.

I try not to think back to the kiss we shared in the study, but it's impossible. I bring my fingers across my lips at the memory of it. It was a spur-of-the-moment thing, and she's probably already forgotten about it by now.

We're best friends. Friends can share a kiss or two. It's no big deal. Plus, she has Vincent, and I'm still figuring this thing out with Michelle.

We meet back in my room and I'm thrown off by the heat that rises up the back of my neck when I see what Beanca's changed into. She's wearing an oversized white T-shirt that goes to just above her knees. This isn't the first time I've seen her in it. However, it's the first time it has an effect on me.

When she crawls over to her side of the bed, her pink underwear is exposed and I drag my eyes away immediately.

What the hell is going on with me?

"So what're we reading tonight?" she asks cheerfully.

I turn to see her getting under the covers, and I'm grateful when she's fully covered up.

I utter a silent prayer.

"*The Little Prince*," I say, clearing my throat when my voice comes out a little gravelly. "It's a children's book, but don't judge this one by looks, because it's actually pretty good."

"Let me see it." She reaches over to get it from me, causing her chest to sway beneath the T-shirt.

This isn't going to work.

From now on when Beanca comes over, she'll have to sleep in a different room.

I climb in on my side of the bed and stay on top of the covers.

She turns to me when she opens the book and frowns.

"Lucas, what's the matter? Why aren't you getting under the blanket? It's cold in here."

"I'm hot actually." It wasn't a complete lie.

"Whatever. Suit yourself."

We read together and I'm finally able to focus on something else entirely. We get done with the book in less than an hour and a half, and I can honestly say it's one of the better books we've read together.

"*But if you tame me, then we shall need each other,*" I say, repeating a phrase from the story. That particular one resonates with me.

"*What must I do, to tame you?*" Beanca asks, repeating another line.

I'm not sure if she's doing it to humor me.

"*I shall look at you … and you will say nothing … but you will sit a little closer to me, every day …*" I finish, looking over at her.

She places the book underneath her pillow, then gestures for me to get under the covers. When I do, she moves closer to me and cuddles up to my side, placing her arm across my chest and laying her head on my shoulder.

I hug her to me and place my lips against the top of her head.

Yet another line plays in my head.

To me, you will be unique in all the world … to you, I shall be unique in all the world.

Chapter Nine

LUCAS

"Shep, do you think you could have your dad pull some strings and look into someone for me?" I pull my duffel bag from my locker and close it.

"Sure thing, just send me the name," he replies. "Is there any particular reason why this is a person of interest?" He removes his gloves and gets started on his padding.

"My mom works for him, and they're going out. He seems like a pretty stand-up guy, but, I want to be on the safe side."

We head to the locker room showers.

After I get out, I text Shepherd a photo of King Bridges's business card.

With that sorted, I head to Ricardo's place for band practice. I have a good handle on juggling both football and the band, and I'm confident about my senior showcase coming up next month.

I pull my guitar from the back seat before jogging up to the garage. When I only see Michelle and Ricardo, I frown in confusion.

"Where's everyone else?"

"You didn't tell him?" Ricardo asks, scowling at Michelle.

"I'm telling him now," she says, scowling back at him. Then she turns to me. "The session's been canceled. Some of the other guys couldn't make it so …"

"Uh. OK." I'm not upset. Although, I don't understand why she'd wait for me to get all the way here to tell me this.

"I forgot to text you about it. It slipped my mind, " she explains. "*But* now that you are here, why don't we grab a bite to eat?"

She walks over to me and takes a hold of my free hand, turning us toward my truck.

"I hope you don't mind if I leave my car here," she says, smiling at me. "I'll just hitch a ride with you for practice tomorrow." She's not asking. She's telling me she'll carpool with me.

I already have two women in my life who command my time. I don't need Michelle adding her demands to the lot. Her car is in perfect working order.

"Uh. Yes, Michelle," I counter. "I do mind. After football tomorrow, I'm picking up a tux for homecoming."

"I don't mind coming with. Besides, it'll give me a chance to see what you pick out so I can choose a dress that complements it."

I didn't ask her to homecoming. But I guess it's expected.

Now that I think of it, who else was I going to ask? We've been hanging out a lot, and it's clear Michelle likes having me around. Resigning myself to having her as my date, I don't object when she hops into the passenger side of my truck.

Michelle is a beautiful girl, her striking auburn hair and bright blue eyes complementing her looks. She's tall and willowy. She's funny. I have a good time with her.

But something is missing in our interactions.

I need mental stimulation, intellectual conversation. With her, I find myself discussing shallow topics. When I try to talk about deeper things, it always reaches a point where she loses interest in the subject matter, choosing instead to move on to another meaningless one.

I get it.

Not everyone is a conversationalist.

"We'll take the Veggie Delight," Michelle says, ordering for us after we get seated at Caesar's Diner, an Italian pizzeria not too far from our school.

She starts talking about one of the girls in her class. I tune her out after a few minutes, because I have an aversion for conversations that involve nothing constructive, and all the other person wants to do is assassinate someone else's character.

"Like isn't that ridiculous?" she asks.

I have no idea what she said but I nod my head. I'm not about to ask her to repeat herself.

The pizza finally gets here, and I immediately dig in.

"Isn't that your friend Jones?" Michelle asks after a while.

I glance behind me in the direction she's indicating, and sure enough, Jones is over in one of the corner booths in the back of the restaurant.

He's sitting with someone. From my angle, I can only see a glimpse of the top of their head. She's a blonde and that's as much detail as I can get.

"Yeah," I say, turning back to Michelle.

"Well, aren't you gonna go over there and let him know you're here?"

"Soon."

What if Jones wants privacy? He clearly chose that obscure seating arrangement for a reason.

Curiosity getting the better of me after a while, I pull out my phone and shoot him a text.

Me: *Hey Jones, what's up?*

I have to wait a while before I get a response.

Jones: *Studying.*

I narrow my gaze and look back at him.

Studying my ass.

Me: *Where are you? Who are you studying with?*

Jones: *Home and nobody. I've gotta focus.*

Oh I bet he's *gotta focus*. Now I'm more curious about who the hell he's trying to keep a secret from the rest of us. I'm about to recruit Michelle to help figure that out, but think better of it.

After about half an hour of debating whether or not I should go over to him, I stand up, intending to do just that. But when I turn to head over to where he was, the booth is deserted. "What the hell?"

Michelle leans her head to look past me and her eyebrows raise. "That's weird. How'd they get past us?"

"They didn't." I stalk over to the back of the restaurant where they were seated and when a busboy comes to clean the table I ask, "What happened to the couple who was sitting here?"

"They left," he replies, looking at me like he wants to add the word *duh* on the end.

"You guys have a back exit for patrons?"

"It's an emergency exit. Most restaurants have one. It's right through there." He indicates a path that leads from where we're standing straight through to the emergency exit.

Jones had to have seen Michelle and me, then. He's dating some mystery chick, and it's to the point he avoided leaving where we could see them.

Interesting.

Chapter Ten

LUCAS

*I*nstead of driving my truck, I decide to take Dad's vintage Jaguar to homecoming. It's a shiny black two-seater with smooth, tanned leather seats.

"Whoa! This car … is beautiful!" Michelle says in awe as she gets in when I arrive at her place. "Luuuke, I feel expensive in this." She leans over, kissing me as soon as I slide into the driver's side.

"Yeah?" This little beast has that effect. "You *look* expensive," I say returning the compliment. It earns me another kiss.

Michelle looks like a million bucks herself in the skin-tight emerald gown she's wearing. Its sleeves encase her upper arms.

We get to the homecoming venue, and I have to admit, I'm impressed.

Paramount is holding nothing back this year. The theme is Midnight in Paris, and as we enter classical French music fills the air. In one corner is a huge Eiffel Tower prop, complete with lights and a Paris skyline.

"They're not expecting us to dance to this are they?" Michelle asks, a look of mortification on her face.

"I highly doubt that," I reply. I don't care either way. I actually don't find dancing to classical music completely unappealing. I keep the opinion to myself. The last thing I need tonight is for her to shift that look of disgust to me.

"Hey," Jones calls to us.

I turn to him as he heads our way with Jessica, one of the cheerleaders.

Well, she certainly wasn't the chick from the other day. Her dark hair is a dead giveaway. She must be the decoy we're all meant to think he's with.

"Hey, bro." I slap hands with him and go in for a brief hug. "We just got here."

"Us too," he says.

"Lucas," Jessica says politely.

"Jessica," I reply. "You look beautiful tonight."

"Thank you. You don't look so bad yourself."

The four of us form a small group in one of the corners of the ballroom. They haven't dimmed the lights yet and we're in full view of the entrance.

"I'm thinking of ditching the afterparty tonight," Jones confesses.

"Seriously? How come?" I ask. It's probably to go be with the girl he actually wants.

"It's lame," he responds, looking toward the entrance. I follow his line of vision, but see no one there.

Another few minutes go by. Our dates make small talk, while Jones and I talk about my upcoming showcase and his travel plans for the fall break.

"I swear that guy is *so* damn hot," I hear a girl whisper nearby. When her friends whisper back in agreement, I look over at them. They're all staring at a spot near the entrance.

I shift my gaze.

Of course.

Vincent stands there with Beanca and Beverly on either side of him. He looks like a damn peacock, all his feathers on display.

My eyes slide to Beanca.

Her hair's been parted down the middle, and pulled back in a low ponytail. The form-fitting black dress she's in reaches about mid-thigh. Two satin straps go from the sides of her chest to an ebony collar of the same material around her neck. The dress leaves her shoulders exposed and her boobs are pressed so tightly together, they're almost spilling over the top.

"Bee looks good," Jones says from beside me.

And it's almost like Vincent hears him, because dude places a hand around Beanca's waist, staking his claim.

"Luuuke, would you mind coming with me to get something to drink?" Michelle asks, tugging on my arm.

I tear my eyes away from Beanca.

Grabbing one of the pastries when I get to the refreshments table, I stuff the whole thing into my mouth before filling a glass of lemonade. I try to turn my attention back over to the entrance but Michelle waylays me.

"Did I tell you how handsome you look tonight?" she purrs, her eyes coy.

"Well no, not yet." I grin at her, taking delight in her words.

"Well, you do." She places a palm against my cheek and brings her lips to mine. "We're a good match, you and me," she adds, after breaking the kiss.

Something about what she said, or maybe it was the way she said it, feels out of place. I look down at my emerald tie, then over at her dress of the same color, the one she'd chosen to match my suit, and the realization dawns on me.

Michelle is doing all of this to be amendable to me, to please me.

Some guys want a girl to fawn over them, jumping through hoops to satisfy them. I've never given her the impression that I'm one of those guys.

I'm the furthest thing from it.

By the time we make it back over to Jones and Jessica, Shepherd and Evie have arrived, along with Chase and a slew of other people.

I look around when I notice Beverly is here with the group, but I don't see Beanca or Vincent. Beanca didn't even have the decency to stay long enough so we could greet each other.

They finally dim the lights and the music changes to pop. We move the group onto the dance floor. Michelle clings to me like Saran Wrap, and I have to wonder if she expects me to stay with her the entire night.

BEANCA

I don't like how Lucas gets when he's around Michelle.

When I got here tonight and we were about to head over to them, he literally looked at me, then stalked off with her. I was on my way over to them at the refreshments table to talk to him, but then they started kissing.

It brought me back to the night I went over to his house after I got my tattoo.

The night we kissed.

I'd only meant for it to be a small peck between friends when I turned my head, but then it … changed.

I don't think back on it often because he's with Michelle and I'm dating Vincent.

Speaking of Vincent, he freaked when he saw my new hair color. He said it brought out 'the gems that are my green eyes,' and of course I ate that right up.

My parents weren't pleased but that was expected. I don't care. *I* like it.

"Beanca, are you listening to me?" Vincent asks, leaning back so my head is no longer on his shoulder.

We're slow dancing and I clearly didn't hear anything he said. I was too lost in my own thoughts.

"Sorry, no. What did you say? It's kind of loud in here." I'm more than capable of hearing him. I just haven't been paying attention.

"One of my friends is playing at a huge house party tonight. I was hoping you would come with me," he says, looking at me, hopeful.

I contemplate for a few seconds. "I don't mind going with you, but my sister's not interested in house parties." When he looks dejected, I say, "Don't worry. I can get Jones or one of the others to take her home."

We start dancing again and I realize there's a problem.

"Wait, I didn't bring a change of clothes." I hadn't planned on attending the homecoming afterparty either.

"Not a problem at all. What you're wearing is perfectly fine." When I look mortified he says, "If it makes you feel better, I'll keep this on." He gestures to his suit. "Sans jacket of course."

"Of course," I repeat, smiling up at him.

The song ends and I look around in search of my group of friends. I spot them not too far from us and we maneuver through the crowd toward them. We get there and I notice the way Michelle is dancing with Lucas, the two leaving nothing to the imagination.

I make my way to Beverly, who's partnered up with Jones.

"Oh great, you two are together," I say. When I tell them of my plans with Vincent, Jones doesn't hesitate to offer to take Beverly home.

"Thanks," I say.

I'm on my way back over to Vincent's side when I hear, "Well, hello to you too, Bee."

Lucas's tone is insolent at best. I shake my head because like I said I don't expect anything less when Michelle's around him.

"Hey, Lucas." I smile despite his attitude, and then keep it moving.

We don't say anything else to each other for the rest of homecoming, and honestly, I don't mind. Michelle's been plastered to him the whole time.

They announce homecoming king, and I cheer Vincent on as the crown is placed on his head.

No one is shocked that he won. He's swept everyone off their feet with his easy charm and smooth personality, not to mention his devastatingly handsome face and sexy accent.

Chase wins for queen. Both she and Vincent dance together. Afterward, he comes to me. Hugging me against him, he plants a kiss on me right in front of everyone.

"Vincent," I protest.

"I know. I know," he says before releasing me long enough to enjoy the last song.

I excuse myself to the restroom before we hit the road.

A few minutes later in the ballroom, as I head back over to Vincent, Lucas stands in my path. It's not intentional. He's in conversation with one of the other members of his band.

I walk by him, and I don't know how it happens but our fingers touch, brushing ever so slightly against each other.

"Later, Lucas," I say quietly. I want to look over at him, to see if he too felt the contact.

I don't get the chance, because Vincent's waving me over. "Let's head out."

We get into his Camaro, and about forty-five minutes later we're at his friend's house party.

I should say *mansion* party.

I don't know the homes of all the people in our school, but I've seen enough of them to say that this is by far one of the biggest mansions I've seen yet. There are a lot of wealthy kids who attend Paramount, but this takes the cake.

"Who lives here? A celebrity?" I ask, eyes wide as I take in its whopping three-story stature, complete with a gigantic fountain in the middle of the circular driveway. The enormous driveway is lined with over fifty cars.

We hop out of his car and I see at least five different foreign cars parked in a detached parking house.

"Pretty much," Vincent replies. "My friend is the cousin of an executive producer. It's his house party."

"Vincent, this is *not* a house. This is a freaking mansion," I emphasize. "You brought me to a *mansion* party."

"Wait. Is that bad?"

"No, it's not bad, per se. I just think we could have probably invited the others." I thought there would be other Paramount students at the party, familiar faces that I would recognize.

"If you're uncomfortable, we can leave," he suggests.

"No, we can stay. We've already driven all the way here anyway."

He takes my hand and we walk the rest of the way to the entrance. We're allowed inside, but once in, I can barely hear myself talk.

"It's loud in here!" I yell up at Vincent.

He looks at me and nods. I'm pretty sure he hasn't heard anything I've said. I observe everyone around me, and though I feel overdressed, it's so dark I don't think people even care.

"Here," Vincent says handing me a drink. I shake my head, refusing it. Someone just handed two cups to him, and I have no clue where they came from. Neither does he for that matter.

He shrugs and as he puts one of the cups to his mouth, I

stop him. He bends his ear to me and I say in warning, "Don't drink that. You're driving us home and you have *no* idea what was mixed in it."

Gosh could he really be that irresponsible?

He instantly looks annoyed, and now I'm starting to regret coming here with him.

People are dancing all on me, and within fifteen minutes of being in here, someone spills a drink down the front of my dress.

"Sorry," the girl who did it mouths.

I groan inwardly.

Tapping Vincent, I tell him what's happened and he gestures to the giant hallway. "Bathrooms should be over there."

I look up at him in confusion.

Is he really not going to follow me? We're in a strange place with even stranger people, and he expects me to go to the restroom on my own.

I take a deep breath and head there by myself. I'm not a baby, so I guess I can manage to find my way.

I walk down one of the huge first-floor hallways. Passing by a door, I push it tentatively, but there's nothing but furniture stacked up in the room. I pull the door closed and keep going down the hall. When I push the next door, I hear grunts and moans and immediately pull it closed.

Gross!

Lock the door if you're going to be doing that!

When I finally manage to find the restroom, I'm so grateful, I push in and close the door behind me, resting against its wooden frame for a few seconds.

Now I get why Beverly doesn't like house parties. Chase's parties are never like this of course, but if this is the idea my sister has of them … I would *never* consider them either.

I pull a hand towel from a rack against the wall and wipe

my dress before wetting the towel and continuing to clean the stickiness off me.

I jump back when someone tries the door.

"This one's occupied!" I yell loud enough for them to hear me from the other side.

The person keeps jangling the doorknob, so I yell again.

"Someone's in here!"

What the hell?

I quickly finish and use the toilet. I wash my hands, dry them, and open the door to get out.

I don't get one foot out before I'm instantly pushed back in by a giant of a man over a head taller than me.

"Excuse me," I say.

He grabs my elbow and hoists me onto the counter before closing the door behind him.

I immediately start screaming.

He clamps his hand on my mouth and I'm forced to peer into his dark grey eyes. "You're a pretty little thing aren't you," he says, leering at me, at my body. I can tell he's on something because the grey of his eyes is almost gone, his pupils are so dilated.

I scream beneath his hand, begging him to let me go.

"Don't worry. I just want to have a little fun that's all."

Alarm bells start clamoring in my head and I bring my legs up hard against him trying to inflict any degree of pain that'll get him to release me.

He grunts and I slip down off the counter. I reach to open the door, but he plasters his body over mine and I scream again. He slaps a large hand over my mouth once more, and this time, I taste my own blood where my teeth meet my upper lip.

"We've got a fighter here. You're gonna pay for that little stunt." He roughly kisses my neck and pulls my hair tie, releasing my ponytail. I try to bang on the door as hard as I can, screaming into his hand.

He grinds his disgusting body against mine, and Dad's words come slamming into my head.

Slut.

Little whore.

I feel tears in my eyes, and I blink them away.

I double down on my efforts, banging on the door, kicking my legs out and screaming so loudly my throat aches.

"What the hell?" I hear a voice outside the door say.

The man must hear it too, because he abruptly releases me and opens the door. He closes it behind him as he walks out.

"Oh hello, sir," a male voice says to him. "You OK, sir? We heard noises coming from this way."

"Nothing I couldn't handle," the man replies.

I don't say anything as I hear heavy footsteps fading.

With numb fingers I bolt the door before fumbling in my purse for my cell phone. I dial Lucas's number without even thinking.

When he doesn't answer the tears build.

I dial again and when he still doesn't answer, I break down, sliding to the floor of the bathroom.

"Lucas, please. I need you," I whisper, hiccupping big sobs.

A couple of minutes go by, and when my phone starts vibrating, I pull it to my ears.

"Beanca, you really have some nerve—"

"Lucas, please come get me," I cry. A sob escapes, and I try to clamp my mouth shut.

"What's the matter?" he asks, his voice now worried. "Where are you?"

I start crying again as I try to tell him where I am.

"Please," I hear him say, his voice now strained. "I can't hear you clearly."

I repeat the name of the place.

"I'm already on my way. Don't hang up, OK?"

I wasn't planning on it. I pull my knees into my chest and lay my head against them.

Dad would say I deserved this. And even though I promised myself I wouldn't give him any more of my tears, tonight …

I forfeit.

Chapter Eleven

LUCAS

I planned on giving it to Beanca, and was about to tell her she wasn't allowed over at my place tonight. For one, I don't like how tonight has gone.

She left with Vincent and didn't come to the afterparty. She was all over him tonight, and that has been irritating to say the least. I can't believe the moron won homecoming king. Was no one else capable of seeing through his veneer?

I shift gears, my heart pounding as I floor it to the Murdock mansion. The place is at least half an hour from where the homecoming afterparty is, but I'll make it there in half that.

I mute myself with Beanca on my line, while I use the phone Michelle left in the car to dial Beverly.

"Hey, Lucas, what's up?"

"Hey could you text Vincent's number to this line?"

"Uh, sure," she says, hesitantly. "Why? What's up?"

"I'll let you know later." I hang up with her and waste no

time as soon as the phone pings with the information I asked her for.

The jerk doesn't answer the first few times I call. When he finally picks up on the fourth try, I'm so peeved I almost yell into the phone.

"Hello?" he says questioningly, probably due to the unknown number.

"It's Lucas. We're on our way there," I grind out, keeping it plural and trying to sound as nonchalant as possible. "Beanca invited us. Will you let them know so that we're allowed in?"

"Beanca invited you?" he asks, sounding confused. "Did she tell you where she is?"

"At the mansion," I deadpan.

"I know that. I mean, *where* in the mansion is she?"

"Are you serious right now, dude?"

"The place is colossal. She went to the bathroom and I can't find her. It's not for lack of trying. I've checked."

"Just let them know we'll be coming."

He asks for information about the car and my license plate number, and I quickly rattle them off.

I hang up and grip the steering wheel, imagining it's his throat.

"Lucas," Beanca says.

Unmuting myself, I try to keep the anger out of my voice, but it's difficult.

"Yeah, Bee."

She's quiet for a spell. "Please, hurry." She sounds broken, her voice so unlike her own, my chest tightens.

"I'm almost there."

When I finally swing up to the security at the entrance gate, I hand him my ID. They check the car, my license plate, my face, and hand it back to me before opening up. I fly up the driveway, park and jump out of my car, jogging up to the door.

Once inside, I follow Beanca's directions as best I can. The place is too damn big.

I don't get lost though. Within a few minutes, I'm standing in front of a door with these intricate serpentine carvings she described.

I knock.

She doesn't open right away.

"You said it had snakes on it right?" I ask.

"Yeah," she says quietly.

"Then I'm here. I'm the one knocking."

When the door opens, I look down to find her on the floor. Her hair is all over the place and her eye makeup has been smeared across her cheeks where she's been wiping at obvious evidence of tears. She has a bruise on her mouth, and angry red marks around her upper arms.

I'm going to kill him.

I go to her, kneeling and hugging her to me.

Sobs rack her body, and I'm completely gutted. I can't go back and undo any of this for her, and every cell in my body wishes I could.

"It's OK. It's OK," I say, trying to soothe her. "I've got you, Bee. I'm here now."

It's *not* OK though, not by a long shot.

"Do you want to tell me what happened?" I ask.

When she shakes her head, I clench my jaw.

I need to know, but I also can't push her to tell me, at least not right now.

I lift her in my arms and stand, carrying her out of the bathroom.

"Do you know where he is?" I ask, in reference to Vincent.

She shakes her head and places her face in the crook of my neck. The wetness of her tears falls against my skin and dampens my collar.

"I just want—to get out of here," she says, her breath shaky.

I don't want to leave here without figuring out who the hell's responsible for doing this to her, but Beanca's making that impossible.

"Bee, I need to know. Did Vincent do this to you?"

She hesitates for a brief moment. "No, but he—Lucas, please just get me out of here." She squeezes her arms around my neck, hugging herself to me.

The confirmation that it's not him, doesn't let the moron off the hook.

On our way to my car, I faintly hear someone call my name. I turn to see Vincent striding toward us.

Well would you look at that.

I get to my car and gently place Beanca inside. I don't want her seeing this.

"Give me a second, Bee."

Whirling around, I intercept Vincent before he manages to get within ten feet of my car.

I don't hesitate. I swing a fist across his jaw.

He holds his face and looks at me, eyebrows raised in shock. "What the hell was that for?"

I throw another punch.

This time he asks no questions. We're full-on scuffling. He gets a few hits in but I end up on top of him, pounding his face in. Only I don't see him. My vision is filled with Beanca's bruises, the marks on her skin.

I keep pounding.

I don't stop until I hear Beanca's anguished voice cry out behind me. "Lucas, no!"

I turn to look at her, and she's leaning against the passenger side of my Jag, looking at me through sad, haunted eyes.

My chest heaving, I lift myself off of Vincent.

He looks up at me and gets to his knees before shifting his gaze over to Beanca. His eyes widen in horror.

"You moron!" I yell going for him again. "Don't you look at her! Stay the hell away from her!"

Beanca is next to me in a flash, pulling at my arms.

"Let's go, Lucas. Please!" she shrieks.

I allow her to pull me to the car, while I glare at the bastard. "We're not done! You hear?! We're *not* done."

Pulling out of the driveway a few seconds later, we speed out of there.

"I don't want to go home." Beanca looks over at me, placing a trembling hand over mine.

I didn't plan on taking her home.

I nod my head, turning my attention back on the road. I wasn't there to protect her tonight.

"Thank you," she says quietly, removing her hand from mine before clasping her hands together in her lap.

I move my hand from the gear shift and squeeze both of hers. I don't want to let go.

"He came after me in the bathroom," she confesses after a while.

I try not to react because I don't want my anger to frighten her back into her shell.

"I just went to get the residue of a drink that got spilled on me off my dress. I wanted Vincent to follow me to the bathroom. But I annoyed him."

I bite down hard as she continues relaying everything that happened to her.

"But that man he—he put himself on me. He could have—"

"Beanca, you're safe," I say in an attempt to calm her. The guy traumatized her tonight.

I can see it.

I don't go back to the afterparty either. I figure out a way for Michelle to make it home via Shepherd. I'll return her phone when I can.

We get to my place at almost midnight. I carry Beanca up

to my room and place her on the edge of the bed. She starts unbuckling her heels, and I help her remove them before placing them in my closet.

"Please, help me with this." She kneels on my bed and turns her back to me.

I help her unzip her dress, then unhook the button at the nape of her neck. I immediately look away when the material starts to slip. Leaving the room, I go in search of a bath towel for her.

When I get back to my room, I pull out one of my T-shirts and a pair of sweatpants for her to sleep in.

She silently accepts the items and goes across to the bathroom.

I go to the bathroom down the hall and get a good look at myself in the mirror. I have a bruise across the top of my nose and crusted blood on my eyebrow. There's also a scar under my right nostril. I'm not too worse for wear, though.

When I get out of the shower and enter my bedroom, I notice Beanca isn't back yet. After waiting for a while, I go across the hall to the bathroom.

I'm about to knock, but Beanca's soft sobs seep through from the other side.

"Beanca?"

It gets deathly quiet.

"Beanca?"

A few seconds later, the shower starts.

I know what she's trying to do. But not tonight. Tonight, I won't allow her to spiral alone. I don't want her hiding from me.

I push the door open.

Beanca is standing over the sink, looking in the mirror at the marks on her arms, on her mouth. The sweatpants I gave her barely hold up on her hips.

She turns to me as I enter, unaware of her state of undress, and realizing belatedly that she doesn't have the T-shirt on. My eyes, damn them, lower to her chest of their own volition. And though her hair mostly conceals her nakedness, I force my gaze back up to her face.

Her red-rimmed eyes lock on mine as I approach her.

I hug her, to hell with everything.

"He called me a slut," she sobs into my chest. "A little whore."

I assume she's speaking of the guy who manhandled her tonight.

"Beanca, his words mean nothing," I reassure her. "He doesn't know you."

"Of course he does," she says emotionally. "He's my dad."

Confused, I first release, then look down at her. "What do you mean he's your dad?" I ask gently, reaching out to take both her hands in mine.

"My dad will say I deserved what happened to me tonight, Lucas," she replies, turning her head to the mirror again to look over at her left arm. "He called me those things, accused me of sleeping around. He doesn't care about me."

My jaw slackens, and I just look at her, trying to come to terms with what I've just heard.

"A *little whore*," she says, her voice breaking. "He said I acted like one … and then he called me a slut. And then tonight that man called me a *little thing* and then he—" She rushes on, hysterical. "He kissed me on my neck, and then he—he slid his disgusting body against mine!" she gasps, then cries out.

I hug her to me again. I hate seeing Beanca like this. Tears of frustration prick my eyes. I feel hopeless about how much she's hurting.

"Those nasty words don't define you, Beanca," I start, turning her face to me so I can look into her eyes. "You're smart, well-read. You're *super* talented. You're strong. You can be stubborn sometimes," I admit softly. "You're nobody's *thing*. And *little anything* isn't a phrase I would use to describe you.

You're amazing. And you're beyond beautiful, on the outside and more importantly, in *here*," I say, tapping the left side of her chest.

She attempts to smile, and I find myself desperately needing for her to believe my words. Using my thumbs, I wipe at the fresh tears that are slowly falling from her eyes. The strong desire to make her feel better rises in me. Leaning down, I place my lips against her cheek.

When a few seconds go by and she finally turns her face to touch her lips to mine, I kiss her the way I should have kissed her in the study those weeks ago.

Lucas, please, come get me.

The note of need in her voice when she'd said those words to me tonight, trigger something inside me, spurring me on. I run my tongue across her lips and she darts hers out to meet mine. The more she reciprocates my advances, the more the kiss intensifies.

I remember the bruise on her mouth, and slow down, breaking the kiss to look at her mouth. I place a finger on the mark on the corner of her top lip.

"I don't want to hurt you," I tell her. "I don't want to ever hurt you."

She turns her lips into my fingers, kissing them as she gazes up at me. An odd sensation swells in my chest and something shifts within me.

I frown in confusion, feeling vulnerable all of a sudden.

"What is it?" she whispers.

I instantly let her go, turning to walk out of the bathroom.

"Lucas?" She tugs on my shirt.

I turn back to face her, my eyes lowering from her face to her chest.

I look away. "Put the shirt on, Beanca." The words come out rougher than I intended them. Then I scowl, upset at myself for saying them the way I did.

She rushes to put the T-shirt on, swiping it off the bath-room counter and pulling it over her head.

"I think it's best if you sleep in another room from now on," I say, feeling awkward still.

Her eyes flicker but she doesn't say anything.

I exit the bathroom and return to my room. Deciding it's best for the both of us, I bring her stuff to the room two doors down from mine.

It's clean, cozy.

Once Beanca leaves the bathroom, I'm already waiting for her in the hallway.

"Hey, you should sleep in here." I walk ahead of her to the room, and when we get inside, I show her where I put her things. Other necessary items she might want to use, like a TV, and books she might find interesting, are on the entertainment unit against the wall opposite the bed.

She doesn't say anything.

"Good night, Bee."

"Good night," she whispers.

I head back to my room and try to get over whatever this thing is I'm feeling.

Beanca's my best friend.

We're friends.

I don't want to mess up what we have.

Chapter Twelve

BEANCA

I leave Lucas's place early, calling for a ride around four in the morning and sneaking out as quietly as I can.

I left a note, apologizing. Apologizing for involving him in the mess that I am. Apologizing for him feeling the need to fight with Vincent on my behalf. And finally, apologizing for inconveniencing him on a night when he should have been enjoying his senior-year homecoming experience.

Lucas won't have to worry about me anymore.

I'll sleep at home.

I'll grin and bear every insult.

And when I graduate, I'll move someplace far away from here.

Last night, when Lucas showed up in the bathroom, all I cared about was that he came for me, that he showed up to comfort me when I needed it most.

I thought only of myself.

I'm not going to lie, I felt discarded. But then I tried, *really* tried to see things from his perspective.

And in the end I did.

I understand now.

I made him uncomfortable. He's in love with Michelle and I disrespected their relationship with what I did last night.

I kissed him because I wanted to. Because *I* thought it felt right.

But I made a mistake.

He's in a relationship with someone else and I'm—I *was* with Vincent.

Two days later, I survive first period with Vincent. It's pretty hard to avoid him completely. Lunchtime comes around, and I fully ditch campus. I don't want to see him and I don't want people staring at me when he's talking to new prospects, which let's face it, he has to be. I don't expect him to mope around hoping he'll get back into my good graces, because that ship has long since left the harbor.

Today will make the second day of skipping out on lunch.

Jones: *Again, Bee?*

Shepherd: *What's up?*

Me: *Something came up.*

Jones: *Really?*

Me: *Yes, really.*

Shepherd: *Whatever you say, Bee.*

Since I left Lucas's place Sunday morning, he hasn't contacted me. I wanted to text him, but thought better of it. He clearly wants space, and I'm more than willing to give it to him. I feel guilty about everything that happened Saturday night and I'm trying to be a better friend to him than I have been.

John comes over to me while we're completing our one-mile run in PE around the track.

"For what it's worth, Vincent is a prick," he whispers while jogging alongside me.

"Thanks, John." I don't care to hear about the guy at all actually, but John means well.

We're jogging along in silence until he slows us down to a walking pace. "Bee, don't get all weird, but I was wondering if you're free this Friday night?"

John's had a reputation for romancing the cheerleaders on the varsity team, and he hasn't been able to live it down.

I look over at him, and I can see that he almost expects me to reject him. I don't know, but something about it makes me want to do the total opposite.

"Yeah. Why?" I ask.

"Do you want to go see an opera with me? I have two tickets to see *Rigoletto*."

I lift an eyebrow.

"Honestly," he adds, "I wanted to ask you out before you and Vincent got serious. That night he kissed you at Chase's place, I was pretty bummed."

When I think back to that night, I vaguely remember him asking if Vincent and I were together. I had no idea John was interested in me at the time.

"I'd like that," I say, accepting his invite.

At first he's surprised, but then he nods politely. "I'll pick you up at your place at seven?" he asks, his tone formal.

"Seven it is," I reply, mimicking him.

We both laugh as we pick up the pace around the track.

After our date, I see John in a whole new light. Besides being a football player, he studies musical theater. I didn't know he was this passionate.

During our date while watching *Rigoletto*, he was mouthing most of the lines.

"How many times have you seen this?" I'd asked him.

"It's an embarrassingly high number. I've seen it in person and online so, yeah."

There's something about seeing someone enjoy what they love. It endears them to me.

I can't unsee John in his childlike delight watching the opera last week.

We're going out again tonight. Only this time, he's invited me to see a few local bands.

When we get to the venue, we find seats super close to the stage and only a few rows up from the VIP section.

The band opening for the night takes the stage. They play their set and we're bobbing along to the music when I catch a glimpse of Mr. Bridges.

He's looking over at me from where he's seated to my left about two rows over. He's with Lucas's mom.

I get an odd feeling when he waves at me, but I manage to wave back before turning back to the stage.

This is a public venue. But why do I have this weird feeling?

I mean, sure, he knows my and Lucas's family, but how do I keep seeing him everywhere?

Maybe I'm reading too much into it.

That's it.

Yeah. I'm overthinking this.

"What's wrong?" John asks when he notices I've gone a bit stiff next to him.

"Nothing," I say, refocusing on the music.

I eventually manage to relax over the next hour as several different bands take to the stage.

"This next band isn't official yet. In fact, they've *just* given me their name," the host announces. "I've heard them play and they're pretty sweet. Give it up for *Fractured*!"

My mouth lands in my lap when Michelle, Lucas, Ricardo, and all the other members of their band step out on stage. I turn to John who's equally as shocked as I am. I look over to Lucas's mom who's screaming and hooting for him.

I open my phone to check the group chat, since I'd put it on Do Not Disturb since last Wednesday. Sure enough, there it is. The group has been talking about Lucas playing a set for this concert.

If John hadn't invited me tonight, I would've missed it.

A small part of me is happy that I'm here for his first public show, but an even bigger part of me is upset and a little disappointed.

Aren't Lucas and I best friends? If he didn't see me messaging in the group chat to confirm I'd be here, why hadn't he texted or called?

I search the audience for Shepherd and Jones. When I spot them a few rows down and to the right side of the stage, I sit back in my chair.

Why had none of them called me?

I'm glum. But I try to muster up the small amount of happiness I feel for Lucas's debut. He sings a trio with Michelle and another member whose name I don't know. They sound amazing. And when Fractured finishes their set, John and I stand with everyone else.

People scream and cheer, and I try to do the same, but I can't help the sinking feeling that's fallen over me.

"Hey, how about Caesar's Diner?" John asks a while later when the concert ends.

I'm willing to go anywhere else right now, so I accept.

We get to Caesar's in just under fifteen minutes and order our food.

"I'm impressed with Lucas's band," John says. "I've never heard them play before, but tonight? Now that was one *hell* of a debut. How come you didn't know they were playing tonight?"

I'm quiet.

"My bad. I just thought you two were pretty close friends."

Wow.

It's so bad even John sees it the way I do.

"We are," I blurt, faking a confidence I don't feel. "We're close. I just must have forgotten he said he was playing tonight." I have no idea why I feel the need to lie. It doesn't matter what John thinks of my friendship with Lucas.

We move the topic to possible plans for our next date, when Lucas's band enters the restaurant. They are followed of course by his mom and Mr. Bridges, as well as Jones, Shepherd, and Evie.

They immediately notice me sitting with John. Jones and Shepherd come over to greet us, while Lucas hangs back, glancing our way before turning his attention to Mr. Bridges and his mom.

"Were you at the concert tonight?" they both ask in unison.

"Yeah," John replies.

"Fractured was the best band there hands down," Shepherd says.

"Fact," Jones agrees.

Evie walks over and slips her hand into Shepherd's. He hugs her into his side and plants a kiss on her forehead.

"You're quiet, Bee," Jones says.

"How come nobody called to make sure I was there tonight?" I ask instantly.

Shepherd and Jones both look at each other in confusion.

"Lucas didn't call you?" This question comes from Shepherd, who looks over his shoulder at Lucas.

I also look as Mr. Bridges escorts Lucas's mom out of the restaurant.

"No, he didn't," I grind out in response to Shepherd's inquiry.

When Shepherd and Jones both look back over at Lucas, but don't say anything, the same sinking feeling from earlier returns.

Jones decides to share a table with John and me, while Shepherd and Evie decide on their own table not too far from ours. Fractured is ushered to a private room.

I try to ignore the voice telling me it was probably Lucas's idea, that he chose a private room so he wouldn't have to see me.

After eating and talking for a while, Jones whispers, "Did you and Lucas have another fight?"

"No, we didn't fight," I say.

"Bee, he said he called you."

What the hell?

I fist my hands into my skirt, wrinkling the satin material. "John, Jones, will you guys excuse me, please?"

John rises from the booth so I can slide out.

I walk directly to the room Lucas disappeared into earlier, because this is bullshit. I'm tired of waiting around for him to contact me. Most of all, I hate that he lied to our best friends about us.

He *called me?*

Called my ass!

I get to the room and when I don't see him, I say in greeting, "Hey! You guys did amazing tonight."

"Thanks," Ricardo says, grinning from ear to ear. "What's up, Beanca?"

"I'm good. Is Lucas here?"

"Do you *see* him anywhere?" Michelle asks sarcastically. I know she's deliberately trying to jerk me around. She's always hostile toward me. I'm honestly not surprised.

"He went to the restroom," Ricardo replies. "He'll be out soon." He shoots Michelle an exasperated look.

"Beanca, what are you doing here?" Lucas asks a few seconds later from behind me as I stand, waiting at the entrance to the room.

I turn to face him. "Can I talk to you for a minute, in private?"

"Yeah. Do you guys mind?" he asks the other members.

"No, not at all. Take all the time you need," Michelle sneers.

"Michelle," Ricardo warns.

Lucas places his hand on my lower back and ushers me from the doorway and some ways down to one of the empty tables.

"I know what this is about, Beanca," he admits, looking disappointed in himself.

"Why'd you do it? Why'd you say you called me when you didn't?"

"Because," he says, sighing heavily, "I didn't want you to feel pressured into coming."

"What?" I ask, shaking my head in confusion. "Lucas, why would you think that?

"You left, Bee," he says, shaking his head. "You didn't let me know you were leaving and you've never done that before. Your letter made me feel guilty for practically shoving you out of my room." He looks down at the table before continuing. "Then you didn't show up to lunch the following week. I thought you were done with me because of what happened. You stopped coming to my place. You—"

"Lucas, I miss you," I confess. I had no idea he thought that way about any of this. "You're my best friend, OK. I didn't show up to lunch not *just* because of what happened with you. It was because of Vincent. Because of the whole thing."

His eyes widen and the despondency there is almost too much to bear.

I reach over and lay my hand over his.

"This is all just a big misunderstanding," I say, smiling at him. "I stopped coming to your place because *I* felt guilty for making you uncomfortable that night. So uncomfortable you had to, as you say, shove me out of your room."

"Are you serious?" His laughter starts off as a chuckle.

"We made such a mess of everything," I add, laughing along with him.

A moment later, we both sober, and he looks at me, his gaze intense. "Beanca Carlyle, you are not allowed to stop showing up at my place, OK? No matter what," he says before breaking out into a grin.

"Lucas Moore, *you* are not allowed to pack me up like some unwanted child and throw me away into some other part of your house," I counter with a grin.

His grin slowly fades. "Don't say that," he says. "You're far from *unwanted*." His gaze shifts from my eyes to my mouth. "But, I don't think we can share a bed again. Not like we're used to doing."

I don't hide my disappointment.

But I understand. He has Michelle to consider.

He must sense my disappointment, because he adds, "We'll just have to continue our read-alouds together in the study."

I smile, then pop up to my feet, suddenly remembering I'm on a date.

"Oh my gosh! I've gotta get back to John." I go over to hug Lucas as he too stands and squeezes me in a bear hug.

When Lucas places a light peck on my cheek, I don't turn my head this time. I won't ever do that again. I never want him feeling uneasy around me.

Releasing him, I wave goodbye before returning to John.

Things are finally right side up in the world again.

Chapter Thirteen

LUCAS

*A*fter three long weeks of waiting, the investigator Shepherd's dad hired to look into King Bridges sends me a report.

Apparently King isn't from Paramount, but attended high school and college here. Just like my mom, Beanca's parents, and Shepherd's dad. He skipped town not too long after. Years later, he made a name for himself in real estate. A name he built into the huge conglomerate it is today, The Bridges Corporation.

There was an apparent rumor that he got someone pregnant while in college, but when no child appeared under Bridges's name, the rumor was discredited.

I open another file in the report, an audio clip. Clicking on it, I listen as I lounge in one of the sofas in the study.

After it ends, I sit in silence for several seconds.

In the recording King is doing an interview. When asked about his family, he mentions that unfortunately he has not found a leading lady, but that he does have a daughter.

When the interviewer asks his daughter's name, he hesitates, and it's clear he regrets having divulged such personal information.

I listen to the interview again.

King Bridges has a *daughter*. And based on the date of said interview, she has to be at least fourteen years old.

The only question is … why keep her hidden?

It could be that he wants her out of the public eye. But it's not like he's some high-profile celebrity who needs twenty-four-hour protection for his family.

My theory that he possibly has a kid attending Paramount is starting to look a lot more solid. The age fits. Plus, he went to the recital. Only Paramount students performed at that recital.

My eyes literally bulge out of my head.

No way.

He's been over at the Carlyle residence.

The recital. The Carlyles …

Beanca.

No freaking way.

Wait. Maybe I'm being too rash. If he's Beanca's father, why would he pretend not to know her? How come *she* doesn't even know?

My head spins with all the questions.

One's thing's for sure, I can't go running to Beanca with this. She'll freak.

I think about homecoming night and all the other times she's been depressed about how her own parents treat her in that house, how she can't wait to graduate so she can get out. I'm hard-pressed not to tell her my theory. I mean, she might be better off.

I need to get solid evidence that King is her dad. And it's probably unethical to get a DNA test done without their knowledge, but I have my ways.

Beanca deserves to know the truth.

"Honey, King is coming over for dinner tomorrow night," my mom announces as she enters the study.

I stand up, close the laptop, and place it on the sofa. "Mom, would you ever lie to me? Have you ever … lied to me?"

She looks at me like I've lost my mind. "Why are you asking me that? Did something happen?"

"No. I'm just curious is all," I say evasively.

"Well, parents lie to protect their children sometimes, to protect their innocence," she explains. "So the times that I've lied to you, that we've lied to you," she says, referring to my deceased father, "were for your own good."

I can see that she really believes lying to kids is some noble sentiment, but it's not. We'd rather our parents be honest with us.

"Some lies can destroy a child," I say.

She looks away, solemn. "That is also true." Walking over to me, she places a palm against my cheek. "What's gotten you so reflective this evening?"

I shrug.

"You're a wise soul, Lucas. Every day, I see more and more of your grandfather in you. It makes me wish you could've met him." She kisses me, then wipes the lipstick from my face.

By grandfather she means her dad. He'd already died by the time I was born. She always speaks of how much light he brought into her life and how his sage advice steered her away from major life mistakes. According to her, I inherited his contemplative nature and analytical mind. I've discovered that they have their advantages and disadvantages. I hope what I'm about to do is advantageous.

"You said King was coming tomorrow?" I ask.

"Yes he'll be here for seven thirty."

Perfect.

. . .

By the time King gets to our place for dinner, I'm fighting a surly disposition. I invited Beanca over but she turned me down. Apparently, she has some date with John tonight.

I have no clue *what* Beanca sees in him. I mean, yeah, dude plays football, and he's a friend of ours, but all last year he was known for sampling the cheerleaders.

Maybe that's what Beanca wants.

To be *sampled*.

She doesn't ignore us like she did when she dated Vincent. I mean, we talk. We hang out. I don't expect to have a monopoly on her time.

I'm probably annoyed that she couldn't be here on this particular night.

"Honey, did you hear me?" Mom asks.

I look over at her expectantly.

"I was asking if you would like any mutton. I know how sometimes it can get to you."

I shake my head. I don't think I can eat any of that tonight. The chef we hire from time to time makes amazing food, but I'm too anxious.

"King, how come you never married?" I ask, after a while.

"Lucas," Mom says incredulous. "That's a bit of a personal question, don't you think?"

"No, it's OK. I'm not ashamed," King assures her. "I had no desire to be tied down. I was a wildcard in my younger years. I had fun, as most young adults do."

"But you're still not married," I say flatly.

My mom frowns at me and then looks over at King. "You don't have to give my son any explanations, King."

"That I am not," he says, chuckling softly. "When I find the right woman, she'll be a keeper."

"Do you have any kids?" I've been dying to ask, and now that it's out in the open, a part of me wishes I didn't. If he tells the truth, it'll confirm all my suspicions, but if he lies, I can't trust him around my mom, or Beanca. That's why I really wanted Beanca here tonight. Her presence would've been an anchor. I doubt he'd be able to lie with her sitting right across from him.

"Yes, I do," he replies, looking me squarely in the eyes.

Something flashes beneath his gaze, and I look away, turning my spoon in the bowl of soup in front of me.

There's no way he suspects that I could know something.

"Let's move on from King's personal life." Mom abruptly changes the subject, and we talk about everything else but King for the rest of the evening.

Close to the end of the meal, when the help comes to collect the plates before setting out the dessert, I excuse myself to the bathroom. Quietly skirting around to the kitchen, I go over to one of the plates King used. I take a napkin and collect all three of his silver utensils, bagging them.

I've already obtained a sample of Beanca's hair since she always leaves her stuff here. I'll send everything to be analyzed for a DNA match.

I haven't thought of how I'll tell her if or *when* I find out she's King's daughter.

I'm just hoping I can cross that bridge smoothly when I get there.

Chapter Fourteen

BEANCA

"Chase, will you finally admit that you and Dudley are together?" I whisper to her as she collects the pizzas from the delivery guy. I grab half the stack as we notice a bunch of cars pulling up into Chase's driveway.

"Thanks a lot, Steven." She takes the last pizza box from the guy and hands him a generous tip before he leaves.

"So back to the question," I say. "Are you and Dudley official yet?"

"We don't want to jinx it. Dudley and I get each other. We're loyal to each other now, and truthfully, we don't need titles or everyone in our business." She's a bit defensive, leaving me to believe the issue of *titles* is a lot more important to her than she's letting on.

"Does he not want to call you his girlfriend?" I'm not dropping it, because something about it upsets her.

We bring the boxes into her kitchen, sorting them by toppings and piling them in three stacks.

"Or is it something else?" I continue.

"It's me OK." She squirms before grabbing my wrist and dragging me to the back room. "He's wanted to call me his girlfriend for the longest, but I just—I don't know. I feel like once we're *official*," she says, putting air quotes around the word, "he's going to expect a lot more from me."

"Like what? I mean, is that a bad thing?" After I ask the question, I feel like a complete hypocrite because I'd been where Chase was a few weeks ago, not wanting to put a title on Vincent and me.

I'm glad I didn't.

"Actually no, you don't have to answer that," I say.

"No, I'll tell you." She pauses and then says, "Dudley is … serious about me, about us. He wants a deeper commitment than just a relationship."

"What do you mean?" I ask, frowning.

"Well, we've talked about getting married after gradua-tion." When my eyes bug out, she continues. "I know, trust me. It's a lot. And he's an amazing guy …"

"But?"

"*But* I don't know if I want to settle down. I mean, we're so young. I want to go to college out-of-state, travel, and see the world. I just think we're too young to talk about marriage."

"I understand."

Love is fickle. Somewhere down the line when they both get older, they'll probably end up growing out of love.

"If you found someone who really loved you, would you marry them this young?" she asks.

"I would have to be sure," I say stiffly, because I don't believe anyone would *really* love me, as Chase puts it.

"What if you *were* sure?"

I sigh. "Chase, I think whatever decision you make will be the right one for you." That's the only answer I can give. I regret asking about her relationship. I'm the *last* person she should be asking for advice about love.

Shouts and cheers erupt from the living room, signaling the arrival of a few football players, and we go out to welcome them. Dudley immediately makes his way over to Chase.

"What's up, Beanca?" he asks when he finally notices me. "I'm *still* trying to get used to seeing you with your hair that color."

"It does take some getting used to," I reply.

"Almost as much as seeing you with John," Shepherd adds, coming up on Dudley's right.

"I'm saying." Dudley turns his head in Shepherd's direction. "Speaking of John, where's Evie?"

"She's got a family thing tonight," Shepherd replies.

His girlfriend spends every Saturday evening with her parents. They always have some family outing, just them.

Must be nice.

I try to avoid every possible outing my parents plan.

People can come from *such* different worlds.

"I resent that," I say in response to their jab about John and me dating. "Isn't John your friend, Dudley? Shouldn't you guys be going to bat for each other?"

John chooses that moment to walk up, coming over to hug me. "What did I miss?" He suspiciously eyes the guys.

"Oh, just your *friends* totally ragging on you," Chase responds. She looks pointedly at Shepherd and Dudley, and they both shrug.

A few minutes later, Lucas and some of the other players show up, and we all go to the back room.

When I realize Jones isn't here yet, I go in search of him, thinking he's probably in the living room chatting some girl up. I look everywhere and find he's not in the house, so I text him.

Me: *Hey where are you?*

Jones: *I'm skipping out tonight.*

Me: *What? How come?*

Jones: *I had plans.*

He never told us.

Me: *OK, who's the chick, and how come we don't know about her?*

Jones: *Lol, good night, Bee.*

OK so Jones is talking to someone. It's not Jessica because he would've just come right out and said he was ditching us for her tonight. He doesn't just *not* show up to a party because of a random chick, especially after a game.

I'm about to text him again but a hand glides over my lower back, and I jump.

"Who're you texting?" Lucas asks, peering down at the phone in my hands.

"Jones," I say, my fingers tapping away at my screen. "He's not coming tonight." I don't get to finish nor hit send because Lucas snatches my phone out of my hands.

"Lucas! What're you doing?" I try to reach for my cell phone, but he stretches his hands over his head where I can't reach it. I bring myself up on tiptoes against him to try and grab it. "What are you trying to do?" I attempt to wrestle it from his grasp, but I nearly fall.

He instantly grabs me around the waist, laughing as my face lands smack in the middle of his chest.

I place my hands on his shoulders, frowning up at him as I lean my torso away. "Lucas," I warn.

He hands my phone back and releases me with a grin. "I know why Jones isn't coming," he says. "He's not going to tell you, so it's a waste of time asking him about it."

I quirk an eyebrow, "He told you?" It annoys me that they sometimes tell each other stuff and leave me out.

"Not really, no. I saw him with her."

"Oh my gosh! So it really is about a girl."

"She's blonde. That's really all I know. I saw them together at Caesar's Diner one afternoon," he says, his attention riveted on my hair. "If you didn't change your hair color, I'd have thought it was you. But then, best friends don't date each other."

"Of course."

Lucas has believed that line for so long, I don't even bother disagreeing.

"It's a written rule, Bee. Stuff like that messes up friendships." He ruffles my hair before placing a few strands behind my ear. "Anyway, by the time I went over to their table, they'd already deserted the place. They went through the emergency exit at the back."

"What the hell? They snuck out!"

He nods.

"Why would Jones need to hide from us?"

"I don't know. But whoever it is, she must be damn important. That or he's trying to play the field."

John comes out of the back room and spots us in the hallway. "Hey, I was just about to come searching for you," he says. "We're playing Never Have I Ever over drinks. Come on." He takes my hand before turning around.

Lucas suddenly grabs hold of my other arm, stopping me. "Dude, you didn't even ask if she wanted to go."

John looks over at him, narrowing his eyes.

"Plus, she drove here didn't she?" Lucas asks, scowling at John. "How's she going to get home if she drinks?"

I didn't know the two of them weren't getting along. "Lucas, I can talk to John myself," I say frowning up at him.

"Dude, is there a problem?" John asks, looking just as confused as I am.

Lucas doesn't answer. Instead, he releases my arm and stalks away.

I follow John to the back room. My steps are hesitant because I want to know what's wrong with Lucas. He seemed perfectly fine before John came to get me.

"Hey," I say once we're there. "Did you and Lucas have some kind of argument?"

"No." He shakes his head then says, "But I don't think he's mad because of me. Maybe something personal? His girlfriend? I don't know." He shrugs, moving into the circle as they start the game.

I'm standing there for a while watching them play, laughter erupting every now and then. My mind is a fog, because I'm worried about Lucas.

I pull out my phone.

Me: *Did you leave?*

Lucas: *No, I'm out back.*

I leave the room intending to figure out what's up with him, but when I get to the back of the house, Michelle's there.

"Oh, I didn't know you had company," I say.

"I bet you didn't," she says, glaring at me.

I'm so not in the mood for her tonight. "You know what? I'll talk to you later." I turn to head back into the house.

"You do that," she says.

"Michelle," Lucas warns.

"On second thought," I say, changing my mind because that was *the* final straw. "No. What's your problem with me, huh?"

One of Michelle's eyebrows raises, and she turns to face me. "I'm not sure you want me to tell you that, little girl."

Michelle is a student at Paramount, and even though she'd been retained for a year, she sure as hell couldn't be a day over nineteen.

"*Little girl?*" I scoff.

"Michelle, I think it's time for you to go," Lucas says, grabbing her arm.

She pulls her arm free and walks over to me.

I stand my ground because she doesn't scare me. When she gets to about a foot in front of me, I fold my arms and glare up at her.

"You kissed him, even when you *knew* he was with me," she whispers as she steps closer.

My eyes falter because I didn't expect her to say that.

"He tells me everything. *I'm* his person. You were just something fun to pass the time."

I drop my arms, backing up a step. My gaze slowly shifts to Lucas standing a few steps behind her.

"I …," I start, my voice quiet. But I don't finish, because her next words break something inside of me.

"How pathetic is it that even after you did all that, offered yourself to him, he still didn't want a little slut like you under him?"

I twist away from her, feeling a lump in my throat. I don't care what she says, I tell myself. I didn't offer myself to anybody.

Didn't you though?

You little slut.

Little whore.

You're a pretty little thing, aren't you?

You were just something fun to pass the time …

I cover my ears. Please, make them stop! I don't want to hear anything.

I hate them all!

Shut up!

"Shut up!" I shriek before racing back into the house.

Chapter Fifteen

LUCAS

Beanca screams as she takes off into the house.

"What the hell did you say to her?!" I shake Michelle.

She looks at me wide-eyed like she has no damned clue what happened.

I let her go and run after Beanca. She's almost to the front door when I finally spot her, and people are staring after her like they've never seen someone run before.

I catch up to her outside in the driveway. She fumbles for her car keys and completely ignores me. Her hands are trembling violently and the keys fall from her grasp. I snatch them from the ground before she gets a chance to pick them up, and she lunges, trying to pry them from me.

"What did Michelle say to you?" I ask, struggling with her frantic movements.

She looks up at me, and the hate and sadness present in her stormy gaze gives me pause. Angry tears fill her eyes, spilling over onto her cheeks. "Give me my *damn* keys!" she yells, grabbing for them again.

"Look, whatever she said to you, she's just upset OK. She's upset because I broke things off with her," I try to explain, moving the keys out of her reach. I'm not letting her drive out of here like this.

She stops trying to reach for them and tightens her fists. She scowls up at me. "I don't give a shit what you two do together," she grinds out. "All I want are my keys so I can get the hell outta here!"

I glance over to find people off in the distance, standing as an audience, watching us.

I groan inwardly.

Beanca suddenly starts hitting and clawing at me to get her keys.

When Chase exits the house and starts coming toward us, I act on impulse. I grab Beanca around the waist and lift her over my shoulder, carrying her over to my truck. I don't put her in on the passenger side because I know she'll bolt.

I get in on the driver's side and hug her to me, placing her so she straddles me, her back to my steering wheel. I start up the engine, and I don't know if it's shock of the moment that's got her or what, but she stops squirming as I back out and start down the driveway.

"Let go of me," she says, climbing off my lap. "I sure as hell hope you're taking me home because I have no interest in setting foot in your house *ever* again."

"Whatever Michelle said to you, it's a lie," I say firmly. I'm pissed that she's mad at me and won't even tell me why.

"Sure."

When she doesn't say anything else, I lose patience.

"*What* did she say to you?" I almost yell the question, fighting my temper.

Beanca doesn't answer.

We're driving on a strip of road with no houses in sight.

It's dark out, but I don't give a damn. I turn off into the grass and kill the engine.

"What the hell are you doing? Take me home!" she shouts, folding her arms in front of her, and staring straight ahead.

A few seconds pass and she refuses to look at me.

I try to place a hand on her chin, but she slaps it away. I try again, and when she swats at me, I grab her hand. When her free hand comes up, I grab that one too.

That gets her to look at me. Her green eyes are almost black, filled with anger and hate.

I don't … recognize this Beanca. "Bee?"

"Don't. Call me that." She clenches her teeth and lowers her gaze to my mouth. "Little slut works just fine." Fresh tears brim at the edges of her eyes as she continues. "Or better yet little whore."

"Stop it."

"No? How about little green-eyed devil whore."

"I said stop it!" I yell, my voice strained. I shake her because she's breaking my heart. "Bee, don't say that about yourself."

She violently tries to free herself from me. "Take me home," she cries, "I want—I want you to take me home."

I use all my strength to pull her over onto my lap.

I hug her to me, feeling myself come apart. I hold her until she finally tires of fighting me.

"Whatever she said to you, it's not true," I repeat, trying to keep my voice steady. "I broke things off with Michelle and she came tonight after I specifically told her not to. There's nothing going on between us. And if I knew she'd do this to you out of spite, I would've never gotten involved with her."

Beanca raises her head and places a hand over my mouth. When she lifts her eyes to mine, I can't read what I see there.

She suddenly replaces her hand with her mouth, and at first I don't react. But when she moves her legs to straddle me and starts moving her lips against mine, I hold on to her upper arms and lean my head back, breaking the kiss.

"Beanca … what?"

She grinds her lower body against mine.

I release her arms to grip her thighs, moving her away so that she's not on my package.

When she places her hand where she shouldn't and starts caressing me, I grab hold of her hand. "Beanca, look at me."

She's clearly not acting like herself. She switches our hands around so that she's holding mine and brings it straight to the apex of her shorts, pressing it into herself there. I attempt to pull my hand away, my breathing unsteady. She wastes no time in bringing her mouth to mine again.

I manage to hold her face steady in my hands and force her to look at me. "What are you thinking?" I ask, hoping she'll snap out of whatever this is.

She reaches for the hem of her T-shirt and when she starts pulling it up, we struggle. She manages to get it off, and one of the straps of her black bra falls down in the process. I clamp my hands down on her forearms. "Beanca, *don't* do things you know you're going to regret," I growl out.

She looks at a spot behind me, her face a mixture of despair, rage and something else.

When I see she's mellowed a bit, I release her arms and go to remove her from my lap. But she suddenly unhooks her bra and lets it fall. I try to look away but not soon enough.

"Beanca," I groan.

"Luuuuke," she whispers as she glides her hands up and around my neck, pressing herself into me. "Please," she continues, pleading and kissing the shell of my ear.

I close my eyes and take in a shaky breath.

Turning into her, I kiss her back—losing myself in the moment as our mouths meld together.

The soft feel of her all over me, makes me want to do things with her.

"*Luuuuke*," she pants against my lips. And then it hits me. What she's doing. What she's trying to get me to do.

No.

Not this way.

This can't happen this way.

I summon every strand of self-control I have left. Holding her by the waist, I lift her off my lap, placing her back in the passenger seat before retrieving the discarded clothes and handing them to her.

When she doesn't take them, I keep my gaze averted and place them beside her.

"You're wrong, Lucas," she says, her voice mocking. "Michelle didn't lie. *Everything* she said is true."

I look over at her, relieved her hair is a covering her chest. But that relief doesn't last because her next words rip into me.

"She's right. I did kiss you. And even though I might have been something fun to pass the time, you still don't want a *slut* like me under you," she says brokenly.

I reach for her, but she leans away from me.

"Beanca—"

"Don't touch me!" She grabs her clothes, opens her door and climbs out before slamming it shut behind her.

I give her a moment before jumping out to go after her.

BEANCA

I pull on my T-shirt, not giving a damn where I'm going.

Within seconds Lucas catches up to me, grabbing me by the waist and whirling me around to face him.

"Lucas, let go or I'll scream," I warn, my vision blurry as I glare at him.

"Go ahead," he says, looking around at the darkened sky.

We're in the middle of nowhere with nothing but trees around us. The only light is from the moon and whatever stars are scattered across the night sky.

But I don't care because my best friend, the person I trusted most out of *any*one else, he ... he'd been *so* uncomfortable, so appalled by my affections that night that he told Michelle I *offered* myself to him.

I didn't.

That was never my intention. And now I know why he didn't contact me those weeks after homecoming. He'd been showing me that my kiss wasn't welcomed. His lame excuse about feeling guilty was a lie.

They all thought of me the same. Lucas, my dad, that disgusting man ...

Screaming is useless so I start clawing at his hands instead. "Get your hands off me!" I yell.

He traps my arms and lifts me against him, holding me so I can't flail about.

"Put me down!" I scream as he starts carrying me back to his truck. I know I'm not being rational because he won't leave me stranded, but I hate the idea of being back in that truck with him.

As soon as he opens the driver's side, I balk, bracing my legs against the doorframe. He grabs one leg but I use my newly freed arm to hold on to the roof with all my strength, still trying to prevent him from putting me inside.

"You're really starting to piss me off, Beanca," he warns. "I'm trying to talk to you and you won't listen. Didn't you say you wanted me to take you home? Well then, why are you being so damn difficult about it?"

"I'll walk home! Let me go!" I shout, my fingers like a vise on his truck. "I hate you!"

Lucas freezes.

I stop struggling because he places me to stand on my feet, both of us in the light of the truck's open door.

"What did you just say?" he asks, a strange look in his eyes.

Some of my anger dissipates at his sudden calm. "I'll walk home," I repeat, my voice less emotional now.

"No. The other part."

"I *hate* y—" I don't get to finish because Lucas lowers his mouth to mine in a soft kiss, cradling my face in his hands. I startle at the suddenness of the contact. He moves a hand to my waist and puts my back against the side of his truck.

I push at his arms when I can't catch my breath, and he frees my mouth.

"There's no part of me that doesn't want you." Lucas's eyes are wild and his voice is unsteady. He punctuates his statement by placing his body flush against mine. "I told you, you can't take other people's words as gospel. Look at the facts." He kisses me again. "Facts don't lie."

I turn my head when he starts moving his mouth toward mine again.

"Yes. I told Michelle what happened between us. But I owed her that at least," he explains.

I don't *want* to listen to him, but a small part of me latches on to his words. I bring my fingers to his mouth, covering it, hoping he'll take the hint. Then he reaches his hand up to my fingers, holding them firmly against his lips, kissing them like I'd done to his fingers that night. That one gesture and the tender look in his eyes tear away at the rest of my resolve.

"I care about you, Bee," he breathes, kissing my neck and moving to the tattoo behind my ear.

My heart lurches.

He lays my hair over one shoulder. Then his fingers smooth over my tattoo, causing me to wonder at his constant fascination for it.

His breathing labored, he kisses my neck again.

My pulse quickens when he licks my tattoo.

"Lu-cas," I sob, my voice hitching as I sag against the truck.

When one of my hands finds its way into his thick hair, he

looks at me, and our gazes lock in the silver moonlight. He then reaches his free hand up my T-shirt.

"We have to stop," he breathes out. "I love being here with you. But I don't want to lose control, not with you," he adds, his voice low.

I steady my gaze on his because I don't understand what he means.

"This." That's all he says then demonstrates for me what he means.

Oh. He's definitely excited.

"Yeah, you should probably take me home." It feels good knowing Lucas is attracted to me, that I'm not the only one affected by whatever this is brewing between us.

He brings his forehead to mine and his chest rises and falls as he holds me against him. He covers my lips with his, kissing me softly before lifting me in his arms and carrying me to the passenger side of his truck. Carefully placing me in, he closes the door and goes around to his side.

The truck roars to life and he looks ahead.

I hesitate momentarily before putting on my seat belt, staring over at him as my throat works. I don't know if this changes things between us. It should, but I know how Lucas feels about getting into romantic relationships with friends.

"*Actions*, Beanca," he says, as he continues staring out the windscreen, his voice holding the note of an emotion I can't place.

Startled from my thoughts, I secure my seat belt. I don't take my eyes off his profile and I don't know what to say.

Without another word, Lucas pulls out onto the road.

Chapter Sixteen

LUCAS

I can't get what happened last night out of my head.

When Beanca threw herself at me, I thought she was acting out in response to what Michelle said, that she wasn't being herself. But when I told her I wanted her, trying to erase any doubts, any pain Michelle had inflicted with her vindictive words, I didn't expect to be so affected by my own words. My attraction and feelings for her are stronger than I realized, and it scares me.

I don't want to mess up what we have.

I'm trying to fight it, trying to resist the growing temptation to put a label on us, but the depth of my feelings for her is creating a void only she can fill.

We can't go back to being just friends. I want more from her than that, and if I'm honest, the realization started creeping in since the night of homecoming when I brought her back to my place. I've been getting in my own way, holding myself prisoner to my own belief that I shouldn't get involved with my best friend, not wanting to destroy a good thing in case we don't make it out the other end of this.

But I wouldn't feel this way if I'd wanted Beanca only as a friend. I wouldn't feel jealous when she spends time with other guys, especially since she still makes time to hang out with me. And I despise it when she wastes her affections on guys who don't know how to treat her right, who don't know the value she holds.

If I wanted Beanca only as a friend, I wouldn't have enjoyed kissing her the way I did last night. I *wanted* to keep going, embracing her, loving on her.

Her reaction to my desire for her was like an aphrodisiac I didn't know I needed … I didn't expect her to be so uninhibited with me. I had to exert self-control not to take it further.

Beanca deserves more than a late-night rendezvous on some old town road. She deserves to be cherished, loved. She deserves the world itself, not the scraps thrown at her.

I want to show up at her place but I know her adoptive dad will be pissed, so I have to be satisfied with waiting until school tomorrow to see her.

That's right, *adoptive* dad.

The paternity results came back within three days of my resource sending the samples in. And as I predicted, the results were conclusive. King Bridges is Beanca's biological father.

I have no idea how I'll break the news to her.

Placing my guitar pic down, I reach for my phone.

Me: *Hey how about lunch off campus tomorrow? Just you and me?*

Beanca: *Yeah, sounds good. Where do you wanna meet up?*

I tell her where I'll be after fourth period, and then I continue where I left off with the song I've been working on, trying to fine-tune the music and correct lyrical pacing.

An hour later, Jones calls me. I lay the guitar on my bed and pick up.

"Hey, what's up? Haven't seen you in a *minute*," I say because it's true.

"I know," Jones says. "You wanna hang out? My schedule freed up." He sounds upset.

"Yeah, for sure." I get up and grab my keys, already heading to the door. "Dude, are you OK?"

"Nothing, man. My girl's dad is such a jerk," he responds, sighing heavily.

He'd finally said it, and I'm not going to let that slip-up slide. "Your girl?"

"Yeah," he admits, but doesn't disclose who exactly she is. "Her dad is a buzzkill, bro. We were supposed to hang out, but she couldn't because of some last-minute plan he cooked up. I don't want to get into it. You wanna meet up at the park? Toss the football around?"

"Works for me. I'm heading out now. And I get it, dude. Bee's dad is even worse." When I think on it, Shepherd has issues with his dad, too, and King isn't exactly daddy dearest where Beanca's concerned either.

I get to my truck, and pull out, cruising down the drive. When I get to the entrance and the electric gate slides open, I see King's car speed through and fly past me.

I make a quick U-turn and head back up to the house, following after him. I get there and hop down before King is fully out of his car. "Whoa! Where're you in a hurry to?" I ask, jogging over to him. He steps out of his car in a formal suit, a scowl on his face.

"*From*, not to. I was hoping your mother was here. I called but her phone kept going to voicemail," he explains.

"What is it?" I know it's not my place to ask but I'm curious.

"People."

"Seems to be happening to everyone this evening," I offer. "My mom's in but it's Sunday so her phone is more than likely switched off, or she's forwarding calls."

When the realization hits him, he looks visibly defeated. "Right," he says, turning to leave. "Good evening."

"Wait." I put up a hand to stop him because knowing my mom, she'd probably make an exception if she were to see the state King's in. "I'll get her."

"No. I wasn't thinking. I—"

"It's fine, trust me." I head back into the house and gesture for King to follow.

I head up to my mom's room, and after the second set of knocks, she opens up. "Honey? What is it?" she asks, already concerned since I tend not to bother her on Sundays unless it's an emergency.

"King's here and I think he needs to talk," I say with a sense of urgency. "Mom, he looks like he's been through it."

Her eyebrows raise and she instantly looks worried. "Oh dear. OK, let him know I'll be down in a minute." She rushes back in to change out of her robe.

I return downstairs and relay the message. I want to stick around and find out what's happening, but I've got to meet up with Jones. He's probably halfway to the park by now.

When I spot Jones, he's by a bench near the entrance of the small park we hang out in every now and then. The place has a running path encircling its perimeter and an azure lake the size of a stadium at its center. It's also equipped with basketball and tennis courts for those desiring to partake in team sports.

Jones has his ear pods in and is squeezing a football between his hands. He turns to face me. As we both approach each other, I notice that the frustration he'd expressed on our phone call less than half an hour ago isn't evident on his face. In fact, he looks happy as hell right about now.

"Bye, B. I love you, too," he says, hanging up and pulling the pods out. He drops them into one of his hands and pockets them.

When did he and Beanca start saying I love you to each other?

"*I love you?*" I repeat, questioning him as we slap hands and hug briefly.

"I do. Plus, she just told me we're still on. Some argument happened at her place so now she's free for our date. We're good for the next hour or so though," he explains.

"Jones, I thought you were talking about Beanca when you said Bee."

"Wow. No," he counters, shaking his head. "Anyway, what's been up with you lately? I heard some stuff went down at Chase's party. And speaking of Bee, what happened? You two had another fight?"

"Something like that. Michelle was rude to her and she thought I was taking her side at the time. That's all." I avoid mentioning further details about Saturday night, Beanca, or me.

"What's up with you and Michelle? You guys still going strong?" he asks, then tosses the football over to me.

I catch it easily, putting more distance between us before throwing it back to him. "We broke up," I tell him. "Well, I broke it off with her. We weren't compatible, and it was becoming more apparent that we're on two different wavelengths, you know?"

He holds on to the ball, contemplative. "*Weren't compatible.*" He repeats my words, then asks, "What do you think makes two people compatible?"

I hold my hands up so he knows to toss the ball. "Common interests, values, you know, those types of things," I respond.

"Do you think parents factor in to a couple staying together?"

When he asks that question, I raise my eyebrows. "Whoa, dude, you're already trying to meet the parents? Have you already met this girl's parents?"

"No. To both questions. I'm trying to figure out if people should break up over their parents not agreeing with who they're dating, especially if it's based on something superficial."

"Define superficial," I say, because I have a feeling where he's going with this, but I want him to come out and say it.

"You know like money, looks, ethnic background ..." He trails off. I know the girl he's dating is White, so his concern is probably that her parents won't approve of him because he's Black.

"Why'd you say her dad's a pain in the ass?"

He thinks for a second, looks like he's going to say something, and then changes his mind, shrugging instead. "I don't know. He just seems like a prick by the way she talks about him." He doesn't say anything else on the subject and we continue with the football until he has to meet with his mystery girl, whose name I now know starts with a *B*.

Blonde and name starts with a *B*, and I assume she attends our school too.

Got my work cut out for me.

If I didn't want to be a musician, I'd seriously consider working for the police force.

Chapter Seventeen

BEANCA

Two nights ago, I put Lucas in an impossible position. I was all over him in some rebellious attempt to prove Michelle wrong. I regret ever doing that to him. He didn't deserve any of it. I know he values me and I should've afforded him the same courtesy.

But the way he'd been with me Saturday night has stayed with me the entire weekend.

Lucas deserves more than someone like me. Someone who took the word of some chick who hates me instead of his. Someone incapable of genuine love.

"Hey, Bee!" Chase shouts, running up to me as I replace the books in my locker, getting the ones I need for third period.

"Chase, what is it?"

"I should be asking you. What happened with Lucas?"

"Nothing much since what I told you happened Saturday night." I went back to get my car from her house the next morning and told her enough details to avoid twenty-one questions. I wasn't proud of my actions with Lucas, so there really wasn't much to say that wouldn't embarrass me.

"I can't believe Michelle thought Lucas cheated on her with you, that it's the reason for their breakup." Chase rolls her eyes, sighing heavily. "I guess some girls don't believe their boyfriends can be trusted around others. Crazy."

"Yeah, crazy," I say, noncommittal. What Chase said hit home, and not in a good way. Lucas and I kissed before he broke things off with Michelle, but I never thought of our kiss as him cheating on her. Is it considered cheating if you kiss someone else by accident? If it happened because you were emotional and vulnerable? If you didn't think while trying to console your best friend? "Chase, what makes you think that? That Michelle thought he cheated on her?" I ask, needing clarity.

"Because of what you told me. Didn't you say she got in your face about spending time with him? Then she called you a *s-l-u-t*," she explains.

I nod, slowing down as we approach my classroom.

"Either way," she continues, "you were his friend *before* she came along, so even if you guys were to get together, no one would bat an eye about it. Later, Bee." She walks ahead and I enter the class.

Lucas and I together. As in, as a couple.

My best friend as my boyfriend.

I should feel good about the idea; in theory, I do, but … I'm messed up. I have issues. And I don't want to bring them into anything romantic, especially a relationship with Lucas.

Throughout the first half of the school day, I keep thinking about the possibility of Lucas and I getting together, and I grow more anxious the closer it gets to us meeting up for lunch.

When fourth period ends and I'm heading to the north stairwell of the student parking lot, I'm full of nerves. I wait for him at the bottom of the stairs.

His black truck pulls around a bend of cars to my left, and my hands get clammy.

Lucas stops in front of me and I walk up to the truck and climb in. "Hey," I say as I swing my bag onto my lap.

"Heyyyy. Did you want anything specific?" he asks. "I was thinking we could grab a couple burgers."

Our school gives us an entire hour for lunch and we can eat either on or off campus, but most of the time we stay on campus.

"I don't mind burgers," I answer, feeling a bit awkward.

He narrows his eyes, but doesn't say anything. We drive for a bit and he says things here and there, but my responses are quiet. When we get to a red light, he looks over at me.

"Are you OK?" Concern is evident in his voice.

"Yeah," I lie. I can't tell him I'm thinking of what Chase said earlier about me being his girlfriend. *That* would make things awkward as hell. "Sorry, my mind was somewhere else. But speaking of, aren't you excited for the showcase?" His senior showcase is coming up this weekend, and I'm looking forward to hearing Fractured perform again.

Lucas's face instantly brightens up, and he looks so cute. My heart does these crazy flips. I turn my attention to the cars in front of us as the light goes green, and as we move off, my stomach infuses with butterflies. I feel odd because this never happened with Vincent, John, or anyone else. Even when I had that huge crush on Shepherd last year, I never felt this nervous.

It scares me. I was always free to be myself around Lucas, and now my feelings for him are making me act weird.

"I can't wait for the showcase," he replies. "I've been preparing for it every day since the beginning of summer."

"I'm excited to hear you guys again. You were awesome at the concert." There, I can be normal with him. That wasn't so bad. "I love your voice. I mean, when you sing. I mean, I love your singing voice."

What the hell am I even saying right now?

"Thanks, Bee." He places a palm on my thigh, gently rubbing it before bringing his hand back to the gear shift. "You've never said that to me before. It feels nice."

The place his hand touched feels warm, and I can feel that same heat inking itself into my cheeks. "Yeah, well it's true," I add, before staring out the passenger side window. I'm pretty sure my cheeks are the color of Snow White's apple right now.

We get to Five Guys and I regain some semblance of control over my emotions. I remind myself that this is Lucas. He's my best friend and we're having a simple lunch together, that's all.

After we order, we sit at one of the tables by the windows. Lucas and I discuss school stuff but the conversation eventually switches to Michelle … and to Saturday night.

"Why'd you let her get to you?" Lucas asks, his brows pulling together.

"I don't know. But I wasn't only thinking about what she said." When his frown transforms to confusion, I add, "She triggered some bad memories. Then I kept hearing all these …" I trail off because I'll sound like a crazy person if I tell him I heard voices repeating those hateful words.

"All these what?"

"Nothing. I just felt betrayed for some reason and I over-reacted."

"Beanca, do you trust me?" he asks, reaching his hands across the table to hold mine.

"Yes," I answer, my brows furrowing.

"Tell me what happened, what you heard."

I feel super vulnerable but I press on. "I …" I falter and he squeezes my hand. The warmth emanating from Lucas compels me to continue. "I heard the horrible names my dad has called me, and … other people echoing them. They were loud even though I know I was the only one hearing them." I try to gauge his reaction after my confession but I see none of the judgment I expect.

"Has it ever happened before?" he asks, seemingly unfazed by what I've just admitted.

It takes me a few seconds to answer his question. "No. Not that intense anyway."

"Do you want to see someone about it? It might just be a one-off and nothing to be worried about but we don't want to risk it."

That's when I remember his mother had seen a therapist a month or so back, when she'd been drinking too much and couldn't seem to get out of her own head.

"It wouldn't *hurt*," I say. "Honestly, I wanted to try talking to the school counselor. I don't know."

Our food comes and he has to let go of my hand, but when he does, I immediately want it back in his again.

"I can get you in to see my mom's therapist, Dr. Spaulding," he suggests as we start eating.

"But I'm not eighteen yet. Won't he need one of my parents to consent to it?" I'm hopeful, but I want to make sure Lucas and his mother don't experience any grief over this. "If that's the case, I don't mind talking to the school counselor."

"If all you do is talk to Spaulding, I don't see a problem. He'll come to the house, so you won't have to be in a clinical office or anything. I'll ask him about it," he offers.

"Thank you, Lucas. This means a lot." I just confessed about something that scared me, and he made me comfortable enough to share it with him. He didn't judge me about it.

"You want to come riding with me this Saturday?" He blurts. When I stare at him in surprise, he rushes on. "I usually go with my mom but lately she's had last-minute things popping up." Lucas never invites us horseback riding with him since it's his time with his mother.

The butterflies from earlier come alive again.

"Bee, I'd really like for you to come," he says, when I don't answer right away.

"Are you kidding?! I'd love that," I say, ecstatic. I've only ridden a horse about three times in my lifetime, but I love horses.

We finish up and head to his truck. Lucas's hand accidentally brushes mine but instead of pulling his hand away, he grasps my hand in his and laces our fingers together. We walk like this over to his truck and when I get in and he jumps in on the driver's side, he reaches for my hand again.

When he doesn't start the truck, I shift my attention from our joined hands to his face. He looks like he wants to tell me something but isn't quite sure how to say it.

"What is it?" Now it's my turn to be worried. "Tell me."

LUCAS

It's on the tip of my tongue to tell Beanca that King Bridges is her real father.

After she told me she kept hearing voices in her head, voices that probably started with the trauma her *dad* clearly caused, I was hard-pressed not to blurt the truth of her paternity. But if I tell her now that King is her dad, that she's been lied to, it could cause more harm than good.

Deciding not to risk it, I put it off until after she does a session with Spaulding. By then we'll know exactly what's going on with her.

I bring Beanca's hand to my mouth and kiss the back of it. "I don't ever want to hurt you, Bee." I stand by those words, I only want good things for her.

Her eyes flicker, then she leans over to kiss me on the cheek.

When her lips touch my skin, I don't think. I turn my mouth to hers, then bring both my hands to her face, holding her to me. She hesitates at first, but then softens and kisses me back. I keep blurring the lines between us but so does Beanca.

The one thing we didn't talk about at lunch was what happened between us on that old town road. At the time I'd wondered if she was acting out because of Michelle, but somewhere along the line things changed, for her and for me. And this is proof of that.

When I latch on to Beanca's top lip, she follows my lead, capturing my bottom one. When I deepen the kiss, she does the same, always welcoming and accepting my advances.

"Lucas," she says, sighing.

"What is it, Bee?" I swipe a thumb across her lips before leaning in again.

She ends the kiss, flips her hair, and turns her head to the side. Her cheeks are inflamed, ruddy and damn it makes me feel good knowing it's all because of me.

I press a hand to her face, and she turns to me. The greens of her eyes are so thin, her pupils taking up most of the space.

"Why'd you stop?"

"Because," she whispers. "I know how you feel about friendships. I don't want to be selfish with you. Let's just go back to school." She brushes my hand from her face and fixes her hair.

I lean back in my seat, glancing over at her as she buckles her seat belt.

Beanca's right. I've always made it clear that best friends should never get involved with each other.

"I'm sorry. For just now and for Saturday night." She averts her gaze from me and mumbles, "I'll make sure this doesn't happen again. I wasn't fair to you, Lucas."

This is what I want isn't it? Anything to avoid messing up our friendship? So why do her words cause my chest to constrict, like she's closing a door on us, a door that won't ever open again.

"Don't—I don't want you to be fair to me." The words are

out before I have time to think about them. "Don't worry about what I've said before."

"Lucas, what are you saying?"

"I'm *saying* that maybe I've changed my mind. Maybe this thing between us is worth exploring."

She looks out in front of her at the few people walking across the plaza parking lot in the midday sun, but she doesn't respond.

"Or not," I say, starting up the truck.

When she still doesn't reply, I turn to her. "Look, I get it. You want to continue whatever it is you have going with John. But let me ask you this. Did it ever occur to you that he might object to us kissing like we just did? And the way we did this weekend?"

"John and I have fun together—"

"And you have drama with me. I get it. You know what? Forget it." I'm about to put the truck in reverse, but Beanca stops me.

"You didn't let me finish, Lucas." Her voice is gentle and when she starts blushing again, I fully turn to face her. "John and I have fun, but it's not like that between us. He's more of a friend to me than anything else."

"You go on dates with your friends?" I can't help the pettiness in my voice.

"What's going on here, Lucas, huh? One second you're kissing me and the next you're trying to pick a fight with me. Just take me back to school." She fixes her arms across her chest, refusing to say another word.

I clench my hands on the steering wheel, intending to back out, but I kill the engine instead.

"I like you, Bee." There I admit it. "I broke things off with Michelle because I have feelings for you. Michelle and I, let's face it, we're not compatible."

Her arms falter and her mouth opens slightly as she stares at me.

"Say something, Bee. Anything."

"You *like* me?" she asks in disbelief. "And when did you realize you two weren't compatible? Saturday night?"

"Beanca, stop it." I don't like how she's belittling what I feel for her.

"It's a little hard to believe considering all the times I've made it known how little she cares for me," Beanca argues. "And all those times you've witnessed her snarky attitude toward me? How come you never thought you two weren't compatible then? What gives?"

Leave it to Beanca to call me out. "You're right. I did notice, but that doesn't mean I condoned it. You know that. Just as you were with Vincent, I was having a good time with Michelle."

"Oh I bet you were having a *good time* with Michelle." She says the last statement suggestively, and I can't help but laugh.

"I knew it. You were jealous. You were jealous the whole time, even last year. Admit it," I say. "That's why you stopped talking to me that one time." She turns to me, open-mouthed and wide-eyed. "You can't deny it, princess. I'm reading you like a book; no page is left unturned."

"Whatever," she says, smiling. "So what if I was jealous. You're jealous of John. You were probably jealous of Vincent since you keep bringing him up."

"I am. I was," I admit easily. "Any guy who sees the girl he wants with other guys would feel the way I do. I'm not saying I'm proud of it. It just is what it is."

"I bet Michelle hates the very air I breathe right now," she says after a few seconds. "She really likes you, *Luuuke*. Gosh, I dislike the way she calls your name."

I don't want to talk about Michelle. "Do *you*? Like me, I mean?"

She doesn't respond.

"Beanca?"

She removes her seat belt and climbs over onto my lap. "Is

that even a question, Lucas?" She brings her lips to mine, softly, coaxing.

I don't hesitate, returning the kiss and hugging her to me.

A few moments pass, and Beanca encircles my neck, pressing into me. "I like *you*, too," she says, breaking the kiss and running her thumb across my mouth.

I place a firm kiss on her swollen lips. "Trust me, princess, not as much as I you."

Chapter Eighteen

LUCAS

"Hey, guys, you're up next," the stage manager announces.

Our band rallies together and we do our usual pre-performance ritual. Michelle and I aren't on speaking turns, but we're professionals, so we keep things cordial for the sake of everyone.

When we get on stage, I can already feel the energy in the room. I love being able to get an audience going. This is supposed to be a simple performance, but that won't be the case with our band.

We take our positions and I try to search for my mom and my friends in the crowd. I spot them in the front section near stage right. Mom looks up at me, smiles, and blows a kiss. I catch it, place it on my cheek, and smile at her. Then my gaze shifts to where my friends are sitting not too far away. When my eyes land on Beanca, I wink at her. She responds with two thumbs up, and starts hooting for us. The rest join her in cheering for us and so do a few other people. It's a Friday evening, so I guess folks are tired from the workweek. At the end of this set, though, they'll all be as energized and pumped as I am.

"We're Fractured and we'll be showcasing three distinct songs this evening," Michelle announces. "If you feel so inclined, do not hesitate to sing and dance along as the music moves you."

Our opening song is the one we performed at the concert a few weeks ago, and it gets everyone excited. The audience claps along and I notice people starting to stand and move to the beat of the music, some singing the lyrics on the second chorus.

The second song is the one I've been working on. When I shared it with the band, they wanted us to play it for the show-case. For this one I'll be singing one of the solos. I'm a little nervous when we start the first few notes and I can't under-stand why. I've practiced this song multiple times, with and without the band, so it's not that I'm afraid of cracking or not getting the notes right. I must have psyched myself out or something.

I look over at my mom, trying to get myself together. She smiles and mouths something to me. I can't read her lips from over here, but I regain most of my composure knowing that I have people here who support and love me.

The song starts and I sing the first verse.

I know it's hard out here
This world is damn cruel, dear
But with you at my side,
Pretty girl, we're down for a wild ride

The chorus starts and the band comes in. Then Michelle sings the second verse with me. When we finally get to the bridge, I put my entire soul into singing the words, feeling the message, resonating with it.

> *You say you'll stick around maybe*
> *But I, I'm someone you can trust*
> *Love is our anthem, baby*
> *They ain't got nothing on us*

While singing the repeat of the bridge, my eyes fix to where Beanca's seated, and it's like that time during her piano recital all over again. Everyone else is a blur and I only see her. The band continues into the chorus again and I'm supposed to sing with Michelle, but I don't. I strum my guitar and stare at Beanca. My lips move of their own volition, and I mouth the words "*I love you.*" Her eyes flicker and I do it again, but this time I accidentally say them into the mic.

"I love you."

I instantly come to my senses as soon as I hear myself echoed. I don't think the words were said too loudly, and I'm pretty sure no one really noticed. I manage to bring myself back to reality. We perform our third and final song for the showcase, then bow and leave the stage. People are cheering and whistling, giving us a standing ovation.

"What was that?" Michelle asks as soon as we get to the back.

"Yeah, dude, why'd you blurt 'I love you' during 'Redemption'?" Ricardo adds.

Clearly they noticed and everyone else probably did too.

"I just thought it went with the music," I lie because what else could I say? That I was confessing my love to Beanca?

Yeah.

I love Beanca.

I can say that now, without fear of what that deep emotion signifies for our friendship. I think I've always loved Beanca, but not necessarily to this level of affection or extent. I realize that I wrote "Redemption" with her in mind, that this song was for her. That's probably why I'd kept it hidden when she asked to see it.

I get out to where the audience is and find everyone waiting for me.

"Honey, you were amazing!" My mom beams at me. She hugs and kisses me, then ruffles my hair before handing me a card with some flowers.

"Thanks, Mom." I feel as proud as I did the night of the concert. Her support means the world to me.

I look over to my group of friends who are waiting and wave them over to join us. "Where's Bee?" I ask when I don't spot her with them.

"I don't know, dude," Shepherd says. "She said she needed to go and that it was an emergency."

I frown and quickly pull out my phone to check if she texted me or something but I have no missed calls or messages.

That's weird.

"You guys are going places. I promise you that," Jones encourages, slapping his hand over my shoulder before hugging me. "Just don't forget us little people when you get there."

"Ha ha, very funny, Jones," I say. My mind is preoccupied with thoughts of Beanca and where she could have gone.

My mom brings me in for a tight hug before leaving me with the group. I turn to them, trying to quickly come up with an excuse for why I need to take a rain check on our plans to chill by Shepherd's place, at least until I find Beanca.

"Hey, I need to head home for a bit. I just remembered I've got something important pending. I'll check in with you guys as soon as I'm done." I don't allow them to ask me about it, and I'm almost halfway to the door before any of them gets to say anything except that they'll see me later.

As soon as I'm out of earshot of anyone, I dial Beanca's number. She doesn't answer so I call again.

"Hey where are you?" I ask, when she finally picks up.

"I'm sorry, Lucas," she replies. "I was there for your whole set though I promise. You guys were awesome up there."

"Thanks, Bee." I notice she avoided answering my question so I ask again, "Where are you at right now?"

"In my car." She doesn't say anything besides that, and now I'm concerned because I thought she told the others she had some emergency.

"Why'd you leave? Was there really an emergency, Bee?"

"I didn't leave, Lucas. I'm still here. I just needed some air that's all."

This time I notice the sadness in her voice, and I'm instantly on alert. "Did something happen to you? I'm on my way out. Where'd you park?"

She's vague as hell when she answers but tells where she is.

A few moments later, she sees me approaching her car and opens up. When I climb in, she has her head down, and I can tell she's trying to hide her face from me.

"Beanca, what's wrong? Tell me," I say, bringing a hand to her shoulder. "Please," I add, when she doesn't look over at me.

A few seconds pass and she utters, "When you said that you loved me, did you mean it?" She looks up when I don't immediately answer. Then she rushes into speech. "If you didn't it's OK. I'm an impossible person to love. I didn't expect you to say that tonight and it caught me completely off guard. You can take it back if you—"

I take hold of her face, turning her to me, and kiss her. "You are beyond beautiful, Bee, especially where it counts," I say, ending the kiss and tapping against the middle of her chest. "Any, and I mean *any*, guy would be lucky to call you theirs, to say the words 'I love you' to you. I'm happy that guy is me."

She brings her lips back to mine, clinging to them before leaning back to say, "I hope, I really hope one day I can believe those words, Lucas. Not because I don't think you believe them. I know you do. I just hope one day they can be a reality for me, too." She leans her forehead against mine, then opens her eyes and stares into me.

"I want us to be together," I admit. I've wanted to say it since the day we had burgers at Five Guys, the day she trusted me enough to confess something personal she's never admitted to anyone else.

A look of hesitation crosses her features, and I kiss her once more. "Look, why shouldn't we be together? I know you trust me, Bee. I trust you too, OK. That's one of the most important things we share. We care about each other," I conclude, before bringing one of her hands to my lips. "I *want* to be there for you, to help you whenever you need it."

"And what have I done to help you, Lucas, huh? I feel like I just keep taking from you and I never really get to do anything for you where it counts," she says, emotional now.

"You don't have to do anything. I told you that love isn't like that, Beanca. I love you because I just do," I plead. I realize Beanca has to learn that lesson herself instead of me repeating it to her. I'll just have to show her through my actions. "Were you planning on going to Shepherd's place tonight?" I ask.

"Yeah, why?"

"Would you like it if we did our read-aloud at my place instead? We haven't done one in a while, and I miss it." As soon as I make the suggestion, I can see the excitement behind her green eyes.

Chapter Nineteen

BEANCA

"I can't believe that was our first time riding together," I say to Lucas, surprised that we've never thought to do this as a group. On one of the weekends instead of going up to Tallulah, we could all go horseback riding together.

"Yeah, well, count yourself lucky that you at least know how to sit on a horse properly," he replies. "You've only ridden a handful of times. Impressive."

"Oh shut up, Mr. *Equestrian*," I say playfully. "Not all of us were born on the back of one."

We return to the stables, and I try to get down from the horse on my own but Lucas comes over and holds me by the waist, lifting me down. He places me on my feet and I rise up on tiptoes, bringing my lips to his.

"What was that for?" he asks before reaching his arms around me, hugging me to him and placing a light peck on my cheek.

"Does there have to be a reason?" I ask, twisting out of his arms and walking toward the stable doors. "I just wanted to kiss you."

He catches me against him and encircles his arms around me from behind. There's nothing hindering him with my hair in a ponytail as he kisses the tattoo behind my ear.

"And I *just want* to hug you." He places his lips against my neck, and I lay my head back, resting it against his shoulder. "Your neck … I could stare at it all day," he admits. His warm mouth brushes against my skin again before he abruptly releases my waist, grabbing my hand, and lacing our fingers together.

"Why? Because of my tattoo?"

"Because it's you," he replies simply. When I look up at him in confusion as we head back to the house, he adds, "It's a tattoo *you* got because *you* wanted to. It's important to you. Plus that one green note draws me in like your eyes do." He emphasizes this by bending and looking directly into my eyes.

When we finally get to the study some minutes later, he grabs one of the volumes from his desk.

"How about *Dante's Inferno*?" He holds up the epic poem by the Italian writer.

I shake my head and head to the sofa.

Lucas picks up another book. "*Animal Farm*?"

"Uh-uh."

He grabs a third book. Only this time, he doesn't allow me to agree or disagree. He walks over to me and sits on the sofa, bringing me close to his side.

"We're reading this one then," he says. "*The Scarlett Letter*."

"I think I've read that one before. A woman has to wear some red letter around her neck in front of people." I'm pretty sure that's it.

"Something like that. I only read the synopsis. It sounds interesting." Lucas opens the book and starts reading chapter one aloud. When he finishes and gets to chapter two, it's my turn.

As I read, he relaxes next to me before eventually laying his head in my lap and staring up at me. I get caught up in the story and the main female character, Hester Prynne. By the time I finish reading chapter two, something inside me connects with her, especially to the trauma the town's people inflict on her with their critical stares and harsh words.

I frown in frustration.

"What is it?" Lucas asks.

"People," I answer, my voice hostile.

Lucas's expression becomes vague as he continues to stare up at me.

"*What*? I just can't stand people sometimes. That's all," I defend. "I mean honestly, what Hester did, it—it doesn't warrant all that. I think if people lived their lives and focused on themselves it would make the world a better place." I get so passionate, I actually surprise myself. It makes me contemplative, and I think back to last year and what I did to Evie, to Shepherd. I shudder at the memory of my own actions. I'd been too focused on their relationship to see that what I did to them was destructive. Hindsight is always twenty-twenty, and I regret ever having done any of it.

"Should we take a break from this one?" Lucas asks, bringing me back to the present. He looks concerned, but a tentative smile curves his lips.

I shake my head. "No, let's keep reading."

When he doesn't make a move to start reading the next chapter, I reach for the book but he shucks it away from me.

"Lucas, seriously we can continue. I'll be fine."

We continue with the next two chapters but I get so upset midway into chapter four that Lucas takes the book out of my hand and closes it.

"OK, that's enough for today, Beanca," he says as he stands. He returns the novel to his desk and drops it into one of the top drawers.

"It's just ridiculous!" I seethe. "How in the world is it even possible to *do* that to someone?" I get up and start pacing across the room. "Over an accidental pregnancy?! It wasn't even like she murdered anyone. That moron, Chillingworth. Ugh!"

Lucas comes over and captures one of my hands in his. "Let's go get something to eat. We haven't eaten since breakfast and I'm hungry."

I want to tell him I'm not in the mood to eat, but when we get to the dining room and I see the spread of sandwiches and snacks on the table, my stomach growls.

As soon as we sit down, I start in on one of the tuna sandwiches.

"Spaulding says he can come tomorrow to meet with you," Lucas says a few minutes into our meal. "Do you think you can make it here by nine?"

"Of course." I'll finally get a chance to sit down and talk to someone. I feel a little nervous about it but want to understand what's happening with me. What I can do to fix it. "Thank you," I add.

"Bee, you don't have to thank me." He smiles over at me as he picks up a blueberry muffin.

We finish the rest of the meal in conversation and as we're getting up, my cell phone goes off.

"Hey, John, what's up?" I reply, placing the phone to my ear as I walk over to one of the dining room's large windows. "Oh my gosh! I completely forgot it was this evening. What time does it start?" It slipped my mind that John asked me to see the opera *Carmen* with him a couple of weeks ago. He bought us tickets, and I'd confirmed. I'd feel super guilty reneging. "OK, I'll be there for seven then. See you there."

I hang up and turn to face Lucas who instantly looks away. He turns, leaving the room.

Damn it.

"Lucas," I say, going after him. "It's not like that. I

promised John a few weeks ago I'd go see this opera with him and I'll feel bad if I bail last minute."

"You don't have to explain anything to me, Beanca. We're not official," he snaps. "Plus, I don't have the right to stop you from going out with anybody."

I can tell he's upset. I close the distance between us once we get to the foyer, hugging him from behind and placing my head against his back. "I'm sorry OK," I say quietly. "Maybe if you come then—"

"No," he states flatly, turning around to face me. "You go hang out with John. I'll just go hang out with the band. It's no big deal."

"Lucas, stop," I say firmly, looking into his deep-set blue eyes. "You and I both know it *is* a big deal because if it weren't, you wouldn't look as irritated as you do now. Don't say I should go 'hang out with John' like something is going on between us."

"Isn't there?" he asks, his face heated.

"No there isn't, Lucas. I told you already that we're just friends. What are you even saying right now? I want *you*. I want to be with *you*."

"Well then, how come just because of some promise, you're going on a date with him?" he asks. When I don't respond, he backtracks. "You know what, Beanca, forget it. Forget I said anything." He stalks off into the study.

I pull my phone out and dial John. "Hey, somethings come up. I'll pay you back the money for the ticket, but it's an emergency."

"It's all good. I'll just get someone else to come with me. Don't worry about having to pay me back." John sounds bummed, but understanding.

I stroll into the study.

Lucas is sitting on the sofa we'd been reading on before lunch. He jerks when I settle myself on his lap and bring my arms up around his neck.

"I'm your girlfriend now, Lucas," I say confidently. "And *I* don't ever want to do anything to hurt you." As I bring my face to his, he pulls my face the rest of the way.

"Say that again," he whispers.

"I don't ever want to hurt you," I repeat.

"No, the other part."

"I'm your girlfriend," I say, kissing him.

"Beanca, you're my girlfriend," he reiterates, kissing me roughly. "*My* girlfriend," he repeats, then kisses me even harder.

"And you're *my* man, Lucas," I state. Something about it makes me want to stamp my name all over him, so everyone knows he's only *mine*. "My man." Our mouths meld together as we get lost in each other. We don't come up for air until I'm pushing him back to lie against the cushions of the sofa.

I reach up and release my ponytail, shaking my hair so it falls messily over my shoulders and down my back. He leans up to kiss me, running his hands through my hair.

He growls as I throw my head back. "Damn, Bee …" His voice is deep now and he glides his lips against the column of my neck. His breathing comes out a bit labored when he stares into my eyes. "Beanca, I love you."

The words break my concentration, and I blink rapidly at him.

He moves his lip across mine before kissing me deeply again. Latching on to my neck, he nibbles at it.

"Lucas, don't keep saying—"

Bringing his lips back up to mine, he silences my protest.

"Give me this year, princess," he says between kisses. "I'll show you love isn't fickle at all."

I grimace at his use of *love* again, but I don't argue. I don't want to spoil the atmosphere we've got going.

LUCAS

Beanca balks any time I mention loving her.

It's crazy to think that this beautiful girl doesn't believe in the sentiment. I would never have thought that after all our years of friendship, she would ever doubt my feelings for her. She likes spending time with me just as much as I do her, but for some reason she doesn't equate it with love. That's exactly what it is. It's in the way she fully accepts me and I her. I want good things for her. I'm devoted to her.

In the experiences we share together, she'll eventually come to accept what we have *is* love. She may cringe at acknowledging it but that doesn't change that I love her. A huge part of me knows she loves me in return, not that I expect her to admit it. Her loyalty is enough.

"I don't want to go home," she whines, hugging herself to my side as we walk to the front door.

"You could always just stay here," I offer.

"No, I have to get back to my house, otherwise I won't hear the end of it," she says, rolling her eyes. "And it's not even like my dad cares. I swear he takes some sick pleasure in getting at least one chance to criticize or insult me daily." She releases me and stops abruptly. "Do you think maybe he needs a therapist, too? That I got this thing from him?"

"Yes, to the therapist. No, to getting anything from him," I say firmly, walking ahead of her.

"I'm serious, Lucas. Maybe it's genetic." She follows me through the door. "Maybe I got my issues from him. Kind of like that Bridges guy says he inherited his eyes from his parents and so on. I think it's possible to pass on mental problems, too."

"Trust me, Bee, you inherited *nothing* genetic from that man."

"Obviously that's not true, Lucas. He's my dad," she counters, frowning as she strolls to her car. "And since I didn't inherit anything in the physical department, maybe I got his temperament."

"Alright," I say, wanting to table the subject. "Spaulding will let us know once you talk to him. Only then will we decide where that part of your temperament comes from."

She nods and gets into her car before I head over to my truck. She drives out through the entrance gate, and we part ways as I head over to Shepherd's place.

Once I get to Shepherd's, I let him know I'm out front.

"Dude, what's up?" he asks as he opens up. "I don't have too much time to hang since you told me last minute you were coming by. Evie and I have plans and she'll be here in the next hour or two."

We head to his backyard. His land sits on a good spread, and a dense forest stretches for miles out back.

"Shep," I start. "I need to ask you something. If you knew something that could change Evie's life, but you felt it could really hurt her once she found out about it, would you still tell her?"

"Depends." His one-word response offers nothing.

"On what?" I ask, frowning over at him.

"Well, when you say it could change her life, is that for the better, or worse? And if I don't tell her is it possible she'll find out some other way? And when she finds out, will I have to lie to her and pretend *I* didn't know that essential piece of information?" He asks the questions, then looks at me quizzically. "Who's this about anyway? Michelle?"

"You already know I broke up with her." I look out at the evening sky, observing the sun as it peeks through the treetops in the distance. "It's Bee."

"Beanca?" His confusion is evident as his eyes narrow in on mine. "What's up with Beanca?"

"We're together," I confess. "As in, she's my girlfriend now."

"It's about damn time." He slaps me on the shoulder, his

grin widening by the second. "You've finally gotten over your tired no-dating friends rule, huh? I swear Jones and I knew something was up with you two. You guys were arguing way too much over the dumbest stuff."

"You done?" I ask, side-eyeing him.

I guess Beanca and I *have* argued over minor issues in the past year, but it wasn't anything we couldn't get past. This thing though, with King being her dad, is a huge deal. I don't want me knowing about it blowing up in my face.

"Well?" Shepherd asks, chuckling. "What is it?"

"I found out about something pretty serious that'll really shake things up for Bee, but I don't want to say anything until I'm sure she'll be able to fully process it."

"What did you find out?" he asks, his brows drawing together.

"It's not my secret to tell." It isn't, and I would feel like a level-ten loser for letting him in on it before telling Beanca.

"I get it," he says. "If I were you, I'd make damn sure that the right time comes, and soon because you don't want her finding out from anyone else. If she comes and tells you about it, you'll have to pretend you didn't know. And I don't know about you but that'll be awkward as hell. You'd have to be a first-rate actor to be able to pull it off."

"I know. I think I can tell her tomorrow. No matter what, I have to, before it's too late." I don't want to be guilty of lying by omission because that's *not* how I want our relationship to start. No matter the results of her session with Spaulding, I have to tell her ASAP.

Chapter Twenty

BEANCA

The first thing Dr. Spaulding tells me to do is to try and relax. I lay back on the upholstered recliner in the dimly lit room, closing my eyes just as he instructs me.

His voice is surprisingly calming as he leads me into a contemplation of past memories of my early childhood. Some minutes later, Dr. Spaulding begins questioning me about specific events and how they affected me, how I felt, reacted. He asks about my dad, about our good times, when they'd stopped, why they'd stopped.

"Don't overdo it, Beanca. Only tell me the things you're comfortable sharing," he says at one point. "Take a deep breath in … exhale. Once more, in … exhale."

The session lasts for a little over an hour, and when we finish, he asks me to comment on it.

"I feel the same way I did before we started, I guess," I say.

"Would you like us to discuss my findings privately or for

Lucas to be here with you? It is of course, completely up to you." He sits peacefully, awaiting my response.

"I'd like him to be here with me," I say firmly.

Lucas enters when Dr. Spaulding knocks twice against the wooden door. He looks right at me, the corners of his mouth turning up as he stands by where I'm sitting. Placing a warm palm against my neck, he gently kneads the tense muscles as we both listen to Dr. Spaulding.

"Ms. Carlyle suffers from post-traumatic stress disorder. Commonly referred to as PTSD. It appears to be caused by a combination of traumatic experiences she's had over the past five or six years, maybe even more. She also seems to have blocked a few memories of her early years, as she can't remember anything before the age of six. PTSD can last for years, but the important thing is to avoid triggers as much as possible. This includes staying away from certain people or places that might induce memories that can cause flashbacks or anxiety," Dr. Spaulding explains. "Beanca, you turn eighteen next month correct?"

"Yes, I do, on the seventh," I reply.

"Good. Well, Lucas," he says. "You can get in touch with me then. That way we can start scheduled sessions for her. By then we won't need the consent of a parent or guardian. We'll keep in touch." With that he shakes both Lucas's hand and mine before heading out.

"PTSD ...," I say absentmindedly, rising from my perch at the edge of the recliner.

"How was it?" Lucas asks, searching my face.

"It wasn't bad. Dr. Spaulding made me feel comfortable, anyway." I feel cheerful for some reason. "PTSD seems like a serious condition, but I have hope." I'd been scared that my condition might've been much worse. "Thanks again, Lucas."

"OK, if you don't stop thanking me I'm—"

"No, I won't stop," I say, interrupting him and placing a brief kiss against his cheek. I don't have this kind of support from *anyone* else, and everything Lucas does for me makes me even more grateful for him.

Taking hold of his arm, I lace my fingers through his and walk us from the room and into his living room. The space has a fireplace, an intricately designed Turkish carpet and brown leather sofas flanking adjacent walls.

"You're genuinely one of the best, if not *the* best person I know, Lucas. I mean honestly, I feel like a leech. I haven't done half as much for you as you have for me," I say, because it's true. "You're sweet, supportive, honest." I release his arm and turn to face him. The reluctant expression on his face gives me pause. "What's wrong?"

"Nothing," he says evasively. Bringing a palm up to his neck, he nervously rubs against it before averting his gaze.

I frown because it's clear that whatever it is, it's not *nothing*. Tilting my head around to his, I place a hand on his chin and turn his face until his eyes are on mine again. "Try again, Mr. Moore," I say. I frame his face between my palms to coax him into spilling whatever's on his mind. "You know you can tell me anything, right? I've been an open book with you and I want that from you too."

His eyes flash, and I swear he's getting ready to tell me something but instead he chuckles and says, "That's the first time you've called me 'Mr. Moore.' Is that my new nickname?" He gently removes my hands from his face and squeezes them in his, before releasing me and moving to sit on one of the sofas across the room.

Distracted, I grin at his mention of what I call him. "Do you like it?" I ask, going over to where he's sitting.

He pulls me down onto his lap, hugging me tightly against him, the palm of his large hand resting against my abdomen. When he brings his mouth to my ear, I turn in his arms and encircle my arms around his neck, leaning in to kiss him.

"I lo—care about you so much," he says after a while,

tapping my nose with his forefinger. "And I guess I can put up with Mr. Moore for now. Makes me feel old, though."

"It's not meant to," I say, playfully patting his chest and giggling at the idea of this teenager feeling like an old man. "But I'll admit that you're more of a man than … well, than the one I've been calling my *dad* my whole life."

After I say the words, he sobers up.

"Anyway," I continue, rising to leave. "I have to go run some errands for Mom today."

"Beanca." Lucas grabs my hands, grasping them tightly as he rises to his feet in front of me.

"What is it?"

My phone goes off and I'm two seconds from telling Lucas I'll just let it ring, but he doesn't let me.

"No, answer it. It's probably important." He releases my hands and blows out a frustrated breath before placing his hands on his head.

"Hey, Mom." I look up at Lucas, regretful. "Yeah, I'm heading to that store now." I mouth "I'm sorry" after hugging him, then make my exit.

I'm heading up the street to my house when I notice an unmistakable black Bentley backing out of our driveway.

King Bridges.

I wonder what he's doing here.

Again.

I slow my car down as the Bentley drives by me. I attempt to look into the car, but the illegal tint on its windows makes it impossible. I'm startled when the horn honks in acknowledgment before the car speeds up the road.

A few seconds later, I park along the driveway, noticing right away that my mom's car isn't in its usual spot. My dad's is still parked in the same spot it was yesterday.

That's odd.

Both of my parents are usually home on Sundays. At this time of the day anyway. It's late afternoon.

I'm even more confused when I walk through the front door and find Beverly's keys missing from the key holder.

I pull out my phone and am about to head straight up to my room, when Dad calls for me from the den.

I jump, because I didn't think anyone was home. I thought for sure he'd have gone with Mom.

I hesitate on the first stair, contemplating if I should pretend I didn't hear him calling me.

"Beanca!" This time he yells loud enough to quell any pretense I could possibly make of not having heard him. By the sound of it, he is not in a good mood. But then again, is he ever when it comes to me?

Great.

I haven't even been home for a minute, and I'm already being summoned by the dragon. I twist away from the stairs and head to the den. When I reach the open doorway, he wastes no time in ushering me into the cave of a room.

He doesn't close the door, which is unlike him when he decides to lecture me.

Is it just me or is it darker in here than usual?

My senses instantly heighten, and although I am not afraid of my dad, goose bumps flush all over my skin.

"Your mother will be out for a while," he says, his voice tense. "And well, Beverly has gone out with a friend for the day. Therefore, I believe this is the perfect time to enlighten you."

"Enlighten me about what?" I say, frowning up at him in confusion.

His face twists in annoyance at my question but the expression quickly vanishes, replaced by a snarl of satisfaction. "This won't take long. Have a seat." He paces away from me, clearing my path to the couch.

"I'm fine right here," I say, hoping he'll just tell me what he has to say so I can leave this room and it's chokingly stale air.

"Suit yourself," he states flatly. "Beanca, I'm not your father."

When I look at him blankly, not quite understanding his words, he repeats himself, the muscles of his face jerking as he emphasizes the hateful words.

"If this is some warped way of trying to say you hate the way I behave and that I'm dead to you, I get it. We *don't* get along." I'm so over this. I know he doesn't care about me, so this stupid conversation or whatever it is he's trying to do is extremely lame right now.

He comes to stand directly in front of me and I back up a bit, tilting my head up to meet his steel-like gaze.

"It's this insolence I can't damn-well stand," he growls, grabbing hold of my upper arms and shaking me.

"Stop it, Dad." I try to shove him away, but he shakes me again. I freeze because Mom's not here and I have no one to defend me.

"When I tell you I'm not your father. I mean it." He releases my arms and walks to one of the cabinets beside the fireplace. I watch as he opens the cabinet on the very top and pulls out a manila folder before heading back over to me, shoving it in my chest. "All the information you need is in there," he says roughly. Turning, he returns to the cabinet and busies himself with organizing other documents.

I slowly open the folder, hesitantly because I don't know what's happening. I pull out a single white document. "What is this?" I ask, confused.

"Don't tell me you've forgotten how to read," he states before sitting on the couch, his eyes fixed on me.

I look at the document's title.

It's a paternity test.

I scan it, and when the information finally sinks in, my mouth opens.

I should be hurt. I should feel distraught over this.

But I'm not.

I don't know if I'm happy because this monster isn't my dad or sad that I'm almost eighteen and the only father I've known turns out to be a complete fabrication.

"Y-you're not my dad …," I hear myself say in awe, trailing off.

"That's right." He watches me. And even though he looks happy about my confusion and apparent hurt over the news, there's also a quiet anger beneath his veneer.

"Well, then who—who's my dad?" I ask, "Does that mean Mom—?"

"I don't know who your damn father is!" he yells, rising from his seat and cutting me off. "That's something you should go figure out. I married your mother before you were born and I *believed* you were mine. It wasn't until that accident you had that I found out otherwise."

The accident in question was years ago.

Why hadn't he said anything then?

"Why tell me now?" I ask.

"Because of your mother. Trust me, I would've told you that day in that very hospital room. I had no desire to keep raising someone else's bastard." His face is flushed and the vicious scowl he's wearing makes me wonder how much of his hate for me carries over to my mother. "I love that woman, would do anything for her, but I couldn't pretend to share my affections for a kid who isn't mine." He turns away from me and walks to the opposite end of the room.

I don't know what to say next. I'm not crying because the part of me hurt over the news is already coming to terms with the truth, and the happier part is growing more ecstatic by the second. This man isn't my dad. I feel a sense of relief at knowing he'd been a moron for his own egotistical reasons. He didn't want a child who wasn't his.

My mind races, almost fog-like, and we stand in the room

for a few minutes before he speaks again. "Who exactly your father is? I don't know and neither do I care. That's something you and your mother will have to discuss," he says, his back still to me.

I don't believe him. I can't imagine Baron Carlyle, who my mom had obviously cheated on, didn't know who the man was she'd stepped out on him with. I don't press the issue, because I'll find out. As spineless as Mom is, she wouldn't deny me the truth.

"Of course, you're welcome to leave this house at your earliest convenience. You barely sleep here as it is." He finally turns to face me, his expression guarded.

Was he seriously trying to kick me out?

Mom is still my mother, no matter how little she shielded me from him over the years, and she is still a part of this household.

"Really, I don't care where you go. I simply thought you wouldn't want to be the bastard child in a family with as prodigious a name as Carlyle," he continues. "Your mother got knocked up before we were forced to marry so who knows what kind of *vermin* she made the mistake of laying with." He says the word with such hatred, it's like he takes personal offense at whoever it was my mom had been with prior to him.

But he doesn't stop.

"It's no wonder you're so different from Beverly. I mean, it's night"—he gestures to me—"and day." He says the last part while looking at Beverly's photo hanging above the fireplace. "Whatever you decide to do, go ahead. I'm more than willing to have the maids help you."

"I'm *not* leaving before talking to my mom." I'm not letting this man run me out of the house before I get answers from her.

"Suit yourself, but you'll only prolong the inevitable and

probably end up hurting your mother in the process," he says, straightening up and striding over to me.

"More than you already have?" I get bold, feeling more confident by the minute. There's something about knowing I share no blood with this man that gets me fired up.

He glares at me, one of his fists clenching at his side. He immediately unclenches it and smiles at me, a smile that doesn't reach his eyes. "Beanca, I tell you what. I'll go for a *long* drive. When I return, be here, or don't. It doesn't matter to me how long you stay gone, hasn't mattered for a while now." He utters his next words in an attempt to twist his knife deeper. "Why don't you go live with one of the boys you've been with? Whichever one or *ones* they may be at the moment. You know, you are the image and likeness of the being who spawned you. A mini whore."

My eyes flutter at his use of the word *whore*. I close my eyes tightly as I utter words to counter any attack that might come. If Baron Carlyle thinks kicking me out and saying those hateful words will break me, I'll fight like hell to prove him wrong.

I'm glad he's not my father, couldn't be happier. I just wish I'd found this out sooner, so I wouldn't have been subjected to this monster for years.

I hear his footsteps as he strolls past me, but my eyes are still closed as I fight to gain control of my emotions.

Mini whore.

Whore.

His words echo through my head, and I slap my hands over my ears in an attempt to quiet them.

The heat of tears spills from the corners of my eyes.

My fate is worse than the black sheep. At least it *knew* its family.

I have no clue who my father is.

Chapter Twenty-One

BEANCA

I drag my clothes from the closet and stuff them into my suitcase. I'm not staying here. As soon as Mom gets here, and I talk to her, I'm getting out.

Lucas finally picks up. "Hey, princess." His voice calms me, a momentary balm to my frayed nerves.

"Lucas," I say, unable to fake a strength I don't feel.

"Bee? What's wrong?"

I don't want to do this to him, but I don't know how to avoid asking. "I don't h—have anywhere else to go." I can barely talk without sobbing into the phone.

"Are you home? I'm heading there now. Did he—did he hurt you?" The anger in his voice is palpable.

I shake my head. I'm hurt, but it's nothing physical.

"Beanca? Answer me." Lucas's keys jingle before I hear his truck firing up.

"N—no. He didn't. I—I just need someplace to stay. I'm not staying here. I can't. Not anymore. N—not after this."

"Baby, you know you don't need to ask. My place is always

open to you," he says, his voice gentle, soothing. "I should be there in fifteen."

I continue packing. My hands tremble as I reach for my shoes and other miscellaneous items.

My tears shift from sadness to anger.

How could my mom do this to me? I asked her so many times why Dad hated me so much, and she'd willingly lied to me, knowing Baron wasn't my real father. That, over anything else, makes me mad as hell. I could've saved myself so much grief and anguish knowing he wasn't my dad. Instead, I've been Ms. Weeping Willow whenever he gets to me.

Today is the last time … *the* very last time that man gets my tears.

"I'm over this!" I yell, stuffing a medium-sized suitcase with the last few items that can fit in before dragging the zipper closed. I don't need much. Just some stuff to get me through the next few weeks.

"Ms. Beanca, is everything okay—?" One of the maids peeks into my room. I look over to the slightly open doorway and find her hand over her mouth in shock. "What are you doing, Miss?"

"What does it look like I'm doing? I'm leaving!"

"Oh dear. I'll call Mrs. Carlyle." She turns and scurries away, probably to go and gossip to the others about more of our household drama.

"Hot off the press! Tell them! Tell them whatever you want!" I yell after her. I don't believe for a second she got out of here that fast just to go call my mother.

I don't care. I'm out of here today anyway.

The doorbell rings a while later, and when Lucas comes stalking up the stairs and into my room, it's to find me cutting my hair into a shoulder-length bob.

"Beanca," he says, jerking my attention away from the mirror.

The scissors are midway to a handful of strands as I toss a

look over at him before returning to the task at hand. "Hey, Lucas." I've managed to control my emotions, and I'm glad my voice comes out normal.

"Why are you … cutting your hair?"

"Because I want to," I say, turning slightly to offer him a smile before looking down at the mass of long black tresses scattered around my feet. Holding the last few strands steadily, I snip them too.

Turning my head this way and that, I can't help but admire my reflection. I didn't do as hatchet a job as I thought, after all.

"Looks pretty good for an amateur, doesn't it?" I turn away from the mirror and bring my attention back to Lucas. The look on his face makes me feel small, like there's something wrong with what I've done. "Don't look at me like that. I actually like my haircut. Even if you don't." I shift my gaze back to my reflection.

"Do you?" he asks, doubtful. He walks over to stand behind me and looks at me through our reflections in the mirror.

I meet his gaze there, then straighten my spine. "Yes, I do," I say firmly, eyes flashing, daring him to contradict my words.

He surprises me when he gently removes the scissors from my hand and begins evening out my impromptu haircut. "Then if you like it, let me help you." As he continues cutting the jagged ends, I stare at his reflection.

His face is focused as his hands take hold of a few stray ends. He's careful, gliding the edges of the scissors across them.

His eyes mist over, but he says nothing.

When the first drops touch his cheek, I whirl around to face him. Lucas's tears trigger mine and I blink my eyes, dropping my face into my hands.

"This is my fault," he says, dropping the scissors. They clatter against the floor as he pulls me into his embrace.

I'm plunged into a deluge of tears I fought so hard to contain earlier.

"Baby, please," he pleads, squeezing me against him as we slide to the floor of my bedroom.

I don't feel the cold tiles beneath us because I'm curled into the warmth of Lucas's body, my face tucked into the crook of his neck.

"Don't cry, please." His voice is broken and strained. Lucas crying causes me to come further apart at the seams. He holds my head, tugging me so I'll look at him. Framing my face with his warm hands, his eyes lock with mine.

I reach my hands up to his face, wiping at his tears with my fingers. "Lucas, why are you—?"

He slides a thumb over to gently cover my lips.

I gaze into his watery blue eyes, mesmerized by the depth I see there. An emotion I can't place. It's heavy. Too heavy, causing my chest to ache at the sight of it. Feeling odd sensations in my stomach, I avert my gaze, attempting to look anywhere but at him.

"I love you," he says.

I freeze, my body rigid as I stare at the floor of my bedroom.

"I love you, Beanca," he repeats.

I try to remove myself from his embrace, but he holds me captive.

"Look at me." Reaching a hand to my chin, he attempts to turn my face to his again.

"Let go of me, Lucas." I lean away, training my gaze on my suitcase on the bed.

Lucas knows how I feel about that word.

"Why are you doing this to me?" I ask in frustration. "Why now with all that's going on with my family?"

"Beanca, you have to know that no matter what happens with your dad, I love—"

"He's not my dad!" I blurt out, pushing hard at him to let me go.

He slides his hand to encircle my waist, still stubbornly holding me against him. "How did you find out?" For some reason, he doesn't seem surprised by the revelation. But I can't blame him. He's probably happy for me, since Lucas has cared even less for the monster, especially these past few months.

"It's all in that folder over there." I indicate the manila folder my dad—Baron gave me earlier. "He's known all this time. *They've* known all this time and never once thought to tell me. I mean, it doesn't matter since I got what I wanted, right?"

He looks away then, seeming a bit uncomfortable.

I narrow my eyes at him. "What is it?"

"Beanca!" My mom yells from the open doorway as she enters my room. "What have you done to your hair?!" When I'd dyed my hair black, I got a similar response from her. Mom doesn't try to hide her horror and disapproval.

I shoot up from Lucas's lap and look down at the lopped off strands strewn across the floor in front of my dresser. "Can't you see, Mom?" I ask, tossing a hand through my hair. "I cut it."

"Why did you do that? Your beautiful hair … why did you —?" She stops short when she notices the folder on my bed. It's open and the paternity results are clear to see. "How did you get this?" She rushes over and pulls the document from the bed, clutching it to her chest.

"He gave it to me. Your husband that is. Then he kicked me out," I snort in amusement. "Some man you have. I'm never marrying anyone. I *never* want to end up like you."

"Beanca, stop it," Lucas says, grabbing my arm and jerking me toward him. "She's your mother."

"No," Mom says, surprising us both. "Let her talk, Lucas."

I turn to look at her.

"I suppose you'll want to know who your father is." She chuckles, almost hysterical.

"This is *funny* to you?" I ask, scowling.

"Mrs. Carlyle, wait," Lucas says warily. "I don't think now is a good time to—"

"The man who came to dinner a few nights ago—" Mom starts.

"Mrs. Carlyle, please." Lucas tries to get in between us, holding his palm up to her.

"Mr. Bridges?" I ask, ignoring Lucas. "Yeah, what about him?"

"King Bridges *is* your biological father," she confesses.

I stagger back and when I feel the softness of the mattress beneath my fingers, I drop myself onto it. Inhaling deeply, I stare into nothingness. Lucas comes to stand in front of me but all I can see are his jeans and tennis shoes. I cover a hand over my mouth when a scream threatens to erupt from me. Squeezing my eyes shut, I ask, "Why did you keep this from me?"

Silence.

"Mr. Bridges? Does he know?" I ask, opening my eyes.

It's rare to find someone else with eyes the same color as mine.

It's a trait I inherited from my father, and he from his father. I reckon you inherited them from your father.

"He knows, doesn't he?!" I yell the question at her, smacking my hands against the bed.

"Yes! King knows!" My mom shouts, her chest heaving and her face filled with more emotion than I've seen from her in years. "He knows you're his daughter, Beanca. He's wanted to tell you but Baron and I ... we thought it would probably be best to wait until ... until you graduated."

I laugh, rising from the bed to face her. "That's a lie. Baron is the one who wanted to wait. You forget I've grown up with both of you over the years. I know what kind of person he is. He didn't want to risk others knowing you cheated on him."

"I never stepped out on Baron! King and I were in love before Baron and I were made to marry. We always—" She stops herself when she realizes she's said too much.

I frown at the unintended disclosure. "In *love?*" I laugh, holding my stomach when I run out of breath. "You and Mr. Bridges *loved* each other? That's so ridiculous. Some love that was, if you ended up here."

"Beanca," Lucas grinds out in warning.

"*Fine.*" I point to my suitcase. "Will you get that for me?" I grab my duffle and bag pack off the bed.

"What—where are you going with a suitcase?" Mom asks frowning.

Really?

"Didn't you hear the part where your *husband* kicked me out?"

She looks at me incredulous. "Baron can't do that. I'm part owner of this house just as much as he." She turns to Lucas. "Put that down. She is not leaving this house."

"What are you talking about?" I ask, confused. "I always sleep over at my friends' houses. You've never prevented me from doing it." I'm annoyed because it's not like her or … Baron have really stopped me from going out. It'll take some time, but I look forward to referring to that man as anything other than Dad.

"That … was before King expressed his displeasure at you staying out overnight without parental supervision. He'd rather have you here with me. However, if you decide to stay elsewhere indefinitely, it'll have to be at his place and under his supervision." She says the last statement with resignation. "Beanca, please don't make this harder than it has to be."

I don't understand how my life is turned upside down in under an hour, and I'm just supposed to go along with all of it.

Hell no.

"Okay so let me get this straight," I say, pausing to gather my thoughts. "I find out that my dad isn't actually my *dad*, and instead some man whom I've spoken to all of three times in my entire existence is my father. But then I'm expected to pick up and go live with said father. I don't even know him, Mom!"

"No one expects you to go live with King. If you were listening to the first part of my statement you'd realize I said you are perfectly fine remaining under this roof. What you will not do, however, is take off to go live God knows where with God knows whom." She pries the suitcase from Lucas's hand and holds it to her side.

"Mom, this is totally unfair. You know Baron doesn't want me here," I complain, feeling defeated.

"That's not his decision to make. You're *my* daughter," she states firmly.

"Where was all this confidence and backbone when he treated me like crap, Mom?" I'm having a hard time believing this sudden change.

"Beanca, please don't put this on me. Baron can be—"

"A jerk. He's said some awful and hurtful things to me. You should've seen him today. He was reveling in the fact that I'm not his. All these years—all these years he's despised me, your little devil spawn."

"Stop it," Lucas grabs me and turns me to face him. "Listen, I get why you're upset, Bee. You have every right to be. But ruminating on the stuff that guy says, it's not good for you." He turns to my mom, hugging me to his side. "Mrs. Carlyle, I understand you want Beanca either with you or her father. But can she stay with me and my mom for the week? At least let her get a chance to process all of this."

Mom stares into my eyes and sighs heavily. "I do love you, Beanca."

"Don't say that word to me. People who love you don't lie to you, not about something like this. All of you have lied to me. I don't even know who I can trust anymore." I remember how much Lucas has supported me; he's been there for me, and he's not even family. I turn to him, "You've been here the entire time. *You* haven't lied and kept the truth from me like …" I don't finish. It all becomes too much to keep thinking about it.

"Let's just table this," Lucas says, looking over at my mom.

She nods at us. "One week. Then it's either King's place or it's back home with us, Beanca."

I avoid looking at her, frowning with my head down. Lucas takes my suitcase and we walk out, leaving her standing there.

It won't be just one week. I turn eighteen in less than two and I'll be damned if I live either here or with Mr. King Bridges. No way am I calling him dad.

No way.

Chapter Twenty-Two

LUCAS

I should've told Beanca.

The past few days she's been with my mom and I haven't been smooth. Partially because of the overwhelming guilt on my part in the conversations and interactions we've had. I want to let her know I had prior knowledge about her connection to King, but I get choked up each time I think I can tell her. It doesn't help that King comes by almost every day to check on or speak with her. All of which Beanca has refused, locking herself inside the upstairs room she's staying in on Mom's side of the house.

Mom trusts me, but King wouldn't have her quarters anywhere near mine.

"Beanca, I thought we could spend the afternoon together." King walks over to where Beanca stands next to a bay window overlooking the back lawn.

I busy myself with sorting through a new order of books that came in yesterday. There are few classics I know Beanca will enjoy. Glancing over at them, I notice she's gone rigid, refusing to look at King.

"When?" she asks, inspecting an invisible speck on the window. "I have school. And most afternoons I'm already very busy. When will I be able to find the time to … *spend the afternoon* with you?" She says the last bit sarcastically.

"That's not what Lucas said," King says flatly, facing me.

I groan.

Great.

Now she'll think I'm on his side.

I drag my eyes to Beanca's profile to find her side-eyeing me.

"It wasn't like that, Bee," I explain. "King asked which days would be ideal to have a talk with you. He means well." I've said as much to her before. King didn't know about Beanca's true paternity until after her accident a few years back. Her mother and Mr. Carlyle had kept the truth from them both.

Beanca inhales, before whirling around to face her father. "Fine. But I want Lucas there with us." She looks up at him, her features sober.

"That makes three of us." King shifts his gaze between Beanca and me. "Lucas, your mother and I will take you both out tomorrow evening." He holds out his hands to Beanca and she reluctantly places hers in them. "I will try my best to make up for lost time."

"Whatever." Removing her hands from his, she shakes her head, not trusting his words.

"That's a promise. I *don't* break my word. If it weren't for a promise I made to both your mother and Carlyle that I'd wait at their request, until you were eighteen, to make my identity known to you, I would've tried taking you away a long time ago. I'm here now and don't plan on letting you out of my sight."

Beanca frowns as she looks down at her hands, twisting them nervously.

"I shouldn't have listened to Carlyle, but I was careful because of your mother. That … man has some sort of hold over her. Always has." King averts his gaze then strides away, his back to us. "I don't know what virtue she saw in him. I mean, I understand. I didn't have money back then. I was a charity case, and no one thought I had a future to offer any woman, let alone your mother." His voice is despondent. "But I love her—" he clears his throat to correct, "—loved her." He turns to Beanca. "I want to take care of you, Beanca. Let me, please."

My attention goes to Beanca.

She's fighting herself. It's evident through her hesitancy to go to him. It's as if she's stopping herself from giving in to the impulse to embrace the true dedication and affection of a father she never had.

King senses it somehow.

"I—I said fine." Beanca turns to me. "I'll be upstairs." She walks past King and stalks out of the living room.

"She hates me," King says flatly, bringing a hand to his forehead and letting out a frustrated sigh.

"No. Trust me. She doesn't hate you." I leave the stack of books and walk over to him. "When she hates, Beanca doesn't waste words." She won't speak to or give attention to the person she hates or dislikes. She doesn't talk to them at all if she can help it. "She's trying to accept and come to terms with everything. The fact that you want to be in her life and are the opposite of how she's been treated by the man she thought was her father, that's what's throwing her off. It's not you."

King looks intently at me then nods. "I know I'll have to give her time. Take care of her will you. And Lucas," his eyebrows draw together in earnest, "you are both still teenagers. I trust you will be respectful and responsible with my daughter."

"Yes, sir."

"Her birthday is next week," he says. "Do you think she'd be interested in a dinner or just something with you guys and her friends?" King is vulnerable when he asks the question. I almost wish Beanca could be here to see it. How he puts her well-being above everything.

"I'll ask her and get back to you," I say.

"Thank you."

King leaves, and I follow him out. As soon as he disappears through the front door, I head to Beanca's room.

A pillow is thrown at my head as soon as I enter.

"I can't believe you!" Beanca yells, coming over to me. "You took his side! Lucas, you are so——"

I silence her next words by pulling her to me and placing a firm kiss against her lips.

She pushes at my chest, but I hug her closer, trapping her in my arms.

"You're not getting away with this. How could you?" She frowns up at me, a slight sadness in her voice.

"Baby, I didn't take his side. I would never do that. I'm for whoever cares about you. *He* does."

"Yeah, well why didn't he take me away like he said he wanted?" She starts removing invisible specks from my shirt. "No one would have stopped me from taking my kid away from a man who wasn't her dad."

"Maybe he couldn't have made you a stable home like you were accustomed to," I offer. "He's never been married, you know that? Maybe … he's still in love with your mom?"

"Some love that is." She removes my hands from around her and sits in front of her laptop on the desk. I walk over to see what she's up to.

She's searching for scholarships.

"I thought you were confident about getting scouted for a music school," I say.

"I am, but you can never be too careful with these things.

I'm going to college no matter if I get scouted or not. And I'm hoping it's far, far away from here."

The way she says that causes a visceral reaction. She doesn't ask if I'm considering leaving town like she did a few months ago. In fact, Beanca's focus on searching for grants, for scholarships, hasn't included me at all. Maybe I'm being selfish for thinking she needs to ask about my future plans after graduation and how they line up with hers.

"Oh yeah," I say. "How far are we talking?" I lift her off the chair and take a seat before pulling her down on my lap. "Does this distance take your boyfriend into account?"

She looks at me over her shoulder as I rake my fingers through her hair, massaging her scalp. Leaning her head into my hands, she sighs. "That feels so good."

I smile, pulling her mouth to mine for a brief kiss.

"I didn't think about how that sounded," she says. "Of course, I thought about you. About Jones, Shepherd." She pecks my cheek before bringing her attention back to the laptop.

Wrapping my arms around her waist, I lay my head against her back. Listening to her steady heartbeat, I rub my face against her, enjoying the feel of her in my arms. I don't want Beanca moving away and leaving me here. "I love you, Beanca."

She stops typing.

"I love you," I repeat, wanting desperately for her to say it back, yet deep down knowing she won't.

Her heartbeat below my ear intensifies and before she gets a chance to tell me she doesn't want to hear the words, I stand with her in my arms. "Let's go," I say, pulling her along. "I want to show you something."

I grin down at her when she looks up at me, confusion etched in her features.

"What is it?" She's suspicious but there's a note of excitement in her voice.

"Wait and see."

BEANCA

Lucas and I pull up to a ranch, and I look over at him in surprise. "Wait, why'd you bring me here?"

He winks at me then hops out of his truck. He approaches my side and opens the door before holding my hand as I get out. "I asked and Mom said I could. I wanted to wait until next week … but something told me to do it now."

He brings me to his side and we walk toward the entrance of what appears to be a large spread of various barns and stables.

The place is luxurious, the atmosphere of wealth and old money palpable as we pass by a few other guests. I'm not sure how to feel, because I know Lucas's family is wealthy, but it's another thing entirely to witness how he can just waltz into this place. Especially at a young age.

"Hey, Green," Lucas says as we pass the security at the entrance.

"It's been a while since we've seen you out here, Moore," Green, the security guy, replies. He's well-built, and much older than us. But with the way he and Lucas talk to each other you would think they went way back.

"How do you know him?" I whisper when their conversation ends, and we continue down the path to the stables.

"He knew my dad. Dad would bring me here, and he'd sneak me pieces of candy and tell me crazy stories about the people who come here." Lucas chuckles at the memory.

I smile up at him, his joy infectious at recollecting his childhood memories.

We arrive at one of the first stables. It's clean and smells surprisingly nice. I expected the stench of animals and horse manure.

A few people are looking through the slats of several stalls, while others pet and feed some of the horses.

I pause, looking up at Lucas, causing him to stop short beside me. "Lucas, why did you bring me here?" I ask for the second time. I thought we were here to watch horse races.

"Princess, let's play a game," he says mischievously. "One objective. The person who finds the best horse, wins."

"Hey, no fair," I complain. "That's easy for you. I mean, you were practically born on a horse."

He grins, "Alright, I'll give you a five-minute head start."

"Deal." I let go of his hand and start hunting down the best-looking horse I can find. I pet, feed and do everything to figure out which horse I like best. They are all so gorgeous that by the time I meet Lucas back at the starting point, I don't know if I can choose just one.

"Lucas, this is impossible! All of these horses look good. I'm probably going to lose, because you'll choose based on actual stats." I pinch his arm in protest.

He smacks my butt.

"Lu-cas." I look up at him sternly before indicating people can see us.

"Nope. It's fair, princess. It's not my fault you didn't ask what specs should be prioritized." He grabs hold of my hand and laces our fingers together. "Well, which one do you choose?"

Even though I said it was impossible, I do have a favorite. Leading us directly to my choice, I stop in front of the stall. "I like him! He's definitely the best one here." I gesture to a stallion with a pristine black coat, as dark as the midnight sky.

Opening a peppermint from one of the stable hands I'd kept during my hunt, I hand it to him. His thick tongue gladly licks then sucks it up from my hand. Chewing on the mint, he allows me to pet him down the bridge of his nose.

"Then, he's yours," Lucas says without hesitation.

I whirl away from the horse to face him. "Wh-what did you say?"

The way Lucas looks at me, the depth of something I can't name present in his softened eyes, makes yet another chink in my fortified armor.

"Happy early birthday, Beanca. He's yours."

I stand there for several seconds, not knowing what to say.

"Congratulations, miss," one of the stable hands says, drawing my attention to him. "Henry is a purebred stallion and one of our best horses."

Turning my attention back to Lucas, I shake my head. "Lucas, you're not messing with me, right?"

He chuckles, "No, baby. I wouldn't do that. Not on your birthday. Henry is yours now." Lucas turns and places a card in the other man's hand.

The man retrieves something, and when he returns, he places a huge SOLD sign on a hook against the stall.

"See," Lucas says, leaning down to place a brief kiss against my lips. "He's yours."

I squeal.

Reaching giddy arms up and around his neck, I lift myself up and kiss him, not caring about the pairs of eyes that turn to us. "Thank you! You are the kindest person I know, Lucas," I say earnestly, gazing into his intense eyes.

I can't believe he bought me a horse!

I'm coasting on cloud nine for several seconds before reality slams into me. "Lucas, wait. Where am I going to keep him?" It's not like I'll live at his place indefinitely. And then there's me moving out of town when I go off to college.

"We'll climb that mountain when we get there. For now, Henry will stay at my place," he explains. "No matter where you are, you can always come see him." Lucas stares into my eyes, and his words, though clear, seem to hold greater meaning than just referring to the horse. It's as if he's trying to anchor me to *him* somehow.

I shake my head in an attempt to dislodge the ridiculous thought. I clearly need to stop overthinking things.

"Thank you, babe," I repeat, kissing him again, this time with all the emotion I feel. I don't doubt Lucas cares for me. Everything he's done and continues doing is proof of that.

It's me I have to work on.

His actions toward me shake me to my core, throwing me out of sorts with my internal beliefs about what I think I deserve.

A part of me constantly worries that as easily as his affections for me are there, they can fade away just as fast. That all I have to do is make one wrong move, and he'll abandon me.

Chapter Twenty-Three

BEANCA

"You and Lucas have gotten pretty serious, huh?" Chase places another scoop of vanilla ice cream in a glass bowl before handing it to me.

I lean over the huge kitchen island to retrieve it. "I could say the same thing about you and Dudley." I point to the ring on her third finger. "That's new."

Flashing her left hand out in front of her, she sighs, her face concerned. "I like him, and we have a great time together." She serves herself a bowl of ice cream before closing the container and placing it back into the freezer. "It's just a ring. I'm not thinking any further into it."

I frown. "Just a ring? I think that's pretty serious."

"I know. But like I said, I don't think Dudley and I should entertain the idea of marriage when we haven't experienced much out of life yet." She sits on the barstool next to mine, and we both look out to her living room where some of our friends are gathered.

They're all watching the NFL playoffs, getting rowdy whenever one of their coveted teams score a touchdown.

"If anything, maybe you can think of it as just a token of how much you mean to him." I shrug. "That way it doesn't seem so serious."

"Bee, he always tells me how much he loves me, how much he only wants me."

I stiffen. Well, this is where I bow out of this conversation. "Will you look at that. Jones is finally here." I look rueful before saying, "Don't worry, Dudley will understand whatever you decide after graduation. Continue this later?"

She nods, staring down at her ice cream.

"Jones!" I head over to him, immediately noticing he's upset. "Whoa. What's up?"

"I'm good." He brushes past me and makes a beeline for the back room.

I follow him. "Clearly it's *something*. What's going on with you?"

"Nothing a good party won't fix."

Jones opens the door and everyone yells, "Surprise!"

I startle.

Jones turns around with a huge grin as they all start singing.

"Happy birthday, Beanca!" Everyone shouts.

I'm shocked when I look behind me and find Lucas with a cake and the number 18 candle lit. We're scheduled for a dinner with my parents within the hour so I wasn't expecting much of anything else, least of all a surprise.

I shuffle over to Lucas and make a wish, blowing out the candles before reaching up and kissing him. "Thank you, babe."

He smiles down at me and then kisses my forehead. "You deserve it." The *and so much more* is unspoken, but there in his gaze all the same.

I turn to look at Jones. "So all that melodrama just now was for this?"

Jones nods. "Guilty." He pulls me into a bear hug and then pulls out a small, wrapped gift from his pocket. "Thought you'd appreciate this."

"Thanks, Jones." I grab it and unwrap it to find a small silver bracelet with musical notes charms of various colors.

"Happy birthday, Bee." Shepherd also hands me a gift. When I unwrap that one it's a portrait of the four us at the start of our high school years and then transitions into us now. The photo has *Always the Four Musketeers* printed over above our portrait.

"This is so cool! Thank you, Shep." I hug him to me, relieved we've managed to get past everything from last year.

"Lemme see," Lucas says, handing the cake off to someone and taking the photo. "That's pretty cool, Shep. Where'd you get this done?"

The two of them are drowned out by others handing me presents.

After a while, we cut the cake and share it out. For the next hour, I'm so far over the moon I'm practically floating in the heavens. It feels great to have all the people I care so much about in one place. We graduate in the next three months and it's times like this I'm definitely going to miss.

King comes to pick me up for my birthday dinner, and Lucas goes to his truck to follow along. It's a smaller, more intimate celebration, so only Beverly and Mom will be there.

I'm taking my time getting accustomed to viewing King as my father.

"King, I want to apologize for the other day at Lucas's place," I say as I get into the passenger seat of his Bentley. "It was uncalled for and undeserved."

"Beanca, no need for an apology. Understandably, you'd react the way you have."

"Still."

"Before we get to the restaurant, I do have something to ask." His hands tighten around the steering wheel. "Have you decided yet if you'd like to stay with me or your mother until you graduate?"

Of course.

In the end, a father is still a parent with his own preoccupation. King is still not happy with me living in close quarters with a guy, especially due to the relationship between Lucas and me.

I take a breath. "Well, honestly, as awkward as I would feel returning to Baron's house, I think it's best if I live with you. If you don't mind."

His hands visibly loosen, the tension leaving his shoulders. "I was hoping you'd say that. My home is always open to you, sweetheart."

"Thank you."

"I've missed out on a lot."

I turn to him. "How long after my accident did they tell you that I was your daughter?" The question has been eating at me for the past week.

"The same year of your fall, when you had the concussion." His answer is honest, and I can see the disappointment in his features. "I know you're wondering why I didn't reach out then, but your mother's husband can be … well, for lack of a better term, a real pain."

"So you found out when I was eleven?" I frown in confusion. "What did he do to keep you away from me?"

"It's what he refused to do," he says in frustration. "Becky wanted to run a paternity test to confirm you were mine so I'd have a legal right to you, but he prevented her. I was the only other man your mother had been with when she got pregnant."

I sit back, stunned.

"When they ran your blood during your time in the hospital, Carlyle found out that your blood type couldn't have come from his and Becky's union. Only then did he know you weren't his child."

"That's why he changed after the accident," I say.

"What do you mean?" he asks.

"Baron, he—he was horrible to me when I returned home from the hospital. After the day I fell from that treehouse it was like I became a stranger to him, worse than a stranger."

"Did he hit you?" King asks, eyes flashing.

"N-no, he never hit me," I lie. "He just said awful things to me over the years." I have no desire to protect Baron from King. I simply don't want more drama in my life.

King is silent beside me, and I have a feeling he doesn't believe Baron didn't lay hands on me. If hate is a vibration, I can feel it emanating from King in waves.

We get to the restaurant and are ushered to the table he reserved. Lucas, Beverly, and my mom are already seated and waiting for us.

"Happy birthday, honey," Mom says, kissing my cheek. She smells amazing and looks beautiful tonight in her black satin top and dark jeans, her hair left to hang loosely down her shoulders.

I'm shocked Baron let her out of his sight. I wonder at the possible lie she had to tell to be at this dinner with King present.

"Bee, finally!" Beverly says coming around the table to hug me. "Happy birthday!"

We all take our seats, Lucas to my right and Beverly to my left.

King takes a seat next to Mom. Looking at the two of them together like this, King in his white button down and her to his left, I shake my head. I don't want to overthink things, but the way my mom is with him and his manner is reminiscent of two people who are clearly still attracted to each other. It's almost awkward how they try to make it look like they have nothing between them.

"Well," King says, a little more straight-laced than he looks. He attempts not to stare at Mom but fails miserably. "Did you order anything yet?"

Mom frowns. "No, we were waiting for you and Beanca."

"Yup. Right." King shakes his head and picks up an empty glass to drink from it. When he realizes his error, he puts the glass down and focuses on me. "Happy birthday."

It's on my tongue to remind him he's already said as much, but I don't. Why beat a horse when it's down on its luck.

Lucas leans over to whisper, "Is it just me or does King seem nervous?"

I turn to him. "It's not just you."

We order, and as the night wears on, the conversation flows in semi-awkwardness. King eventually mellows, and everything smooths over.

"So, Beanca, have you decided which music school you'll accept?" Mom asks.

"No, I'm still waiting to hear back from a few."

"It's their loss. Those recruiters at your recital should have scouted you on the spot," King says after wiping his mouth. "You were phenomenal."

"I had a feeling you were there because of her," Lucas says.

We all look at him.

"What I mean is, obviously you were there for her," he clarifies. "Not that we would've known at the time." He reaches for his glass of lemon water and downs half of it.

"Yes, well. I agree with King." This statement comes from my mom.

My next words bubble up and pop out before I can hold onto them. "How would you know? You weren't there."

Mom's jaw slackens and her brows furrow.

Lucas nudges me.

King looks from Mom and then over to me. "Beanca, I

believe if it were up to your mother she would have been there."

Mom places a hand on his. "Don't," she says before looking over at me. "Again, I'm sorry I didn't make it that night. I've let you down more than I can ever make up for."

"Hmm. At least you know," I say.

Everyone's eyes fall on me.

I feel like a mole, like I'm the mean one.

"Sorry," I grumble.

The dinner goes on in silence for a little, but we return to some semblance of flow after a while. The restaurant staff come out with a huge cake made into the likeness of a piano and everyone, including the other patrons, sing happy birthday.

"Whoa!" Beverly looks at the cake with wide eyes. "Now that is freaking … I've *never* seen a cake this big. Ever!"

It's true. The staff have to roll it over to us on it's table.

King comes over as they sing to me and drapes an arm over my shoulders before bending to whisper, "I'll always be there for you, sweetheart. I will do whatever it takes to make up for lost time." He hands me a set of keys. "These are for my place. You are welcome home as soon as you want." He kisses my forehead and joins everyone in singing for me.

"Thank you." I faintly smile up at him and offer him the biggest of hugs for making me feel the most special I've felt on my birthday.

Lucas pulls me into his arms once I let go of King. "I'm happy for you, princess. I hope this is the beginning of many more awesome things coming your way." He kisses me, hugging me tightly against him.

When the kiss lasts too long for their liking, King and Mom clear their throats.

"Sorry. I'm sorry," Lucas says, releasing me. "I have another surprise for you," he whispers for my ears alone.

"What is it?"

"You'll see."

I spend the rest of dinner curious about Lucas's additional plans for tonight.

LUCAS

When we leave the restaurant, I take Beanca up to Tallulah. It's a clear night out and the weather's chilly, but I came prepared.

"Do you remember how much we used to fight with each other?" She laughs at the memory. "We were like an old married couple."

"Speak for yourself. I'm not old, remember," I tease.

She slaps my thigh.

We get comfortable after I've spread out thick blankets, covering a grassy patch overlooking the valley below. I pull Beanca into my arms and drag a huge quilt over us. She stares out into the distance, watching the tree branches rustle in the wind.

"Isn't it crazy how much has changed in less than a year? I have a new dad and ...," she says, trailing off.

"Yes, and still changing," I add. Bringing my lips to the side of her neck, I inhale the scent of her perfume. "Mmm. You always smell so good."

"Thanks. Wish I could say the same for you, babe," she teases.

"Oh, yeah?"

"No! Lucas," she shrieks, trying to leap from my arms when I start tickling her. She laughs uncontrollably. "S-stop. L-Lucas."

I finally let up as she tries to catch her breath. "That's what you get."

"I'm thinking of attending a New York school," she blurts out after she's managed to settle down. "It's the perfect location if I want to play professionally. I'm still waiting to hear back from a couple of schools, but I'm pretty sure I'll get into one of the music schools I applied to there."

I'm quiet.

I know Beanca wants to go away. It makes the most sense, but it still doesn't lessen how much impact it'll probably have on our relationship.

"You can always come and visit me." She turns to look at me, placing a palm against my cheek. "And I'm not opposed to coming back to town just to spend time with you."

I meet her eyes.

"Lucas," she says, kissing me softly. "Don't sulk. We can go on trips together during the breaks. Think about it. It'll give us something to look forward to."

She manages to cheer me up.

"I'd like that, actually," I say.

"See."

Swallowing at the sudden dry lump in my throat, I reach into my pocket for the gift I brought for her.

Beanca frowns when she sees the small navy-colored box. "Lucas?"

I open it and remove the ring before holding my palm out for her hand.

She places her hand tentatively in mine, hesitant at first.

I place the golden ring on her finger. It's a thin band with a teardrop emerald surrounded by small diamonds. It cost a small fortune, but it reminded me so much of her and how much she means to me.

"It's just a promise ring, Bee," I say, my voice strained. "I'll always care about you. I want you to remember that no matter where you decide to go after graduation." I'm careful not to use the word *love*.

"Lucas, did you and Dudley plan this?" she asks, smiling as she offers me her hand.

"What do you mean?" I carefully slide the ring onto her finger.

"Chase had a ring on today." Her eyes narrow, a glint of mischief behind them. "Dudley gave it to her not too long ago. Just wondering if you two have been comparing notes."

"Seriously?" I ask. I had no idea Dudley gave Chase a ring.

Her attention now focused on her third finger, she frowns.

I look away from her. "Look, if you don't want it, all you have to do is take it off and give it back."

She reaches for my chin, guiding my face back to her. "Lucas, stop. Of course I'll wear your ring. It's not that big a deal."

It is a big deal, but I don't say it. I just stare at her.

She stretches out her hand, flexing her fingers and carefully observing the ring before bringing her gaze back to mine. "I like it. It's beautiful. Thank you, babe."

"I know you don't like to hear the word but for what it's worth, I love you, Beanca. And I always want to be there for you. If you'll let me."

To my surprise, she doesn't go rigid like she usually does at hearing the word, giving me hope.

"I want to be there for you too, Lucas. We're best friends first, and that means a lot to me. I trust you."

I pull her into me for a kiss. "Happy birthday again, princess."

Chapter Twenty-Four

BEANCA

"I don't think I'll ever get used to this," I say, exhilarated.

Lucas steers his horse and bends low, passing under another tree branch.

He's taken us out on a trail near his house. I'm not a seasoned rider yet, so on a lot of the paths he guides us through, he ends up having to hold on to Henry's reigns.

There's a ravine coming up, and Henry is a little skittish about it.

"You think you can get him through the water?" Lucas asks, trotting ahead of us.

"I can try. He seems nervous, though."

Lucas wades through the water before turning on his horse to watch me guide Henry. We trot through the water, but Henry's front right hoof gets stuck in the mud when we get to Lucas's side of the ravine.

"Dang it! He can't move, babe." I try to pull hard on the reigns but my horse doesn't budge.

Lucas jumps down from his horse and comes over to help. "He needs a little more guidance that's all. Here, let me have those."

I hand him the reigns then climb down. I lose my footing and land ass down in the mud. "Ugh!"

Lucas laughs. "Why didn't you wait for me to help you down?"

He holds a hand out to me and I slap it away. "Laughing like that, it's a wonder you would've helped me at all."

"Aawe, princess. Did I hurt your feelings?" His sarcasm only serves to annoy me more.

I manage to get up on my own and after I brush the mud from the seat of my pants, I take a muddied finger and swipe it across his cheek. "There. That'll teach you to laugh at me."

Lucas doesn't look at me, but chooses to focus instead on freeing Henry from the rut he's in and then guiding him up onto the other bank. He falls when he turns and tries to reach for me. His boots and pants become caked in the mud.

I can't stop myself from bubbling over with laughter.

Lucas gets up and tries to grab for me again. "Come here."

I manage to leap away from him and over next to Henry. The sudden movement spooks my horse and he takes off.

"No! Henry, come back here!" I yell after him.

"That won't work, Bee." Lucas chuckles before grabbing me around the waist. "Here, get on Dandelion." He lifts me up and onto the back of his horse before jumping up behind me. Then we take off after Henry.

The thighs of his muddied pants brush against mine, marring my ivory riding pants. "Lucas, you're ruining my pants."

"Not much more than they already were," he counters.

I twist my head around to him, but he snakes a hand around my mid-section and pulls me against his chest, causing my head to knock against his chin.

"Ow!" I immediately reach my hand up to rub against the tender area near my temple.

Lucas kisses it, dispelling my annoyance.

"Henry!" I call out.

"Shhhh," he says.

When he starts whistling, I frown. "What's that gonna do? He's my horse, remember? Hen—!"

He covers my mouth with one hand and whistles louder.

To my surprise, a few seconds later, a rustling sound comes from the bushes up ahead. Henry reappears and slowly canters over to us. When he gets close enough, Lucas collects his reigns and guides him alongside Dandelion.

I notice we take a different way back to the house, one that doesn't require us to scale a ravine.

"Why didn't we just take that path to begin with?" I ask Lucas as we stroll back into the house a little while later.

"And miss seeing you with mud all over your ass? Hard pass." He laughs loudly, then lunges away from me when I try to swat at him.

"Not funny, Lucas."

"Not funny, but fun." He reaches for me and pulls me in for a bear hug. "Let's wash up."

I go to the room he and his mom have prepared for me whenever I visit. I shower, change, and head to the study before Lucas arrives.

New mail must have come in since the last time I was here. I'm hoping to hear back from at least one of the music schools I've applied to and I'd used their address on my application at the time.

There's a stack of unopened envelopes atop the office desk. I sift through them and almost squeal when I find three addressed to me. Opening the desk drawer, I leaf through some papers for a letter opener.

When I find neither, I go to close the drawer when the words Paternity Results arrest my attention. I shuffle the document free of others and pull it out of the drawer. The results show a paternity match with Patient A and Patient B. I flip the paper this way and that, looking for names but finding none. Was Lucas's trying to find out his own paternity, too? Why?

"What's that?"

I jump at the sound of Lucas's voice from the open doorway.

He walks into the room and nods to the mail and the paper in my hand.

"Hey, I just found this in your desk while searching for something to open my mail." I hold up the paternity results. "Is this yours? I thought I was the only one around here with a long lost parent." I fan the paper out in front of me.

Lucas's eyes widen and he comes over to me, snatching the paper from my grasp. He doesn't say anything, but rubs a hand over his neck.

"What is it?" I ask, frowning at his odd reaction.

He pauses before looking at me, his expression sober. "Beanca, I can explain."

"Explain? You look like the kid that just got caught with his hands in the cookie jar." I chuckle, then place my fingers in the loops of his jeans. "Explain what?"

His brows knit together and he stares down at the paper. His throat works and he attempts to speak but no words come out.

I sober up too, removing my hands from his belt loops and smoothing them up and down his upper arms. "Lucas, what's wrong? You know you can tell me anything."

"I—," he pauses and averts his gaze, contemplating his next words. "I knew King was your father."

Confused, I look from him to the paper in his hands and back up to him. "What do you mean you knew?"

"This, Beanca." He holds the paper up to me, and my hands fall away from him. "I had a DNA test done for you and King when I suspected you were his kid." He stares down at me, looking contrite. "I wanted to tell you before it all came out but I never got the chance."

I grab the paper from him and peer at the date.

No way.

This can't be true.

My stomach feels queasy and my heart lurches, beating like a gong against my chest. "I—I don't understand. How did you—?"

"I used a hairbrush you left here and when King came for dinner one night … well—," he pauses, not finishing the statement. "I'm not proud of what I did. I just wanted to help."

"But this is dated *weeks* before I found out from Baron." The despair in my voice must trigger him, because Lucas grabs a hold of the paternity results and tosses the paper to the floor.

He takes both arms and places them around his waist, hugging me to him. "This doesn't change anything, princess."

I try to push away from him, but his embrace tightens, anchoring me in his arms. "Let go of me, Lucas."

"Beanca, I care about you. That's why I did it." He moves his hands to the planes of my face and wipes at the corners of my eyes. I didn't even realize I was crying. "Please, don't cry. None of this changes anything."

"Lucas, of course it does" I say, my voice despondent as I brush his hands away from my face. "You lied to me. You knew for weeks that that *jerk* wasn't my dad and you never even told me. Why—why would you do that? Why would you keep that from me? You knew that it was hell for me living with that man."

He closes his eyes and lets out an unsteady breath. He tries to reach for me again.

"Don't, Lucas. Don't." I step back, putting some distance between us. "Answer me. You could have chosen any time to let me know that you knew before I did. You didn't, and now … now I don't even know what else you're keeping from me."

"I'm not keeping anything from you," he pleads, stepping closer.

I hold my palms up and step back once more. "I can't trust that. If you supposedly *love* me as you say you do, you wouldn't have kept the truth from me." Realization hits me that he could have come clean after I'd found out. "You never did look shocked that day I found out King was my father."

He's hesitant and looks guilty as hell.

"You knew before I did, before my mom confessed to me that afternoon." When he just stands there, I lose it. Going over to him, I shove at his chest. "This is bullshit, Lucas! I can't believe you. I can't believe you knew!" He captures my wrists, and I pull free from his grasp. "What? Did you think I was too much of a fragile flower to handle it?"

He doesn't say anything.

"Of course. I'll answer for you. I was losing my mind, and needed a therapist. You didn't want me going *crazy*. Fine, I'll give you that. But what about after that, huh? What about all this time that's passed in between? You *still* didn't tell me?"

He just stares at me.

"Say something, damn it!" I shove at him again. When tears of anger and frustration blur my vision, he grabs my arms. "You! You're unbelievable!" I scream, jerking my body and trying to get him to let me go. "I'm sick of people lying to me all the damn time. I'm over this!"

"Beanca," he says though gritted teeth. "You're—I did nothing different than what you did when you kept the truth about Evie from Shepherd."

His words are like a slap in the face.

Last year when I didn't tell Shepherd about the video Evie secretly filmed of her and his dad together, it was purely to keep Shepherd and his dad from getting into a fight over a girl I didn't think was worth it at the time. I was trying to protect my friend. Initially, I kept the truth to myself for his own good, but in the end, I came clean.

That's not the case with Lucas and he knows it. Him keeping the truth from me only caused me to suffer longer under the roof of a monster who cared nothing about me.

For Lucas to throw what happened last year with Shepherd and Evie in my face, lets me know he doesn't regret his actions.

I sober immediately, going rigid in his arms.

"Bee, I didn't mean that. I'm sorry," he says, releasing me. Stepping back, he rakes both hands through his hair. "What does it really matter when I found out, huh? I was going to tell you, but you found out the truth before I got the chance, so it doesn't matter anymore."

I grow even colder, the numbness spreading throughout my entire body. I am not interested in continuing this conversation.

Lucas reaches an arm out, and I shove it away.

"Then we have nothing else to say to each other, Lucas. I thought you were someone I could trust. Turns out I was wrong. Let's try and end this without ill feelings towards each other." My voice is flat, emotionless as I continue. "I'll remember you as an amazing friend I once had. I'll see you around."

I attempt to walk past him but he shoots a hand out and stops me. "You're breaking up with me? Beanca, are you serious? Over something that's not even an issue anymore? You realize how ridiculous that is, right?" He glares into my eyes, anger souring his features.

"I don't care if you think I'm *ridiculous*. You made a decision without me, and now I'm making one without you. This *relationship* or whatever you want to call it, is over. You lied, and if I didn't find this paper by accident," I bend to pick up the discarded paternity results, then continue, "you would have never told me." I place the paper in his hand, and he unblocks my path.

"Fine," he says flatly, not bothering to come after me as I

walk away. "Suit yourself. We're not together anymore. Don't get upset if I take my newfound freedom with ease."

I pause, close my eyes, and inhale.

He said those words to hurt me. Maybe he's wanted me to end this, to free him so that he could be with other people. It's funny really, how in the end I always do end up abandoned.

I look down at my left hand, at the promise ring he'd given me. The emerald teardrop stares back at me. Slowly removing it, I place it on one of the bookshelves near me. Strengthening my resolve, I don't look back when I say, "Do whatever you want, Lucas. You always did anyway …"

I quicken my strides and stalk through the study doors and out to my car.

Once in, I slam the door, start the car and speed through the gates. Leaving Lucas Moore to the *freedom* I've kept him from.

LUCAS

I walk over and retrieve the ring Beanca left behind, the ring I gave her. I promised to always be there for her, and she promised me she'd do the same.

Some promise that was.

My chest hurts like hell and the emotions I tried so hard to suppress burst out of me like a geyser that's been freshly tapped.

Beanca broke up with me and for the life of me, I can't figure out how our conversation went from me confessing that I knew King was her father to her walking out on me, on us.

I would go after her but it's impossible to reason with Beanca when she gets like this. Instead, I message the guys for an emergency meet up at Caesar's Diner.

Not more than half an hour later, they show up for me.

"What's up?" Jones asks.

"Beanca broke things off with me."

"What?" Shepherd and Jones ask in unison.

"What'd you do?" Shepherd asks.

"Remember that thing I told you I knew but didn't feel it was my place to disclose?" I ask Shepherd.

Jones looks between us. "Oh, I see how it is."

"Uh." I clear my throat. "Are y'all gonna help me or what?"

"My bad, bro," Jones says. "You and Bee fight all the time. Y'all will be back together before the week's out."

"No. It's different this time. She gave me the ring back."

Shepherd's eyebrows raise. "That serious? What did you know?"

My throat thickens. "I knew King Bridges was her dad before she found out. It was that favor I called in from your dad, a DNA test I asked for help with." I put my hand up when Shepherd and Jones open their mouths. "Don't ask how I got what I needed for the test. The results came back, confirming that King and Beanca were a match, that he in fact was her real dad."

"That's pretty serious," Jones says. "I mean, I probably wouldn't have been that invested. You know, going so far as to get a DNA test done on any of my friends."

"Dude, you didn't tell me you went that far," Shepherd adds. "That's pretty personal."

Great. Just what I needed, my friends telling me I crossed a line. "I just wanted to help her. Beverly's dad was being awful to her, I just …"

"I get it, man," Jones says. "In more ways than you know."

"Look," Shepherd chimes in, "for what it's worth, now she knows that you were aware. Give her some time to stew about it and like Jones says, she'll eventually get over it."

The server brings the pizza to our table and they dig in.

I don't have much of an appetite. I just needed to talk to them about Beanca. For some reason, this feels different. They say she'll get over this, but I'm not feeling it this time.

I train my gaze through the panes of glass, looking out to the sidewalk and parking lot, contemplating how I'll fix this mess with Beanca. That's when I spot Beverly. Only, she's with Vincent of all people.

He's the last person I want to see today.

"Look at this idiot," I say, nodding to Vincent as he enters the diner, Beverly at his side.

Jones and Shepherd look in their direction. Jones immediately returns his attention to the slice of pizza on his plate.

"What the hell?" Shepherd asks. "When did those two get together?" He turns to me. "Does Beanca know?"

I frown. "Not that I know of. If she had she'd have said something to me, for sure."

Jones is quiet, eating and swiping through his phone.

"Jones, did you know about Beverly and Vincent?" I ask. Jones hangs out with Beverly from time to time but never let on about this.

"Bro, I don't have time to think about her personal life." His voice is strained, almost as if he's upset. "What she does is her business. It ain't got nothing to do with me."

I could comment on that but I don't. I have my own problems and I may need Beverly's help to solve them. She's currently glued to Vincent's side though, so I'll have to get her to help me later.

Shepherd signals to me, and then nods over to Jones. He frowns, silently asking about Jones's sudden change of mood.

I shrug and shake my head.

Jones suddenly starts laughing then shows us a clip of some college football fumbles. "I swear, how they got recruited is beyond me."

"Speaking of," Shepherd says. "Lucas, have you decided yet if you're staying in town with the band?"

I sigh heavily. "Yeah, I'm focusing on my music."

"That's what's up." Jones clicks his phone closed and looks at me. "It's not even like you need to go to college. It's not for everyone. I happen to like college football and got signed. *That's* why I'm going."

"Well," Shepherd chimes in, "as y'all know I'm heading up with Ev. I decided on NYU so we could stay together. I mean, I wasn't going to play football forever and I'll eventually have to take over my dad's company when he retires."

"Good for you, Shep," I say, unable to keep the note of anguish from my voice.

"You and Evie have been solid since you got together," Jones says. "First comes love, then comes marriage, and then something about a baby carriage, right?"

"Whoa!" Shepherd says. "Don't let Ev hear you say that."

I narrow my eyes. "Why? Is she not interested in tying the knot?"

"Dude, it's whatever. We're about to graduate and she's more focused on getting an education."

"Yeah, it's understandable, knowing Evie." Jones finishes off the pizza and throws an arm over Shepherd's shoulder.

My phone goes off, and when I look, it's Beanca calling me. I pick up without hesitation. "Hey."

"I've got all the stuff I borrowed from you in my car and wanted to come get my stuff, and … say goodbye to Henry. Just let me know when is a good time for you so we can make the exchange." Beanca's voice is emotionless, like none of this means anything but a necessary transaction.

"Yeah, sure," I say stiffly. "I'll let you know." I hang up, put the phone down, and then look at the guys. "She's done with me. I just know it. She's …"

Jones sighs. "All this happened today, right?"

I nod.

"Beanca's blowing off steam, man. I'm telling you."

"She's just upset, dude," Shepherd reassures. "She'll come around like she always does."

Jones looks over his shoulder at where Beverly and Vincent

are sitting, cozied up beside each other. "Hey, do y'all mind if I head out?" He drops a few bucks on the table and stands.

"What? Where?" I ask.

"Anywhere but here," he mumbles. "Look, for what it's worth, I always thought you and Bee made a good couple. Don't let a small fight ruin everything. Y'all make sense together." His gaze shifts to Beverly again and he adds, "While some of us don't."

Chapter Twenty-Five

BEANCA

I'm still upset and I have every right to be.

For Lucas, I tried. I really did. I tried to believe love was about fully trusting someone else and doing things for them that indicated you cared. How could Lucas have said he loved me when he so easily lied to me? He completely broke my trust and put a shadow over what we had. Never once had he tried to tell me he knew about my paternity before I found out.

That, more than anything, hurt most.

I don't want anything to do with him. As far as I'm concerned, we're not friends. Friends don't do to one another what he did to me.

He's just like the rest of them. Mom, Baron … They all kept the truth from me. And like a band-aid over an unhealed wound, Lucas ripped it off before I had the chance to fully recover.

I swipe at the fresh tears escaping from the corner of my

eyes, gritting my teeth against the force of emotions forming a pulsing ache in my chest.

I can do this.

Lucas and I haven't been on speaking terms for the past two months since graduation. I reassure myself that I'll continue to survive without him.

I rise from my seat when they announce that my group should line up at the gate for boarding.

I'm flying to New York today. Except for Mom, Beverly and King, no one knows I'm heading out of town early.

It's better this way.

If I had told Jones, Shepherd, or any of the others, it would have eventually made it to Lucas's ears. I still feel vulnerable when it comes to him and I don't want to be sucked back into that vortex.

After an hours-long flight, I finally land and I'm excited to get to my new apartment in Manhattan.

"Beanca Carlyle," I say to the worker at the front desk. Placing my carry-on next to me, I fish for my ID before handing it over to her.

She taps away at her computer before handing me my set of keys. She then directs the guy hired to help me with my luggage to the hallway on the right. "The elevators are right through there."

King set me up pretty well. And although we're not the daddy-daughter pairing of the year, I'm grateful for him. He doesn't over do it or forcefully dote on me. It's enough that he tries.

I enter my apartment on one of the highest floors of the nearly twenty-story building, and I'm in awe. The place is spacious with two walls of floor-to-ceiling windows, providing an amazing view of the city's skyline.

"Whoa! King you are freaking amazing!" I squeal, barely able to contain my excitement.

I rush to pull my phone out and send him a quick message

of appreciation before proceeding to take myself on a self-guided tour of the place. There are two bedrooms, one small one and a larger master, complete with a sizable walk-in closet and a to-die-for adjoined bathroom. Staring at the jacuzzi-like bathtub, I daydream about the bubble bath I'll take as soon as I can get out of these clothes.

Walking back into the living room, I sigh dreamily, then swing my legs over the edge of one of the cream-colored sofas lining its parameter.

I get lost in my thoughts, but instantly flip upright when the intercom at the front door goes off.

I walk over to look at the video feed, only to see the face of a guy I don't recognize fill the screen. I turn, intending to return to my spot on the sofa and ignoring the stranger, when the intercom signals again.

Ugh.

I whirl about and hit the button. "Can I help you?"

"Beanca?" he asks, his voice low. He doesn't seem much older than me. His sandy blonde hair is tapered down the sides and his brown eyes seem friendly enough.

"How—who is it?" I ask, confused as to how he already knows my name.

"Hey, it's Jason. Look, I live next door to you. King wanted me to check on you to see if you needed anything."

I frown. King didn't tell me he set a watch over me. I mean it's a kind sentiment, as I don't really know anyone in Manhattan.

I open the door. "Jason?"

He's quiet for a moment before visibly shaking himself. "Jason Collin. A pleasure meeting you." He reaches out a hand.

"Thank you, Jason. I just got here really, so there's not much I'll be needing."

He looks over my shoulder, then back down at me. "How

about dinner? I'm guessing you haven't gotten the chance to get groceries yet."

He's right about that.

"One second." I close the door, leaving him waiting on the other side while I call King to verify this guy's identity. I'm not taking any chances.

"Jason. Yes, he was meant to be discreet." King mumbles something under his breath before continuing. "He's one of my employee's sons and is quite honest and reliable. I wouldn't have him look out for you otherwise."

I hang up with King, grab my purse, then reopen the door. Sure enough, Jason hasn't moved.

"Good to go?" he asks, a genuine smile softening his features.

"Yes, thank you."

LUCAS

"Beanca moved to New York," Jones says. He looks over at me as he drops the last few boxes into the back of the U-Haul he's using to head out to his college campus today. "I didn't talk to her for long," he continues. "I'm not gonna lie. I was annoyed with her for keeping us in the dark, only telling us she's gone once she was already out of town."

I don't say anything.

If I say anything, it'll come out wrong. I'm over whatever it is Beanca and I had. She and I weren't supposed to happen anyway.

"She didn't tell you she moved, did she?" Shepherd asks, standing next to me and placing an arm over my shoulder.

"Dude, it's whatever," I say, shrugging him off and busying myself with securing one of Jones's boxes in the U-Haul. "Beanca and I haven't been anything for a while. You guys should've gotten used to it by now. She's gone, and I'm here. Soon, you'll both be gone too."

Shepherd and Evie are heading out within the week. They'll be at NYU, not too far from Beanca's school. At least she won't be alone up there. She'll have Shepherd to look out for her when she needs someone.

"You sure you don't want to pack up your guitar and head up with us?" Shepherd asks. "Who's gonna keep you company down here?"

"I've got other friends. Don't y'all go thinking I'm gonna be Lonely Lucas down here with nothing but my band and music to keep me company. I'll manage."

"*Lonely Lucas*?" Shepherd throws his head back in laughter.

"It's got a good ring to it," Jones joins in. "Bro, I'll know where to find you. Paramount's just a couple hours from my campus."

We hug it out. "Yeah, well, I'm not saying I'll stay here forever. Michelle, the boys, and I are considering going on a debut tour this year. We just have to call the necessary people and organize a schedule of venues."

"Keep us updated, OK?" Shepherd says.

Jones slaps hands with him and then turns to salute us both. "See you guys in a few months, or whenever Lucas sends us those tour dates."

Jones's dad comes out then and nods at us before the two hop into the U-Haul and drive off.

Shepherd and I head over to my truck. "Want to tell me what's really going on in that head of yours?" He always could read me like a book.

"Nothing much. If Beanca never speaks to me again, I deserve it."

"Bullshit. Beanca is being selfish." Shepherd looks over at me, anger in his voice. "So you kept some DNA results from her. So? She found out anyway. What does it matter all this time later?"

"For her it matters a whole damn lot," I grind out. "I

never should have dated her, man. What the hell was I thinking getting involved with her?"

I thought I'd buried my feelings, but moments like this make me realize Beanca's actions affect me more than I let on.

"I don't want to talk about it." Starting up the truck, I pull out of Jones's neighborhood.

"I'm sorry for bringing her up."

I'm the one who should be sorry. Sorry I ever let myself *feel* anything for Beanca. Sorry I ever let myself *have* anything other than a friendship with her.

I regret all of it.

Chapter Twenty-Six

One Year Later

BEANCA

The soft melodies of Chopin's Nocturne op.9 No.2 flow from the piano as my fingers glide along the keys. Closing my eyes, I allow the vibrations to sway me as I move with the intensity of the music.

I play the last few notes and stand to a round of applause from an audience of my peers.

"You are a sight for sore eyes," Jason says once I finally get seated next to him in the front row of the small auditorium.

I'm in an off-the-shoulder, silky black gown with a train. The open design at the front of the dress perfectly displays my legs. Black stilettos round out the look.

"Stop it, Jason," I say, giving him a friendly swat on his thigh. "I should say the same for you." I'd given him advice on his attire for this evening and he'd completely gone overboard with the glam, showing up in a full tuxedo as if he were one of the music students performing tonight. "I mean, you look great."

The other audience members are mostly in either business casual or streetwear.

"I always do," he says, grinning at me.

I roll my eyes, and at the start of the orchestra, we both refocus our attention on the stage.

Two hours later, the other performances are over. I return to the stage with everyone and we all bow before dispersing into the crowd again.

Jason and I are heading down a sidewalk to the cars, when a bouquet of indigo blossoms are thrust into my path.

"Sweetheart, for you," King says, appearing stealthily from the shadows on the sidewalk.

"Oh!" I jump back startled, looking up at him with my hand slapped against my chest. "Dad! Don't do that again, you almost scared the life out of me."

I clasp my hand around the bouquet and accept his hug.

"I thought you said you couldn't make it tonight." I hadn't made a big deal about it because few students were lucky enough to have family fly in for this small, in-house performance.

"I pulled a few strings," King explains, not going into further detail. "Jason, good evening."

"What's up, King?"

The two nod at each other and King falls into step with us. "So where were you two headed? Let's have dinner."

"Can't," Jason says. "I have other plans with Dana tonight. I was planning on dropping Beanca home first." By Dana, he means his current girlfriend. The two met through their gym a few months back.

I swat him on the shoulder. "Really? No wonder you wore *this*." I smooth my hand over the sleeve of his tux. "Dad and I will be fine without you weighing us down," I say playfully. Turning to King, I add, "Won't we?" I've grown comfortable in his company. Over the past year, he's proven to be more of a father to me than I've had all my life. The first time I called him *Dad* it slipped out like it was the most natural thing, and we both just went with it.

We separate from Jason and go around to King's car.

"How come you're here?" I ask, curious as to why he'd shown up when he'd initially said he wouldn't be able to make it. This wasn't the first time my school's had these informal recitals, and it's been difficult for family to attend due to distance and scheduling.

"Like I said, sweetheart, I made a few arrangements. Once I arrived, I came straight here," he says vaguely.

"OK, Dad. If you say so." I look forward to enjoying the rest of the evening with him. It's not often that he can fly in to spend time with me.

We get to an upscale Italian restaurant near my school, and I'm not surprised that even though they are booked, they just happen to have a table available for King and me. He has a lot of pull wherever he goes. Come to think of it, there isn't really much that remains closed to King Bridges when he wants it.

It's not long before we're ushered to a table with more settings than necessary.

"Will there be someone else joining us?" I ask, curious.

To my surprise, he nods, further piquing my curiosity. "Yes, if you don't mind." He pulls out my chair. "Someone will indeed be joining us."

I'm curious and it's on the tip of my tongue to ask, but before I get the chance, I glance over to my right and freeze.

I blink rapidly, trying to ensure my eyes aren't playing tricks on me.

I don't think I breathe for the next few seconds.

"Beanca, sweetheart, what's wrong?" King asks.

I whip my head to back to him. "No—nothing." My heart is pounding in my ears.

Not more than two tables over is Lucas, Shepherd, Evie and some other girl, all having dinner together.

Lucas …

"Hey, Dad, I'm—I need to use the ladies room." I shoot up from the table, and not knowing where I'm going, I walk in the opposite direction of their table.

When I eventually get to the restroom, I stare at my reflection in the mirror.

Over the past year, I've let my hair grow out. I've kept it dyed black, deciding I prefer it this way.

The first tear falls against my cheek and I'm a goner. The restroom doors open a minute later and I scurry into the large private stall behind me.

"He's super cute, Evie. When you and Shepherd said you set me up with a friend, I had no idea he'd be this hot!" The girl's high-pitched voice assails my ears.

I instantly decide I don't like her.

"Yeah, well, Lucas is an even better person on the inside," Evie says. "He's always been extremely intelligent. And remember I told you, he has a band he's on tour with right now."

"You said they're playing here, right?" The girl asks, her over-the-top excitement evident.

One of them enters the stall next to mine. I can't make out Evie's response to the girl's question, because the tap goes off as someone washes their hands.

I remain where I am until I'm positive everyone's left. Only then do I decide to leave the restroom, giving myself a quick once-over before I do.

On my way back to my table, I stop dead in my tracks. Not a few feet ahead and standing at my table talking to King, are Lucas and Shepherd.

"Oh, there you are, sweetheart" King says, drawing everyone's attention to me. "You were gone so long, I was beginning to get worried."

My legs become sticks as they carry me the rest of the way to the table.

"Hey, Bee," Shepherd says, coming to hug me.

"Lucas was inviting us to a show his band will be playing tomorrow night," King says, standing to clap a hand over Lucas's shoulder before looking at me again. "I thought maybe you and Jason would care to join."

My eyes connect with Lucas's at the mention of Jason's name, and I instantly regret it. His eyes are cold, calculating almost.

"Lucas, how've you been?" I manage.

We haven't talked since I left Paramount. In all that time since I moved away, he never texted or called me.

It's what I'd wanted.

I didn't want him contacting me, coming after me.

I didn't need him.

I wanted time to myself, to take care of me. I'm comfortable with who I am. It's taken over a year to discover myself and love me; honestly, I don't need him in my life. And I don't need these feelings for him resurfacing and trying to mess up the balance I've curated for myself here in New York.

"Do you really want to know that, Beanca?" He asks, pulling me from my thoughts. His voice is flat, cynical. "Or are you just asking because you have to?"

King and Shepherd both turn to look at him in surprise.

"Lucas?" Shepherd asks. "Don't, dude."

King raises an eyebrow, looking between Lucas and me.

"No problem here," Lucas says. "You know, that uh, that invitation. It wasn't communal." He glares at me while attempting a smile that doesn't reach his eyes. "Beanca and her boyfriend can find other things to do. I'm sure he wouldn't appreciate going out to watch her ex-boyfriend's band."

"Come on, dude," Shepherd says.

"I don't have—"

The waitresses choose that very moment to arrive with our food, and Shepherd steers Lucas away.

I awkwardly reclaim my seat, glancing at their retreating form.

Seated across from me, King becomes pensive. "Beanca, what exactly happened between you and Lucas?"

I look down, tightly clasping my hands together in my lap.

"You don't have to answer, if it makes you uncomfortable."

"He lied to me," I say without hesitation, my emotions getting the better of me. "He knew you were my father before I did and he never told me."

"Wha—?" King's attention shifts over to Lucas's table.

I follow his gaze only to witness what I'd dreaded seeing since I first spotted them this evening. The girl Shepherd and Evie set Lucas up with is practically falling all over him, and he's eating up every piece of it. He allows her to touch him, giggle at him. I mean she's practically sitting on his lap.

I look away.

"Yeah, he knew who you were and didn't tell me," I continue. "We broke up when I found out and we … eventually stopped talking. I couldn't trust him anymore; honestly, I wasn't in a good place before leaving town. I don't want him back or anything. I just wish he didn't hate me the way he obviously does now."

When King doesn't say anything, I look up to find him looking at me in the oddest way.

"What?" I ask.

"Are you sure?"

"Sure about what?"

"Sure you don't want anything with Lucas." He raises an eyebrow and shifts his gaze back to their table.

I keep my attention trained on King, refusing to keep watching *that* show. "Oh, I'm sure. I've had enough lies for a lifetime."

"People make mistakes, sweetheart. They grow and change." His eyes soften as he continues. "I'm sure we've all made our fair share of mistakes, but we apologize and we try to move on."

I grit my teeth.

"Lucas didn't apologize?" he asks.

"No. I mean, yeah, he did." I'm even more emotional now and don't want to discuss this anymore. "Hey, can we just eat?"

"Sure. Whatever you want."

"Anyway, are the other people coming who you said would be joining us?"

"I'm not quite sure that's a good idea anymore." King's forehead creases as he watches the other table.

I can feel eyes on me, but I pretend nothing phases me. I try, but fail, because when I turn my head, I find Lucas staring back at me.

LUCAS

I can't keep my eyes off her.

It's been a whole damn year without Beanca in my life. I thought I'd put her out of my mind. Out of my heart. And all it took was one meeting at a restaurant.

Maybe you and Jason would care to join.

Jason?

Who the hell is Jason?

She obviously has a boyfriend. King prevented me from making a complete fool out of myself. I should be happy.

But I'm not happy damn it!

I'm livid.

How dare Beanca move on from us like that?

Then to come here tonight and find her like this.

Beanca is still as beautiful as ever. But even with all that, she's still as selfish as ever.

I look over at her again, nauseated by this chick Shepherd and Evie thought it a bright idea to set me up with.

Beanca must feel my eyes on her because her gaze suddenly meets mine.

I take an unsteady breath when she doesn't look away but keeps her eyes locked on mine.

She mouths something but I can't make it out. When I frown, she mouths it slower this time.

"*I'm sorry.*"

I turn to the chick next to me, chuckling to myself.

It's a little too late for apologies. If she meant she was sorry for not contacting me this past year, she has a phone.

"So how long have you been playing?" the girl beside me asks.

I can't even remember her name. "About three years."

"That's so cool! I wish I could play an instrument or at least sing."

"Lisa, you're gifted in other ways," Evie offers. "Opposites attract. I'm proof of that." She kisses Shepherd on the cheek before he bends to sign our check.

"Where are we off to?" Shepherd asks as we all stand to leave.

"How about a club? I feel like dancing off these carbs I just ate," Evie says, placing her hand in Shepherd's. They both walk ahead of us.

We pass King and Beanca on our way out.

"Have a good evening, kids," King says.

"You too, King," Shepherd says.

"Later," I say, my gaze falling to Beanca's shoulders. I instantly close my eyes, shutting myself off from the curiosity that piques when I notice she's added more musical notes down the side of her neck and along her shoulder.

"Hey, are you good?" Lisa asks.

"Yeah," I say, my voice strained. It's then that I realize I've stopped just behind Beanca's chair, my hand resting on the back of it. Her soft ebony hair brushes against my knuckles when she turns to look up at me. I can see her tattoo fully now, and my hand itches to smooth over the trail of notes from her shoulder up to my favorite green one behind her ear.

"I hope you're enjoying your time here, Lucas." Beanca says this before staring pointedly at Lisa, and then turning her attention back to the food in front of her.

"That I am, princess."

Before I can make an ass of myself, I remove my hand from her chair, say my goodbyes and make long strides to catch up to Shepherd and Evie.

"Princess?" Lisa asks. "Evie told me her name's Beanca."

I bring a hand to my face and close my eyes. "Freudian slip."

"What's that?"

"Nothing," I say.

I message the band's group chat to meet us if they're free. A few of them have other friends in New York. Michelle has an aunt she's visiting with in Queens and won't be back in Manhattan until tomorrow.

By the time we get to the club, I know I'm not staying for long. None of my bandmates can make it and Lisa isn't the kind of company I want to keep this evening. Shepherd and Evie have all but left us to our own devices in here. It's dark and the music is too loud. It's not even the kind I like to listen to. The crowd is a buzzkill, too. If you can even call it a crowd. There're barely a hundred people here tops. I've seen house parties livelier than this. But I guess it's to be expected since it's still early.

About an hour goes by, and I'm dancing with some girl I don't know. This woman comes out of nowhere and flashes me a grin.

"I don't believe it. Are you Lucas Moore?" she asks.

Confused, I frown. "Who wants to know?"

"I can't believe I ran into you tonight. I've seen photos and heard some of your band's songs, but you're even more good-looking in person." The woman turns to some other dude she's with and whispers in his ear.

The guy looks at me and smiles. "You're one of the lead singers in Fractured?"

I chuckle. "Yeah."

"Oh my God! It's so freaking crazy to actually meet you. I'm Dana, this is Jason." She holds a hand out and we shake.

Of course her friend's name is Jason. Anything to keep *her* a constant in my thoughts.

"We've got tickets to your concert tomorrow night. Could you sign this for me?" Dana pulls out a ticket to tomorrow's live show and hands me a pen from the pocket of Jason's tuxedo. Dude is a little overdressed for this place but I'm not judging.

Lisa tugs on my arm as soon as I finish signing the ticket. "I didn't know you were famous." Her face lights up and she pulls me away from the others. "I'm sure you both won't mind if I steal him back."

She proceeds to ask me question after question. I barely respond to one before she has another one ready to fly.

"How long will you be here?"

"Just another two weeks," I say.

"How long have you been on tour?"

"For months now—"

"Why'd you decide not to go to college?"

"I've got my reasons."

"Are you interested in anyone?"

I groan inwardly. "Hey, what about you? How long have you known Shepherd and Evie?" I deflect.

"We just met this past year. They're new to our Christ Fellowship group on campus."

My brows knit together. "Christ Fellowship group?"

"Yeah, it's a Christian organization that ministers to believers in the faith."

"Interesting."

When the song ends, I search for Shepherd and Evie. Spotting them, I walk over, Lisa beside me.

"Christ Fellowship, huh?" I ask Shepherd.

His gaze shifts to Lisa then back to me. "Yeah. Evie went and eventually invited me to join her."

"Hmm."

"It's something you have to experience for yourself, Lucas," Shepherd says.

Evie places her arm through the crook of Shepherd's. "Yeah, we can't fully describe what it's like, the sense of fulfillment you get in knowing Him for yourself."

My next question just begs itself to be asked. "And yet all three of you are here tonight."

"Grace doesn't stop at the club's entrance," Lisa adds. "It's not where you are. It's where your heart is."

I snort. "Whatever. Look, I actually came to let you guys know I'm heading out. I'm beat."

"Aww, but we haven't been here that long," Lisa complains.

"It was nice meeting you, Lisa," I say. "Shepherd, Evie, see you tomorrow." I salute the three of them and make my exit.

Chapter Twenty-Seven

BEANCA

I shouldn't go tonight.

I should dig in my heels and tell King he's more than welcome to got to the concert without me.

But I can't.

I want to see Lucas play. I didn't know he was touring. I didn't even know he was in New York. There's a lot of things I don't know about him anymore.

Then again, it's not like I tried to. I have no one to blame but myself.

I treated Lucas like crap after I found out he'd lied to me. And then I also turned around and blamed him for not reaching out once I moved away.

I've had moments where I missed Lucas like crazy, but I would tell myself we were better off not talking. If we'd stayed in contact, we would've probably ended up back in each others arms. I couldn't handle that then. I needed time before entertaining being with him again.

I miss him.

Seeing him last night brought on a wave of emotions. And the feelings I thought I'd buried deep within me, shot right up to the surface.

The connection we have is still there, and I owe it to us to at least try fixing things back to some semblance of normalcy.

Grabbing my phone before I think better of it, I message Shepherd.

Me: Hey do you know where Lucas is staying?

Half an hour goes by before I get a response.

Shepherd: Yeah, why?

Me: Can you send me the address and room number?

Shepherd: Beanca, are you sure that's a good idea?

Me: Shep, I messed up, OK. And I'm the only one that can fix it.

He sends me the information.

I take a quick shower and am out of the apartment before noon. With any luck Lucas is still at his hotel.

When I get to the Hampton, I fly through the double-glass doors in the lobby, and head straight for the elevator. Everything is a blur around me. I should have called him but I didn't want to risk him avoiding me.

I get to Lucas's room and knock lightly. After a half a minute without a response, I pound on the door. "Lucas. It's Beanca. Open up."

A few seconds go by before the lock clicks and the door opens.

My eyes go wide when instead of Lucas in the open doorway, I'm staring at a woman.

"He's in the shower," she says, flipping her ebony hair over her shoulder, leaving it to cascade down her back. She stands a head taller than me and sports a dress that barely leaves anything to the imagination. "What'd you say your name was again?"

When I just stand there gawking at her, she furrows her brow.

"Beanca," I reply flatly. "I'm here to see Lucas."

"Beanca," she says, repeating my name while eyeing me curiously. "Why don't you come in, Beanca?"

I falter. "Never … mind. I—" I'm about to turn and leave when I spot Lucas walking out of a bedroom with only a towel around his waist. His wavy brown hair a wet mass sticking to his head.

"Esmerelda, will you—" He pauses mid-stride when he notices me at the door with *Esmerelda*. "Beanca?"

I awkwardly look between him and the woman. "Hey," I say, my voice weak. "This is obviously not a good time. I'll see you around." I whirl around and make a beeline back to the elevator. It's not far from his hotel room, so I get there within seconds. I'm about to press the arrow down button when Lucas grabs a hold of wrist, pulling me away from it.

"Why—how come you're here?" he asks, his eyes staring into mine. "How did you know where—? Shepherd." He comes to the correct conclusion all on his own, then frowns at me. "Why didn't you tell me you were coming? My phone still works, you know. Not that you—"

I pull my wrist free from his grasp. "Mistake. Won't happen again." I shift my gaze to his bare chest, refusing to make further eye-contact.

"Beanca. It's not what it looks like."

At his words, my eyes fly back up to meet his. "You don't have to explain anything to me."

The mere fact he's trying to, makes me feel silly. Lucas can be with whomever he chooses. I don't have any hold over him. Especially after the way things ended between us.

He chuckles. "I guess you're right. I mean, you're in a relationship."

It's on the tip of my tongue to clarify that I'm not, but I don't get the chance.

"Look, Beanca, for what it's worth, I truly am happy for you. I just wish you'd have—"

"I'm sorry, Lucas," I say, interrupting him. "I'm sorry for

the way I treated you last summer. I was angry and I was hurting. You made a mistake, and you apologized, but I decided to completely discard everything we had. It was selfish. I was selfish."

When he opens his mouth to speak, I hold my hand up.

"Let me finish, please. This past year, I've gotten to know myself better. And I'm happy I did. Away from the watching eyes of the people I've known all my life. It was necessary, and I'm grateful for the time I had to really be with me, you know." I pause, mustering up the courage to say my next words. "But I have one regret. And that's letting all this time pass without ever reaching out to you. You didn't deserve that."

"Beanca—"

"No, please. I understand. You've got your own thing going on. Umm." My throat thickens and I work to say the last few words. "Good luck at your concert tonight." I manage a weak smile before turning to the elevator and pressing the down button.

Hands encircle my waste from behind, startling me. "Princess," Lucas says, pulling me into him. "Please, don't. Don't cry."

At his words, I realize belatedly that my face is wet. Swiping my hands across my cheeks, I cover my face, mortified at my overreaction at seeing a woman in his hotel room.

Lucas hugs me to his chest, his face in my hair as he inhales deeply. The feel of his arms around me is the warmth I didn't know I needed. I let myself feel him, his skin, his scent, not caring about anything or anyone else.

Reality sets in the moment his lips graze my neck and brush against my tattoo.

I gently push at his arms, but he doesn't release me.

"Lucas, we can't," I say, my voice barely a whisper.

When he doesn't let up, but kisses my tattoo instead, I freeze. He does it again, and again.

The sensation of having him so close to me, having him still want me, it does something to me. Turning in his arms, I bring my mouth up to his. I pour a year's worth of pent up anger, frustration, despair over missing what we had into our kiss.

Lucas coaxes my lips apart and deepens the kiss. Framing my face in his hands, he moves his lips roughly across mine, kissing me with such heat, such intensity that I lose myself in the moment.

The elevator dings, and only then do we pull apart.

"Lucas?" A male voice asks.

We both turn to the elevator.

"Beanca?" Ricardo, his band mate, looks between us and starts grinning from ear-to-ear. "About damn time!"

"Hey, Ricardo," I say with a shaky breath. Feeling awkward as hell, I face Lucas again. His cheeks are flushed and his gaze is still locked on me.

"Well, don't let me interrupt," Ricardo says as he walks past us, winking and whistling as he heads to their hotel room. "Esmerelda is waiting on her morning coffee, and *I'm* anticipating my reward."

Oh.

Esmerelda is *Ricardo's* girl.

Lucas reaches for me again when he realizes I've figured that part out. Tightening his arms around my waist, he lowers his head to mine.

I cover his lips with my fingers. "Lucas. We—"

He abruptly lets go of my waist and I have to find my footing.

"Right. I forgot. You've got a boyfriend," he scowls. "I wonder what Jason would say if he knew you kissed me like that."

I roll my eyes. This is the Lucas I know. I've successfully managed to draw him out. "I'm not dating Jason, Lucas. You assumed that."

He straightens and frowns down at me. "He's not your boyfriend? If you two aren't dating, why'd King—"

"First off, Jason's like a big brother to me. Second, you were the one who *assumed* from what my dad said that we were dating."

He rubs a hand over the back of his neck.

"So am I invited to your concert tonight?" I ask. "Or do I need to do more groveling?"

He sobers up and looks at me intently.

"I'm sorry," I say again. "I feel like a part of me hoped you'd reach out again after last summer. When you didn't, I resigned myself to the idea you wanted nothing to do with me anymore. And I thought if you decided that, then we were both better off."

He sighs in frustration. "Beanca, last summer you didn't respond to my texts nor answered my calls. You weren't at your house anymore and forget asking King anything. He insisted you needed your time and space."

Wow. I really did make a mess of things. "I guess at the time I did."

"I didn't call you after that. Not after I found out you'd moved away and didn't tell me." He walks over to the fake, potted plant by the elevator, busying his hands with its leaves. "I blamed myself for getting into a relationship with my best friend, which was what I promised myself I wouldn't do. When you left like that, it solidified what I'd always feared. And I guess I just accepted that our friendship was done then, too."

I don't know what to say.

Lucas turns to face me. "I was—I am really sorry, Bee. If I could have made that decision again, I wouldn't have gotten involved where King was concerned."

"I know." I walk over to him, bring my arms around his waist and lay my head on his chest. "I miss you, Lucas. I miss us."

He hugs me tightly. "*That makes two of us.*"

I lean my head back and smile up at him, hopeful. "Does this mean you forgive me?"

He places a soft, firm kiss against my lips. "Rome wasn't built in a day, princess."

My mouth falls open.

He snakes a hand up to the neck of my blouse and pulls it to the side. "These?" he inquires, smoothing the pads of his fingers over the tattoo of musical notes trailing along my shoulder.

I grin up at him. "You like 'em?"

Lucas lowers his head, softly kissing a path from my neck down to the very last shoulder note. "I love 'em."

"Lu-cas," I warn.

"Come on," he groans, hauling me back to the hotel room.

"You didn't answer my question," I say. "Am I invited to Fractured's concert tonight?"

When he suddenly picks me up in his arms, I squeal. "Lucas! No! What are you doing?!" Laughing, I clasp my arms around his neck for balance.

"I don't know. Should I let you in tonight?" His eyes soften as they stare into mine.

"Tonight … and every night after that," I say before leaning into him.

LUCAS

This moment feels surreal.

In just a day so much has changed.

When I came to New York this past week, I didn't do it to see Beanca. A part of me had hoped for it, but with the way we left things, I didn't know what to expect if and when we *did* finally see each other.

Beanca not only reentered my life, she singlehandedly

turned my world upside down, or I should say, right side up again. After almost a year of silence, she comes bulldozing in after weeds had grown in, almost choking out what we had.

Correction.

What we have.

I don't think Beanca and I were ever just best friends. We lead ourselves to believe that, but there was always something there.

At least for me, anyway.

I always expected more from her ... more than a mere friendship could afford.

If nothing else, there's one thing I'm sure of.

I want her back, for keeps this time.

I'm addicted, desperate, and I want to be sure she'll stay. No more *coulda, shoulda, wouldas* with us.

"We're Fractured, and we're glad y'all have come out to share tonight with us!" Michelle shouts, getting the audience pumped.

The small concert hall is packed with a little over three hundred people. The audience cheers and hoots with a few screaming, "*We love you!*"

I look out to find Shepherd, Evie, King, and Beanca among our friends and family in the row directly in front of the stage.

Throughout our performance my eyes constantly find their way to Beanca. She and everyone else show their appreciation by standing and swaying along to the music from time to time.

When we get to *Redemption*, the song I wrote at the beginning of senior year, I pull my mic closer.

"Initially when I wrote this next piece," I say, "I tried to hide it from someone who means a lot to me. I wasn't brave enough to tell her at the time that she'd inspired it." My eyes are trained on Beanca and our gazes lock. "Well now I'm telling her," I confess with a wink.

I signal for the band to start playing and I sing with all that's in me. Not for the audience, not even for the performance, but for us … for Beanca and me. I change one line in the lyrics to the original words I'd written. It's what I'd intended then, but was too freaked out by what it meant.

I know it's hard out here
This world is damn cruel, dear
But with you as my wife,
Pretty girl, we're down for a wild ride
You say you'll stick around maybe
But I, I'm someone you can trust
Love is our anthem, baby
They ain't got nothing on us

I haven't taken my eyes off Beanca once when the song ends. Everyone is loud, whistling, screaming …

"I love you." I say the words into the mic. This time with more confidence than I'd said them when she'd been at my showcase our senior year.

"We love you, too!" the audience screams in response, thinking I've said the words to them.

My heart on my sleeve, I gaze into Beanca's eyes, waiting for a reaction.

More than I'd hoped for, she says what I could only wish she'd say. "*I love you.*"

I don't hear the words over the audience and the music, but I can make them out, the words and the makeshift heart she forms with her hands.

My eyes go wide when she repeats the words again, louder this time. "I love you, Lucas!" Beanca is equally as shocked, quickly covering her mouth when Shepherd, King, and a few others close by angle their heads toward her.

I grin, winking at her, a surge of newfound energy coursing through me.

We finish the rest of our performance with more passion than I had at the start.

Beanca doesn't run away this time.

"You guys did good." King joins in congratulating us.

"Appreciate it," I say, offering him thanks before my eyes shift to Beanca. "You're still here," I say.

"I'm still here." She surprises me when she boldly reaches her arms up around my neck and pulls me down for a kiss, in front of everyone. Beanca is not into public displays of affection, and yet here she is, initiating it in front of others. "I'll be by your side, Lucas. For as long as you want me."

I stare into her eyes, searching for any doubt that could belie her statement, hoping there's none.

Her eyes soften, and I have my answer.

"For as long as I want you, huh?" I ask. "What if that's longer than you expect?" I kiss her firmly, tightening my hands around her waist and pulling her softness into me, feeling her warmth. I get caught up in the moment, but I manage to stop when I notice King, Shepherd, and Evie looking anywhere but at us.

I make an apologetic gesture to King, but he brushes me off. "There's no one I feel more comfortable with around my daughter, Lucas. As long as Beanca is happy, protected, and feeling her best, I have nothing to worry about." King slaps me on the shoulder and holds an arm out to Beanca. "Where are we off to to celebrate your reconciliation, sweetheart?" He winks at Shepherd, and the two exchange meaningful glances.

That's when I finally realize it. They'd planned the whole *chance* meeting last night.

I chuckle to myself, shaking my head.

I should have known.

"*Daaad.*" Beanca blushes, hooking an arm through his. "Excuse him, Lucas."

"What?" I ask, feigning ignorance. "It's nice to know I have King's blessing. I'll need even more of it soon."

"Lu-cas," she warns, side-eyeing me.

"Is there another guy I should be worried about in your life?" I inquire, quirking an eyebrow.

She smacks my shoulder. "Of course not. You know that. We're together."

Good.

And if I have it my way, there won't ever be anyone else.

Chapter Twenty-Eight

6 Months Later

LUCAS

I drive us out to where it all started
That old town road.

The road where Beanca's destiny forever became more deeply intertwined with mine. On that night, she awakened in me a deeper desire for her than I knew I had. A desire to love her and be loved by her in return. To want what's only good for her, no matter the cost to me.

It was dark the night we stopped off here after Chase's house party, so it's difficult to gauge where the exact spot was.

I pull my truck over about halfway between Beanca's old house and Chase's place.

"Umm, Lucas. Today is my last day of Spring Break," Beanca says, her brows furrowing in confusion. "*This* is where we're choosing for our date?"

I turn to her and kill the engine. "Yup."

"I thought we'd at least go to Tallulah, babe." She looks out through her window in disappointment. "There's nothing but trees and grass out here."

"Exactly. The perfect spot for a picnic." I grin at her before hopping out and heading to her side. Opening the door, I lift her down.

Lacing my fingers through hers, I watch her as I walk backwards into the tall grasses.

"Do you remember that night, princess?"

At first she looks around us, then back at the truck.

It takes Beanca a few seconds, but realization dawns on her when she looks from the truck to the road, and then back over to me. "Why'd you bring us out here?" She tilts her head in curiosity, her eyes narrowing.

"Wait and see." I pull her into me and start slow dancing with her, using the wind as my melody.

"That's your favorite line, isn't it?" she asks, laughing as I twirl her around before bending her backwards over one knee.

"No," I say, grinning down at her. "My favorite line is this dress you're wearing." She looks amazing in the red, form-fitting number complete with frilly off-the-shoulder sleeves. The same frills are designed in the hem at her ankles.

"Wow," she says, throwing her head back in laughter.

I don't fight the urge to kiss the column of her neck where it's exposed. I nibble on her there, and she immediately brings her head back up, giggling at the contact.

"I mean it. I love this on you."

She places a hand at the nape of my neck and pulls my mouth down to hers. "Thank you, Mr. Moore. A certain someone got it for me." She kisses me then, satisfied with my gift.

"I love you," I whisper in her ear. I'll never tire of telling her how much she means to me. Spinning us around, I crush her against me as we continue dancing.

"Sometimes," she says quietly. "I can't understand how

you remained loyal to me after all I put us through … all I put *you* through."

"Hey, I'm not without fault here," I mumble. "I'm no saint."

"Yeah, well, compared to me, and for as long as I've known you, you've always been good to damn near everybody. Well, except Vincent, of course."

"Oh so we're measuring sainthood by the ability to be *good* are we?"

She smacks me on the shoulder before placing her head on my chest.

I turn us in slow circles, resting my head atop hers.

"I honestly don't get what my sister sees in Vincent," Beanca sighs. "She refuses to listen to me about the guy. He always had a self-centerdness that only you saw from the start."

"Maybe Beverly got him to reform. I don't know."

"Maybe."

"That wasn't a slight to you." I realize my words may have come across harsh.

"What? No. I don't care anything about the guy. I just wish Bev never gave him the time of day. And I'm happy I never did put a title on whatever we had."

"Can we talk about us?" We've given Vincent way too much real estate in our conversation.

"Us?" Beanca looks up at me in confusion. "We're nothing like them. Vincent's character leaves a *lot* to be desired. I'm not much better than him, but at least I don't hide who I am. I'm me, flaws and all."

I look wide-eyed at her. "*Flaws* and all." I grin and lean away when she playfully slaps my chest.

"Hey."

I sober up and straighten my stance. "Princess, as messed up as you believe yourself to be, I love you. No matter what, I'm loyal only to you."

"Oh, yeah? I seem to remember you threatening that you'd date other people at one point."

I capture one of her hands in mine and head back over to my truck. "I spoke out of anger then. I never meant that."

"I know," she admits, her voice softening.

"And you don't have to worry about me choosing someone else, because I've already chosen you. Two lifetimes from now, I'll still choose you, and only you." I walk us to the very spot near my truck where I'd kissed her that night. The night I'd felt and admitted for the first time that I wanted Beanca as more than a friend.

I place her against the side of my truck as I'd done that night, and leaning down, I cover her lips with mine. Framing her face, I deepen the kiss, while sliding a hand down to my pocket.

I remove the ring before breaking the kiss. It's the same promise ring I'd given her almost two years ago.

Beanca gasps, covering her mouth when she instantly recognizes the green teardrop in a bed of smaller diamonds.

Taking her left hand in mine, I get down on one knee and gaze up into her beautiful green eyes. I say the next words with my heart open and bare to her.

"I love you, Beanca Carlyle." My throat thickens with each word. "Will you marry me?"

BEANCA

Lucas is my forever.

I don't hesitate when he asks me to be his. "Yes! A thousand times yes!"

Lucas places the ring on my finger and lifts his eyes to mine. The way he's looking at me causes my breath to catch. He shifts his gaze to my lips, and I automatically look to his.

Slowly rising to his feet, he brings his mouth to mine. At the contact, my eyes flutter closed. My heart fills with an intensity I've never felt before, bursting through every single pore.

Lucas releases my lips only to brush feather-like kisses across my cheeks, dismantling my tears as they fall down my face. Using the pads of his thumbs, he wipes at them.

My throat closes up, and I can't bear it when his eyes become reddened and he succumbs to his emotions. I wipe at his face with the palms of my hands. "Lucas," I say brokenly, "I—"

His lips instantly cover mine, and we get lost in each other.

"I love you, Lucas," I finally manage to say moments later. "I love you," I repeat, more confident this time, rising to kiss him again.

He looks at me, his heart in his eyes. "You have no idea how much I love hearing those words coming from your lips." He places a feather-light kiss against my mouth before walking to the back of the truck. He opens it, and I stand close as he removes a few supplies and a duffel bag.

Lucas takes a hold of my hand and we walk a little further out from where his truck is parked. I help him set up the picnic blanket under one of the huge oak trees sprawled across the field. With the sun low on the horizon, we don't have much time before it's dark out.

He thought of everything: sandwiches, drinks, dessert, you name it.

"Wow. My fiancé is impressive," I tease.

"All the best for my woman." He reaches for me, pulling my back against his chest as he leans against the oak's wide bark.

I grab a turkey sandwich and unwrap it. Turning to him, I hold it in front of his mouth. He smiles then takes a bite before nipping my cheek. I giggle before taking a bite of my own.

After a while, I relax into him, my head falling against his shoulder as we watch the soft golden-orange glow of the setting sun.

"I have something else," Lucas whispers, his lips against my ear. He sits up a little, moves a hand through his duffel bag and pulls out a book.

It looks familiar and when he places it in my hands, I immediately smile when I see the title. *The Alchemist* is the book he'd suggested to me before the beginning of our senior year at PSA.

He taps a finger on the purple tabs placed throughout the book. "Read, princess." He pulls me closer, cocooning me into the warmth and protection of his arms.

I flip to the first tabbed page and find a section of the book highlighted in purple. I clear my throat before reading the words. "*No heart has ever suffered when it goes in search of its dreams, because every second of the search is a second's encounter with God and with eternity.*" I fumble the words when I flip to the next tab and start reading. "*So, I love you because—I love you because the entire universe conspired to help me find you.*"

Lucas places a soft kiss behind my ear, on my tattoo, before whispering again. "I choose you, Beanca. I'll always choose you."

My heart squeezes, then fills with him and everything he's come to mean to me over the years. My vision blurs as I look at the pages of the open book. I remember reading a section those years ago when he'd recommended it. It's a section I didn't particularly understand at the time, but thinking on it now that things have come full circle with us, I flip through the book, desperate to find it.

"What is it?" he asks, leaning his head over my shoulder, his cheek rubbing up against mine.

My hands continue to leaf through, hoping my memory serves me correctly and I can find the words.

After several seconds of searching through the book, my eyes land on the quote I've come to understand.

"Read, babe." I point him to the section.

He gazes into my eyes, then presses his lips firmly against mine before turning his attention to the book. "*When you are loved, there's no need at all to understand what's happening, because everything happens within you.*"

I turn in his arms, hugging him to me. "At first, I didn't understand why people used the word *love* when they did nothing or had nothing to show for it. I witnessed people just throwing the word around, never actually understanding it, never embodying what it really meant to love someone." I loosen the hug and look at him, trying to gauge his reaction.

Lucas's brows knit together, but it doesn't take long before understanding lightens his features.

"I needed to take that time, Lucas. To figure things out, to be away from you and from everything and everyone here in Paramount." I slide my arms from his shoulders to his torso, placing my head on his chest. "I realize now that I had to go away to become a better me for myself, for you and for the people I care about. I wouldn't have understood the significance or depth of love without first finding out how to love myself." I lean my head back and gaze into deep-set blue eyes. "I love you and I'll always choose you, too."

Lifting my lips to his, I become the peace of knowing I'm where I'm supposed to be and with the person I'm meant to fulfill this journey with.

Much like Santiago from *The Alchemist*, I realize that the place I'd been searching for, the place I'd be happy, where I would finally feel at home, feel wanted, loved …

I already possessed it.

That place … is in me.

Deleted Scene

BEANCA

Parents aren't supposed to play favorites.

They aren't supposed to treat one child like the prodigy, and the other like the black sheep.

Key words there are, aren't supposed to.

I guess mine happened to have skipped out on that lesson.

"Beanca, you are so forgetful." Dad sighs, picks up his cell phone from the kitchen counter and dials Mom. "I swear most of the time you act as if you don't have half a brain." He directs his next words into the phone. "Becky," he says to Mom, "Will you pick up Beverly? Beanca seems to have somehow forgotten that she's returning today."

Beverly, my younger sister, is coming back from cheer camp, and it completely slipped my mind that I was responsible for getting her from the airport.

We attend Paramount School of Arts together, and while this upcoming year will be my senior year, she'll be a sophomore. She didn't make our school's cheerleading team, so Mom and Dad thought it a good idea to send her to Tisch

Cheer Camp up in Wisconsin for the past six weeks this summer.

Twirling my ponytail around my fingers, I intentionally ignore Dad's insult, strolling away from him and into the study.

I truly had forgotten that my sister would be coming home today, but it wasn't my fault. I had a lot on my plate. I volunteer with the Boys & Girls Club in Paramount and I'm also involved in PSA's Reading Rangers, an organization that pairs high schoolers with kids in middle school and elementary school who struggle with reading. Throughout the summer, I've been enjoying the time I spent working with different groups of kids. I especially liked helping the struggling readers. I feel connected to them in some way. For one thing, I find that we share the lack of parental support and devotion in our development, so I guess I have a vested interest in wanting to see them succeed.

If Dad had reminded me that Beverly was supposed to come home today, that would have fixed the current dilemma. If he cared to talk to me instead of constantly criticizing me, maybe this wouldn't have happened.

I glide a hand across one of the many bookshelves lining the four walls of the study. This is my favorite place in our house. Well, besides my bedroom. I could lose myself in here, spending hours engrossed in one of the volumes. I crook a finger when my hand reaches the book I'm currently interested in, The Alchemist.

Lucas recommended it. He's one of my best friends. There are four of us in our little circle. But, it's been more of a trio lately since Shepherd, our fourth man standing, decided he wanted nothing to do with me. I get it, I was a bitch to his girlfriend and almost ruined their relationship. But seriously, I helped him because I care about him. I hope one day he'll see it and forgive me for the shady way I went about everything.

After reading almost half of part one of The Alchemist,

I'm hooked. I want to keep going but I need to practice for my recital. I slide out of the loveseat and over to my favorite thing in this room, the piano. My parents never doted on me, and honestly, if they hadn't bought this for the prestige and aesthetic it brought to the house, I doubt they'd have purchased it had I asked them crawling on my knees over broken glass.

It wasn't always like this with them. There was a time when they'd loved Beverly and me equally. As equally as parents can love two very different children anyway.

Things started changing around my eleventh birthday. I'd had a nasty fall from one of the trees in our backyard. I'd broken my arm and had suffered a pretty awful concussion. When I'd finally woken up and interacted with my parents, I noticed my dad acting distant, almost like I was a stranger to him. I'd chalked it up to him having been scared shitless that I possibly could have died. But his behavior didn't return to normal. After a few months, my mom had changed toward me too. She definitely wasn't as bad as my dad, but it had been evident that her affection for me had waned considerably.

Beverly became the prized princess at our house. The venerable Queen B. She could do no wrong. Anytime something occurred that wasn't to my parents' liking, I was always the one to blame. And anytime something praiseworthy happened, they'd find a way to commend Beverly, even if it was clear I'd accomplished it. For example, if I'd get straight As, they'd say Beverly's study habits must have rubbed off on me. If I'd start helping out around the house, with small tasks the maids didn't finish, they'd say Beverly must have been the one to do it, because I was too selfish to think of anyone else.

If I'm selfish, it's because I've realized for a while now that I'm not lovable. People's affection for me never lasts. They'll always find someone more deserving of their time and attention. Even when I'd tried being more like Beverly, acting like her, copying her style, attempting to imitate her personality, nothing ever worked.

Don't get me wrong, I love my sister.

I only wish we were born to two different families. That way she could occupy a space where she received her own affection, and I … would have mine. Two parents actually loving me, seeing me, spending time with me.

As my fingers glide across the keys of the piano, and the notes of Prelude in E Minor by Chopin fill the room, I close my eyes, feeling the music.

I play the piece over and over again, as I let the inevitable tears flow freely. They fall to my hands, my lap, and the keys of the piano.

I can't stop them. They've become me in this house.

One more year.

Just one more year and I'd be out of here.

I should be happy about it.

I am happy about it.

Maybe if I tell myself often enough, I'll eventually feel it.

"When It Ends"

Sneak Peek: PSA Book 3
"When It Ends"
Jones and Samantha's Story

JONES

I roll my head, attempting to relieve the knot lodged in my neck. I didn't sleep well last night. I try to convince myself it has nothing to do with running into Beverly and Vincent at that house party.

My fists clench at the memory. At his cocky disposition and their blatant display on the dance floor.

What the hell does she see in Vincent anyway?

The dude dated her sister and moved on to Beverly the moment he got the chance. He's a straight-up selfish prick who only cares about his image.

"Earth to Jones. Bro, what's with you?"

I open my eyes, desperately trying to keep my lids from closing again. I look over at Zeke, one of my good friends. I've known him since Sabbath School days. We always snuck out of our youth services at church, giving the excuse we needed to use the restroom when we really just ended up escaping to the play park adjacent to our churchyard.

"Sorry, bro. Were you saying something?" I ask, shifting my gaze from him and to our Spanish teaching assistant.

She's in the middle of a lecture, explaining the use of the verb *gustarse*. Several students are confused and still another few with their hands raised.

"Yeah," Zeke replies. "Listen, there's a party this weekend that a couple of frat guys were telling me about. Said I could invite whoever. You down?" Zeke eyes me, daring me to refuse.

I don't have anything against fraternities. It's the groupies that'll most likely make up the majority of the scene that I don't particularly care to be around. Whenever I go to parties, I'm always pressured to take advantage of what those girls throw my way. And after what happened last night, I'm just tired.

I frown, fixing my mouth to turn down the offer, but Zeke speaks before I can.

"Bro, don't," he says, sounding disappointed already. "I know what you're thinking, and I promise it won't be that bad. I'll stand as guard. How about it? Keep the chicks at bay."

"You said the same thing about last night, remember." In his defense, it wasn't Zeke's fault I had a run-in with my ex and her douchebag of a partner.

"How was I supposed to know she'd be there? Beverly never used to go to house parties. She was always a bit antisocial. I guess she just needed the right person to open her up to—"

"I'll go," I say, interrupting him. I don't want to talk about Beverly or the ... *replacement*. They've occupied enough of my thoughts since yesterday's ill-fated run-in.

"You sure? Or are you agreeing just to get me to shut up?" Zeke asks suspiciously.

"Both."

When Spanish is over, Zeke and I head over to one of Paramount University's campus cafeterias. I have to admit the food is good nine times out of ten. It's a plus that Zeke is on Paramount's basketball team, because we get to sit in the room designated for athletes only. The cafeteria is loud most of the time, a cacophony of people talking and eating. That's why I appreciate the more reserved area where only a handful of athletes eat at once.

We grab our food from an unlimited buffet of choices. When we select a table, we spot Brian, Zeke's cousin, who's already seated at one of the window seats with a friend. He waves us over and I follow Zeke to sit with them.

Apparently they're talking about some chick. Although I wouldn't usually mind the topic, I've had enough of one particular girl to last me a week. I snatch a few fries off my plate and focus on my food as the conversation flows.

I'm quiet almost the entire lunch as I eat and try to drown out the conversation. I don't have much luck the last few minutes though because I'm dragged in when Zeke turns to me.

"Jones, what do you think?" he asks.

"Huh?" I take the last bite of my burger and wipe my hands on a napkin.

"Brian's got this chick in his accounting class he's into. Studies with her in a small group during the week. I'm telling him to ask her out if he likes her, and he's being a wuss about it. Claims he doesn't know if she's interested."

I look over at Brian. "Does it matter if she's interested?" I ask. "When did you suddenly become shy around girls?"

Brian's always been confident and outgoing. Girls are into him. I'm surprised he's doubting himself.

"Yo, who said I was shy?" he asks in annoyance. "She's just not like other chicks, man. She's … different. I don't know. There's something stoic about her."

Zeke laughs and slaps a hand over his shoulder. "*Stoic?* Cuz, what the hell kind of books have you been reading?"

"Whatever," Brian counters, rolling his eyes. "Laugh all you want, but I'm serious. There's something about her that stands out. Makes me want to take my time, you know. Get to know her from afar."

"Except you're not doing it from afar, are you?" Brian's friend pipes in. "You're in the girl's study group. If I were you, I wouldn't hang around waiting for an opportunity to ask her out if she's so *stoic*. Who's to say there aren't other guys hanging around her. Don't wait around, or you may just lose her to someone else. Life and time wait for no man."

I reach for my ginger ale and take a huge gulp, nearly halving the can.

Ain't that the truth.

I thought Beverly and I would've been able to last, but life and time had other plans. I wonder, if I could go back now, would I change anything? Do anything differently?

Would I have went out with her at all?

I honestly wish I hadn't, because then our breakup wouldn't have caused such a deep rift between us. I liked us when we were friends. We should've never crossed over into being anything else but that.

"Whoa! She's beautiful." Zeke takes the phone from Brian's hand and pinches the screen zooming in. "Wait. She looks …" He trails off and frowns at the image, scrutinizing it.

"What?" Brian asks, looking over at Zeke.

"Jones, you've got to see this."

"Nah, I'm good," I say, rising to my feet. "I need to go drop off a book at the library, anyway. I'll check in with you later."

"Bro, no. You've got to look at her."

"Dude, I'm good. I promise." I frown at him and pick up my tray. The last thing I need is to look at some girl Brian's into.

I exit the room, drop the tray off, and head to the library.

After I return the library book, I walk to my dorm. It takes me about fifteen minutes to get there, but I need the fresh air and the exercise. Anything to help clear my head.

"You're really cute," some girl says to me as she walks by.

"Thanks," I reply, noncommittal. Don't get me wrong, I appreciate the compliment. I'm moody right now; the last thing I want is attention. I just want to go to my dorm room and stew.

Of course you're here. How many girls have you had tonight?

Those words, like a knife, cut deep. I'm not used to that version of Beverly. And even though she said those words to me, I can't hate her. I have nothing but love for her. I guess that's why the level of hatred in her words, and worse, in her eyes, gets to me.

I hold my building key up to the reader and the door beeps before I pull it open. Heading to the second floor, I tap my hall badge against the lock and open the heavy metal door. Intending to go straight to my room, I pause when I'm confronted with an unexpected guest in the middle of the hallway.

It's not often I find a girl in the middle of our male-only floor, especially not so bold and out in the open in the midafternoon.

She stalks in my direction, her face downturned. Her curly hair sways from side to side, slapping against her face.

I draw my brows together when I notice something familiar about her. I don't know if it's in the way she's walking or a certain aura about her.

The moment she looks up, I stop short, a muscle in my jaw tensing at the sight of her.

Samantha Rosenthal.

She's grown even prettier through the years since she left Paramount. Her short hair now rests just past her shoulders. The once black strands now a mixture of browns from honey to dark chestnut. She's gotten taller, too. Definitely not the "Tiny Thal" I used to tease when we were kids.

"Samantha?" I call to her, hoping I'm not making an idiot out of myself if I'm wrong, and it's not her.

She stops.

That's when I notice a girl behind her.

They both direct their gazes to me, and I know without a doubt she's the same Samantha I had a crush on my freshman year of high school.

Her eyes widen, her face creasing in confusion. "JJ?" she says, her voice tentative. A wan smile briefly appears before disappearing behind another emotion.

She's about to say something else, but stops short when a guy bursts from one of the dorm rooms and jogs toward her.

"Sam, wait!" he yells as she whirls around to face him.

When he gets to the girls, he grabs hold of Samantha. She brushes him off, but he tries holding on to her again.

"Get off me, Taye!" She slaps at his hands, attempting to shove them away from her.

The other girl just stands there, doing nothing.

The moment Samantha starts struggling with the guy again, I move over to them pushing him off her.

"Who the hell are you?" he scowls, nostrils flaring.

Bro, today is not the day.

Also by Sasha-Marie Marshall

<u>Embers of Hate</u>

Paramount School of Arts Book 1

There's no cure for heartbreak. Or the need for revenge…

Shepherd Buchanan is not your average high school junior. Attractive, popular, and athletic, he goes through life as if the whole world belongs to him.

Every heart at the Paramount School of Arts sure does.

He's the guy featured in every girl's dreams. The best wide receiver their football team has seen in years. The son every family would be proud to have.

The only thing he can't handle is the very idea of a relationship…

Enter Evelyn Richards.

The enigmatic new transfer student he can't seem to take his eyes off.

On the surface, Evelyn is smart, confident, and unapologetically herself. Deep down, she's still struggling with the childhood trauma that almost tore her family apart.

Just because she survived it, it doesn't mean she'll let it go.

Not when she discovers that Shepherd is tied to her past and the tragic event that changed her life forever.

Not when she finally gets a chance to right this wrong.

Certainly not when her feelings for Shepherd start to get in her way.

She wants retribution, and she'll sacrifice anything for it. Including her own heart…

Sasha-Marie Marshall is an emerging author. *Fractured Redemption* is the second book in her Paramount School of Arts Series, preceded by its first title, *Embers of Hate.* She made the leap from years in education to author of inspirational novels and existing in the eternal now, living out her dreams one story and one endeavor at a time.

She currently resides in the USA and always looks forward to her next adventure.

To keep updated on her upcoming releases, sneak peeks and extras, you can sign up to her author newsletter at her website: www.sashamariemarshall.com

9 798987 521724